BAH Humbug

AN ANTHOLOGY

Conglomerate Ink

PO BOX 512 Shelbyville, TN 37162

www.RayneshaPittman.com

ISBN: 978-0-9967856-8-6

table of CONTENT

Bah Humbug Individual Stories Synopsis

❖ **Holiday Homicide** by C.J Hudson- After serving just two months of a life sentence for bank robbery, Eugene "Butch" Conway concocts a scheme to break out of prison. His plan is to gather up the cash from the heists he's pulled and head for the boarder. But before he does, Butch vows to get even with everyone who was involved in him being imprisoned. Driven by revenge and rage, Butch sets his date with revenge for Christmas morning. Ready to gift a dose of yuletide lead from the barrel of his gun he wasn't prepared to receive a gift in exchange so devastating, it would shatter him to the core.

❖ **Everyone Comes Home for Christmas** by E. Raye Turonek- This holiday suspense thriller takes you on a journey through the psyche of John Henry Butcher. With a volatile mental state and no signs of recovery, due to a malicious act fueled by the jealousy of his older sibling, at the age of thirteen John Henry was committed to a psychiatric hospital. Spawning from those of affluent lineage, he was afforded the best care. Psychiatrists have made phenomenal progress, identifying Butchers many personalities, but will

i

they be able to keep them under submission long enough for John to be released?

Although he has his regular visitor, John gets especially lonely around the holidays. It's been over twenty years since he'd been home for Christmas. This year John has plans to return. Will the memories brought back from the past push John's alternate identities to boil to the surface one after another exacting their revenge on his loved ones? Unlock the secrets of his family, then watch them atone for their sins in this delicious thriller.

❖ **Release Date** by Tito M. Bradley- Ed Wilson an inmate in an Ohio correctional institution has come up for parole right before Christmas. While battling his demons with gambling, he is trying to stay out of trouble until he has his hearing. His baby momma is giving him a hard time and his mother will only allow him back in her home if he returns to her strict religious lifestyle. Without a place to stay he can't get paroled. If he doesn't get parole, he may never leave prison. How far will Ed go to make his Release Date?

❖ **The Gift We Didn't Want** by Danielle Bigsby-Christmas is supposed to be a fun-filled, joyous occasion full of laughs and gift exchanges but what happens when that's just not so? What happens when the one gift you're given has no return policy and comes riddled with pain?

"The Gift We Didn't Want" gives a whole new meaning to exchanging gifts for better ones and after one reads this tale, Christmas will never be looked at the same way again.

❖ **Christmas Memories** by Juan Diaz-It's no secret that Julio hates Christmas. Haunted by the memory of his seven year-old son Ray becoming disabled by a bullet to the head as a toddler, Julio wants nothing more in the world than to make his son happy by buying him the coveted video game console the Funtendo Station. With nothing but poverty and despair in sight, Julio decides to aid his friend Big Mike with contract killing that has been set up by the infamous Ismael Zepedas.

❖ **A Cold December** by Nisha Lanae-Christmas is a time for family, joyous memories and love. For Detective Shanae Shaw it's a constant reminder of the day her life was torn apart. Twenty years later, the tragedy of that day still haunts her. The hole in her heart remains as large as a football field. The only thing that'll come close mending that hole is finding the people responsible for the loss of her mother and father. With everything on the line including her life Shanae realizes that everything she thought she knew she didn't and those she thought she could trust she can't.

Will Shane's fight for justice give her that or will it only add to the turmoil life has thrown her way.

❖ **Daddy Christmas** by Raynesha Pittman- That New year, New me saying made its way down the country side to Mayhem, Tennessee and into Monica's salon and boy, did it leave its mark on her mind. But how will she make it past Christmas day with daddy issues stemming from Santa Claus of years ago and an unhealed love war wound that she uses smothering her son to cover as a band aid. Will asking Santa for a new daddy really fix all her holiday problems or will daddy Christmas gift her with more than she could see coming?

Holiday Homicide

$\mathcal{B}$oom! Chunks of drywall shattered and crashed to the floor. Hysterical screams bounced off the walls and echoed throughout the lobby. Instinctively, all eyes pivoted toward the menacing figure dressed as Santa Claus. Smoke leaked from the end of the double barrel shotgun he held tightly in his clutches.

"A'ight, muthafuckas! Y'all know what the fuck this is! Run that bread and kiss the muthafuckin' carpet! And by the way… Merry muthafuckin' Christmas!"

Immediately, the place fell as quiet as a morgue. The only sounds that could be heard were from the twenty-something year old Caucasian woman nodding her head and singing along to whatever music was coming through her headphones. Because her eyes were also closed, she neither saw nor heard the gunshot nor the screams from the other customers. Her high pitched, off key vocals sounded so bad that the gunman briefly entertained the thought of putting the barrel of his gun in her mouth and pulling the trigger just to shut her the fuck up. Instead, he opted for a more practical approach. He calmly walked over to her and tapped her on the shoulder. When the young lady opened her eyes, her breathing nearly stopped. A sinister smirk was on the gunman's face as he ripped the headphones off of the girl's ears and held them to his own. A disgusted frown slowly found its way onto his face when he discovered what she was listening to.

1

"The fuck you doin' listening to this bullshit?" he asked, just before slapping her viciously across the face with the butt of his shotgun. The young lady crumbled to the floor. The area that she was sitting in wasn't carpeted, so when her head hit the floor, it made a sickening crack. The gunman then walked to the nearest teller and pointed his weapon in her face.

"Run that bread, bitch," he demanded.

Out of the corner of his eye, the gunman noticed a slight flinch from one of the customers in the bank, causing him to swing the gun in that direction. The man, who was a regular customer, foolishly thought of sneaking behind the gunman, but the twin barrels that were now aimed at his rotund frame changed his thought process.

"Don't be a hero and miss ya' next meal, fat boy! I'll put so much lead in yo' thick ass, Superman won't be able to see through you! Hurry up, bitch," he yelled, turning the gun back on the teller.

The terrified woman quickly began stuffing money into a large bag. The woman had contemplated taking the day off and now she wished she'd followed her first instinct. Yet, here she was, smack dab in the middle of a heist. After filling the bag, she carefully placed it on the counter. She didn't want to make any sudden moves while being in the crosshairs of a madman. She did, however, make a stupid move. After opening the bag and peering inside, the gunman drew back and punched her in the face.

"Bitch! You think I'm fuckin' stupid? Dump this fake shit on the floor and fill this damned bag with something that won't explode!"

As tears leaked from her eyes and blood poured from her nose, the woman fearfully complied. She wondered if trying to be slick was going to cost her, her life. She filled the bag with real money, sat it on the counter, and took a step back.

"Thought you were dealing with a rookie, huh, bitch? I should shoot your stupid ass for that shit! Dumb bitch; this ain't even your fuckin' money," he yelled, as he snatched the bag off of the counter and headed for the door. On his way there, he noticed an elderly white woman lying face down on the carpet.

Her face was wrinkled, like a used bedsheet. She was in no way attractive to look at, but what was beautiful to Butch was the watch hanging around her wrist. Butch walked up to her, bent down, and yanked her up from the floor.

"Okay, old bitch, check that watch in." Immediately, the woman began to cry. The watch meant the world to her. "Bitch, if you don't shut the fuck up, I'm gonna take my dick out and beat the shit out of you with it!"

"Please, sir, don't take my watch. It was the last thing my husband bought for me before he perished."

"Bitch, I don't give a fuck if the Almighty himself gave it to you! You've got five seconds to un-ass that bling or you're gonna be the quietest bitch in church this Sunday!"

The woman foolishly thought about calling the gunman's bluff, but the evil look in his eyes told her that he meant every word he said. She loved that watch, but she loved breathing much more. She reluctantly slid the watch off her wrist and handed it to him.

"Thanks, grandma," he responded, just before shoving her back to the floor. Without missing a beat, he shot the teller in the face and then sped towards the door. Taking aim, he fired into the locking mechanism. The gunman wasn't a rookie. He knew that the teller hit the silent alarm, causing the front entrance to lock automatically.

Five shots later, the lock shattered. The gunman then kicked the door opened and ran out of the bank. A large smile was plastered across his face. He knew he had to hurry and get to the getaway car before the police arrived. He sprinted halfway down the block where a black Dodge Charger awaited his arrival. When he got within ten feet of the car, the passenger's side door flew open.

With the dexterity of an acrobat, the gunman leaped into the front seat, tossing the shotgun into the back of the car. Before the door was even closed, the car was screeching down the street.

$$$

Detective Wayne Morris sat at his table, nursing a cup of lukewarm coffee. Still photos from the crime scene were scattered across his desk. This was the fifth bank robbery in the last two months. Because there weren't any discernible patterns to go on, the Cleveland Police Force was having a hard time zeroing in on the culprit.

"Damn, this coffee is nasty as hell when it gets cold," he spat, before getting up and walking over to the microwave. He'd been concentrating on the photos for so long that his hot coffee had practically turned into iced coffee. After heating up his caffeine, Detective Morris walked back to his chair and dropped down. He was getting frustrated. He'd been assigned the unenviable task of putting a stop to the robberies and so far, his investigation hadn't yielded any results. Reaching into his desk, the detective took out the reports of two previous robberies. He laid all of the photos in conjunction with the other ones and stared at them intently.

"I'm missing something; I know it."

"I'm missing something, too," a sweet voice said, upon entering the room. "And I hope that you're in the mood to give it to me." Detective Morris continued to stare at the pictures. He didn't even have to look up to know who the voice belonged to.

With all the sex appeal she could muster, Melissa sauntered across the room. Although she was wearing her uniform, her perfectly proportioned body still stood out to the naked eye... Her butter light skin was smooth to the touch. Her light brown eyes held a glint of lust as she stared at Detective Morris hungrily. Her short cropped hairstyle may have seemed masculine to some, but the Detective knew all too well that she was all woman. When it came to her job, she was all business, which led a few of her coworkers to question her sexuality.

Detective Morris scoffed at this insinuation. The two of them had been screwing around for the better part of six months. Even though they'd tried to keep their dealings with each other secret, rumors had begun to circulate throughout the precinct. In order to not incur their Captain's wrath, the two of them tried to have as little contact as possible. Today, however, was different. The Captain had a family funeral to attend to, so he wasn't going to be at work.

"Melissa, not now. I'm trying to concentrate on these crime photos," he said, sternly. Like he knew it wouldn't, the tone of his voice didn't do anything to deter her from dropping to her knees and reaching for his zipper.

"Melissa, did you hear what I just said? I'm busy right now."

"Yep, I heard what you said. But, I also hear what he says," she purred, nodding toward the Detective's hardening manhood. Detective Morris opened his mouth to protest, but the objection got caught in his throat when he felt the warm grip of Melissa's hand wrap around his dick. Looking up at him with a lustful smile, she slid her hand through the slit of his boxers and took his sex tool completely out. Slowly and seductively, she ran her tongue across the bottom of her top lip. She knew just what to do to put him at her mercy.

"Wait; go lock the door."

"I already did," she said, just before swallowing his six and a half inches whole.

Detective Morris gasped as she slowly pulled her head upward, flicking the head with her tongue the entire way. She teased and toyed with him, removing it from her mouth and reinserting it. When she was done playing around, Melissa went to work.

"Oh, fuck, that feels good," Detective Morris said, beating on his desk. After another forty-five minutes of the intense blow job he was receiving, the Detective was ready to fuck.

He reached down to try to help Melissa to her feet. He couldn't wait to bend her over his table and give it to her doggy style.

"Come on, baby, get up. I'm ready to hit that pussy."

Disappointment registered on his face when Melissa wiggled her finger, letting him know that intercourse wasn't an option at this time. Truth be told, she wanted to fuck just as badly as he did. But because her menstrual cycle had started, Detective Morris would just have to settle for a suck and swallow. Detective Morris could feel his nuts tighten. It wouldn't be long before he exploded in her mouth. His hand instinctively gripped the back of her head. As Melissa began to suck even harder, the detective began to thrust in and out of her mouth.

"Oh, shit, baby, I'm 'bout to cum!" He hadn't meant to yell, but it felt so damned good to him, he just couldn't help himself. Not even five seconds later, Detective Morris' babies were on the D train to Melissa's stomach.

"Shit, baby, that was incredible. Be a good girl and let me get back to work now, okay?" Pouting like a small child, Melissa got up and crossed her arms.

"Oh, so after using me for your sexual whims, you're just gonna kick me the fuck out, huh?" Detective Morris frowned.

"You know you enjoyed that just as much as I did; so don't front."

"Ain't nobody frontin'. I just want to make sure that you're not starting to think of me as just some common whore or jump off."

"What? Come on, Melissa. You know better than that."

"Do I?" Detective Morris studied her facial expression. He could tell that there was something on her mind.

"Okay, Melissa. What's going through that pretty little head of yours?"

"Well, since you asked. Wayne, we've been dating for some time now. Don't you think it's time for us to get a little more serious?"

Detective Morris sighed. He was afraid of this. When the two of them first hooked up, he'd made it perfectly clear to Melissa that he wasn't looking to be in a relationship. At first, she seemed to be content with it. But as time moved forward, Melissa began to get extremely clingy.

"Melissa, we had an agreement that neither of us would…"

"No, you had an agreement, Wayne. I don't ever remember saying that I wanted this relationship to stay in the same place forever."

Relationship? When in the hell did I give this dizzy broad the impression that this was a relationship? He wondered.

"Melissa, look. You know as well as I do that what we have is not a relationship. You give me release; I give you release. So, please stop acting like we're engaged or something."

Melissa's eyes turned into slits. She stared at the detective like she wanted to cut his throat.

"Oh, so that's all I am to you, huh? Just a quick nut?"

"Melissa, you need to calm the fuck down. Like I said, I'm not ready to be in a serious relationship. You need to respect that."

"Oh, I'm going to respect it. I'm also going to tell your ass goodbye. I ain't got time to be fuckin' around with someone who just wants to keep me on as a fuck buddy!"

"Look, what I said, I meant. So if you can't deal with it…"

"Fuck you," Melissa screamed, storming toward the door.

$$$

Butch's toes curled so much that cramps were starting to set into them. He was more than happy, however, to endure the pain that it caused since it was offset by the lustful pleasure that was provided by his girl's mouth as it see-sawed up and down on his dick. She was a pro in the art of fellatio. Swallowing his eight and a half inch monster was no small feat, but the cocoa skinned beauty did it with ease. The thing that made her so great at giving head was not her extra-long tongue, nor was it her vacuum type lungs. No, not at all. The thing that made her dick sucking skills so fantastic was the fact that she absolutely loved to have a penis slide between her lips. To her, sucking dick and swallowing cum was the best shit a bitch could ever do. She loved it so much, in fact, that she often came all over herself just from giving a blowjob. Butch instinctively grabbed the sides of her head as he pumped in and out of her hungry mouth. His eyes began to roll to the back of his head as Hershey continued to work her magic on his joy stick.

"Oh, shit," he moaned loudly, as he felt his nuts tighten. A satisfied smile formed on his lips, knowing that in a few seconds his ride or die bitch would be doing for him what every red blooded American male dreams about during a blow job.

"Oh, yeah, baby, get it all," he begged. Both of his legs stiffened as he felt his eruption travel from his sacks to the tip of his dick. Hershey moaned in self-satisfaction. The feeling of Butch's semen shooting into her mouth and making its way down her throat and into her belly pushed her over the edge also. A lustful scream emitted from her mouth as she squirted and sprayed the bed sheets with her juice. Butch looked down at her and grinned. The sight of her cum rushing out of her vagina combined with the fact that she still held his dick in her mouth caused his penis to remain hard. That was a good thing, too, because he was ready to fuck. As soon as the last drop was in her mouth, Butch picked her up and dumped her backward onto the bed.

Before he could even make another move toward her, Hershey had already grabbed her own legs and pulled them back towards her head. Her slightly hairy pussy looked so delicious that he couldn't help but sample a taste before he started fucking her. Butch licked his lips hungrily and dove in, head first.

"Oh, fuck!" Hershey screamed, as Butch's wet tongue made contact with her clit. Her right leg began to quiver and, within a matter of a few minutes, she was cumming again. Then, like a lion crawling onto its prey, Butch mounted her. The heat radiating from their bodies caused the room temperature to spike. As his dick sank into Hershey's dripping wet love station, Butch lowered his lips onto hers to allow her to taste her own sweet juices. The two of them kissed for a few short seconds before Butch broke the lip lock and buried his head in her shoulder. With Hershey's legs pulled so far back, Butch had access to every inch of her mound of paradise. His hips began to rotate slowly, causing his partner to purr softly. As he was stroking her, he kissed and nibbled on her neck, turning her on even more.

"Come on, baby! Give it to me hard," she yelled, wrapping her legs around his back and crossing them at the ankles. Butch was all too happy to oblige. He started pounding into her like her's was the last piece of pussy he was ever going to get.

"Oh, hell yeah, baby, that's what the fuck I'm talking about! Pound that pussy!"

Hershey liked it rough and hard and Butch never disappointed her. From the first time they crawled into the sack, the chemistry was electric.

Their attraction to each other was damn near as strong as the earth's gravitational pull. Their respective sex organs seemed to be specifically designed for each other. Butch continued to dig deep, his eight and a half inch tool disappearing in and out of Hershey's juicy womb.

"Uuhhgg, oh my God, baby, I think you just hit bottom on me!"

Hershey's face twisted into a mask of pleasure and pain. Butch had always been able to bring her to the fringe of tapping out and today was no exception. Five seconds later, she squirted out another load of cum. Feeling her warm liquid flow from her body rendered Butch powerless to control his own bodily functions. He was trying as hard as he could to hold out and enjoy her moist, warm pussy, but the sensational feeling his dick had caused by her orgasm was too much to overcome. After releasing his load, Butch collapsed on top of his lover. The two of them seemed to melt into each other's arms as they both lay there trying to catch their breath Hershey was the first one to break the silence.

"So, was that my early Christmas gift? Because, if it was, you can give me that every year."

Butch laughed. He loved her sense of humor, although he wasn't completely sure if she was joking or not.

"Nah, I got you something extra special."

"For real? Run that shit then, nigga," she said, excitedly.

"Nah, you gonna have to find it," he said.

"Find it? The fuck kinda hide and seek shit you on today?"

"The kind that says if yo' ass don't find it, yo' ass don't get it," he teased, grabbing a handful of her bare left breast. "All I'mma tell you is that it's in the bedroom."

Hershey sighed heavily. After the sexual marathon the two of them had, the last thing she wanted to do was roll out of bed to do anything; but, for the sake of being blessed with a gift, she played along. As Hershey searched high and low for her gift, Butch would periodically tell her when she was getting warm or when she was getting cold. His dick jumped to attention when she bent over to look in the bottom drawer. Hershey was thick in all the right places.

Her ass was perfectly proportioned to her thin waist and her titties sat up like they were being supported by kick stands. Her smooth, dark skin reminded Butch of a chocolate bar, which is why he'd nicknamed her Hershey. The way she gracefully moved around the room made him want to grab her and pull her back into the bed; but first, he wanted to see the look on her face when she found her gift. Hershey was about to give up when she looked down at his jeans lying on the floor. She wouldn't have given them a second thought had she not noticed the bulge in the pocket. With a smile starting to creep onto her face, Hershey slid over to where they were and picked them up from the floor. She glanced at Butch, who was now smiling back at her. She reached inside and pulled out the most beautiful piece of jewelry that she'd ever seen in her life. Holding it up to the light, she stared at it for a good ten seconds.

"Now you can tell time in style, baby," Butch said, suddenly feeling mighty proud of himself. He loved to see his woman smile. Hershey was downright giddy as she slipped the diamond encrusted Rolex onto her wrist.

Tears formed in her eyes as she continued to stare at the expensive piece of jewelry.

"Merry Christmas, baby," Butch said, proudly.

Tears leaked from Hershey's eyes as she crawled into the bed with her lover and snuggled up next to him. Butch wrapped his arms around her and held her until she fell asleep. He had never loved her more than in that moment. Being the thug that he was, Butch never thought that he would ever find the yin to his yang, but Hershey proved to be more than his complement. As Hershey slept peacefully, Butch couldn't help but reminisce when their destinies became intertwined.

$$$

Butch sat in a 2015 Toyota Camry, eyeing the confrontation between a thick, mocha-skinned woman and an overweight security guard. An amused look was plastered on his face as he watched the feisty young woman give the rent a cop a piece of her mind. In a sly attempt to ear hustle, Butch cracked the window slightly. It became even more comical when he was able to clearly hear the young woman's tirade.

"Nigga, fuck you, this punk ass job, and that faggot ass branch manager," she bellowed.

"Look, you need to calm the fuck down. You act like it's everybody else's fault that they caught your dumb ass stealing. You should be thankful that they are just firing you instead of pressing charges," the security guard said, before turning to walk away.

"Fuck you! I ain't got to steal shit from this low budget ass bank!"

The security guard continued to ignore her rants. As far as he was concerned, it was over. He'd done his job by escorting her from the bank and defusing a volatile situation. He'd just opened the door to return to his post when the fiery young woman hit him with a gut punch.

"That's why me, my man, and Sylvia had a threesome last night! What? You didn't know that yo' bitch liked to suck dick AND eat pussy? After my man smashed her ass, she ate me out! That bitch sho' do know how to lick a clit!"

The security guard's head snapped around. His eyes shot daggers at the young woman. Sylvia was his off-again, on-again girlfriend. They were currently on the outs so he had no idea if the young lady was telling the truth or not. Of course, the young lady didn't know if Sylvia went both ways or not. She just said it to get under the security guard's skin. Butch's eyes followed her as she stormed to her car and got in. She was still laughing as she slammed the door shut. Butch couldn't tell from far away, but to him, it looked like she had lit something and started smoking. Butch just shook his head. He was glad that he wasn't going to have to deal with her on this job.

There was no doubt that the young woman was beautiful and quite possibly the sexiest woman that he'd ever laid eyes on, but he needed to get his head back in the game. He needed to focus. There was paper to be made and he had every intention of getting his share. By hook or by crook, Butch was going to get paid. Working for minimum wage had never appealed to him, so he decided a little over a year prior to try robbing and stealing as an occupation. He started off by robbing corner hustlers and soon graduated to sticking up convenience stores. His thirst for more wealth lead him to conducting armed robberies of check cashing places and small banks. In all, he'd accumulated more than one hundred and fifty thousand dollars in cash from his heists. He'd known all along that he couldn't rob banks forever. His long term goal was to dive headfirst into the dope game and make a king-sized splash, but he didn't want to deal in small quantities. Butch tore his gaze away from the young beauty long enough to take inventory of his surroundings. He'd chosen this time of day because foot traffic was almost nonexistent around this time and today was no exception. He frowned when he saw a couple of knuckleheads sitting at a bus stop passing a blunt back and forth. Butch gave serious consideration to canceling his plans, but ultimately, his paper chase won out. Pulling the strings of his black hoodie tightly to further conceal his identity, Butch slid on a pair of dark sunglasses and got out of the stolen vehicle. He smoothly tucked his .45 into his waist band and headed for the bank. As soon as Butch walked into the bank, he spotted the security guard who'd been arguing with the pretty young lady. A strange feeling suddenly swept over him. For some reason, he felt the need to teach the guy a lesson for disrespecting the young beauty. Before anyone could yell a warning to him, Butch ran up to the security guard and cracked him upside the head with the butt of his pistol. The guard's lights went out immediately, which disappointed the hell out of Butch. He wanted to punish and embarrass him. Butch then fired two shots into the ceiling.

"Stop looking at me all crazy and shit and run that bread," he yelled to one of the tellers. The woman froze with fear, an action that got her slapped across the face. A large gash opened on her cheek. The woman cried out in pain as her blood splattered across the counter.

"Louise!" One of the tellers shouted.

"Nigga, shut the fuck up! Ain't nothing wrong with that bitch! And since you wanna be Captain Save a Hoe, I'm gonna put yo' punk ass to work! Fill that fuckin' bag up with dough before I blow yo' muthafuckin' brains out!"

The man was scared shitless. He tried to move, but his feet felt like they were stuck in cement. All that changed when Butch cocked the hammer of his heater. This got the man to moving quick, fast, and in a hurry. After filling the bag, the teller nervously handed it over to Butch. Butch was in such a hurry to leave the scene, that he tripped over the fallen security guard on his way to the door.

"Fuck," he shouted, as he got up from the floor. "Get the hell out of the way, you fat muthafucka," he yelled, before kicking the man in the ribs. The impact from his kick brought the guard back from the land of the unconscious. Butch snatched open the door and sprinted toward where he'd parked the stolen car. But, there was one problem that he hadn't counted on. The car was no longer there. Someone had stolen the car that Butch had stolen himself. Butch's eyes immediately traveled to the bus stop. The two young hoodlums that he'd seen sharing a blunt were gone and there wasn't a doubt in his mind that they were the ones that had taken the car.

"Fuck, fuck, fuck!" He shouted. He looked in the direction of the bank he'd just robbed and saw the door opening. The security guard stumbled out and ran toward him.

Damn, I shoulda kicked his ass in the head, he thought. With no other options, Butch slung the bag of money over his shoulder and headed in the opposite direction.

After running a block and a half, he looked back and was surprised to see that the security guard was still hot on his ass.

The fuck wrong with this nigga? I got something that'll slow his fat ass down! Butch slowed up just enough to pull the gun from his waist band. He

16

was just getting ready to aim and pull the trigger when he heard someone call out to him.

"Hey! Get in!" Butch did a double take when he saw who it was risking their freedom to help him escape. Unless his eyes were deceiving him, he was now staring directly into the face of the brown-skinned beauty that had been thrown out of the bank for allegedly stealing. Butch didn't have to be told a second time. He was damn near out of breath when he got to the passenger's side door and aggressively yanked it open. Butch barely had time to get in and close the door before she peeled off. He looked in the side view mirror and was amused to see the security guard bent over with his hands on his knees breathing heavily. After his shits and giggles, Butch turned to look at the woman who'd helped him escape. When the two of them locked eyes, it was love at first sight. From that moment on, it was them against the world.

$$$

Hershey began to snore lightly, snapping Butch back to the here and now. Slowly and carefully, he inched his body away from her's. Butch had one more lick to hit and that would be it for his bank robing days. He would take the money he'd stolen, dive headfirst into the dope game, and become a king pin. Butch leaned down and kissed his lady on the forehead before throwing on his Santa costume, grabbing his gun, and walking out of the door to do one last job. It would be a piece of cake...or so he thought.

$$$

Melissa drove down the street at a snail's pace. Angry motorists gave her the finger as they sped past her, but Melissa clearly didn't have any fucks to give. The last thing on her mind was the attitude of other drivers on the road. She was still in her feelings from the way the detective had treated her.

"Fuckin' asshole," she shouted.

Some of her fellow officers had warned her about getting involved with him but she didn't listen and now her heart was paying the price. What started out as two consenting adults just having fun had turned into one of them catching feelings and wanting a relationship. Melissa was so pissed off that she considered inviting him to her apartment for one last fuck and "accidentally" blowing his brains out while they were role playing cops and robbers, but she quickly shook that thought off. No matter how in love she was, she wasn't about to throw her life away for any man. A wicked smile creased her lips as she thought of a devilish scheme. Her heart was hurting and she was determined to make him feel the pain she was feeling.

"So, he don't want this pussy no more, huh? Well, I know for a fact that one of our fellow officers do," she said, grinning evilly. Melissa was referring to Richard Green, an officer on the force and a close friend of Wayne's. Even though he knew that his friend was smashing Melissa, Richard still lusted after her. He wanted her in the worst way and wouldn't hesitate to hop in the sack with her once he found out that she wasn't sleeping with Wayne anymore. Melissa picked up her cell phone as she was driving and gave a voice command to call Richard. The only reason she had his number in the first place was because he'd used the oldest trick in the book to give it to her.

"What kind of phone do you have? Let me check it out," he'd asked her. Before she knew what was going on, he'd used her cell phone to call his, thus ensuring that he had her phone number. Melissa was pissed, to say the least, but the damage had been done. Now the sneaky maneuver turned out to be a blessing in disguise.

"Hello?" Richard answered in his annoyingly, high pitched voice. He wasn't all that handsome and didn't turn Melissa on in the least, but because he and Wayne were such good friends, he was perfect for the job.

$$$

Richard couldn't believe his good fortune. For months, he'd been trying to figure a way to talk Melissa out of her pants but hadn't been able to come up with a solid plan. Wayne was his boy, true, but he just had to have some of Melissa's sweet pie.

"Hey, pretty lady. Whatchu up to?" Richard asked. He prayed to God that her calling him had nothing to do with Wayne. His prayers were answered as soon as she started speaking.

"Not much. What's up with you later on? Are you busy?" Richard paused. If he didn't know any better, he would think she was hitting on him.

"Whatchu mean?"

"Just what I said. What time do you get off duty?"

"Uh, I get off in an hour. Why? You and Wayne wanna double date or something?" He asked, slyly.

"Hell nah! And I don't wanna talk about that nigga! You busy or not?"

"Nah, I ain't busy at all," Richard quickly answered. His dick was already getting hard in anticipation. But, he had to make sure that Melissa wasn't just fucking with him.

"What did you have in mind?" He asked.

"Well, for starters, I was hoping that you could help me finish off a bottle of Henny I got. Then, provided you don't do or say anything to fuck it up, it's Netflix and… Well, you know the rest," Melissa said as she hung up.

It really didn't matter what Richard said. Melissa had already made up her mind to give up the pussy anyway. She just didn't feel like hearing some dumb shit come out of his mouth. Richard was so happy that he nearly came on himself sitting at his desk. His joyous mood turned sour when he realized that he didn't have her address. Thinking that she was screwing with his head, Richard was two seconds from calling her back and cussing her out when a text message containing her address came through.

"The hell you smiling so hard for? You got a hot date tonight or something?" Wayne asked, as he walked past Richard's desk. He was on his way to get something from the vending machine and saw his old buddy sitting with a smile on his face a mile wide.

"Yeah, something like that. Hey, why don't you and Melissa come with us?" He asked. He was wondering why Melissa got so heated when Wayne's name was brought up and here was his chance to fish for information.

"Nah, you go ahead and have fun. I've got my hands full with these bank robberies."

Wayne walked away without saying another word. Richard noticed how he'd tensed up when he mentioned Melissa.

Oh well, he thought, figuring that Wayne's loss was damned sure going to be his gain. After dicking around with some minor paperwork for the next hour, Richard walked out of the precinct like he'd won the lottery. His strut had an air of bravado and his confidence soared. Although Melissa had given him the good news over an hour earlier, Richard's dick was still hard. Then a sudden thought entered his head.

Maybe I should jack off one good time before going to her place.

Even though Richard had faith in his pipe game, the last thing he wanted to do was bust a nut as soon as he penetrated Melissa. Unchartered pussy had a way of doing that and pussy that a man had lusted after for months could definitely make that happen. As soon as he got home, Richard jumped in the shower, got cleaned up, and took a nap. He wanted to be well rested for his fuck session. In her text message, Melissa told him to be at her place at six o clock, so he set his alarm to go off at five. It was only going to take him fifteen minutes to get to her house, but he didn't want to risk being late and blowing his golden opportunity. When his alarm went off nearly an hour later, the first thing Richard did was reach for his cock. His first release of the evening was going to be on his sheets, but the rest was going to be emptied into Melissa. After washing his dick, Richard got dressed and headed out the door. All while he drove, his dick was hard. He pulled into the complex's parking lot and searched for Melissa's car. When he couldn't find it, he took out his cell phone and called her.

"I'll be there in ten minutes," she told him. While waiting for her to get home, Richard played around on Facebook. Time flew by as he scrolled and read some of the fuckery that people posted on their timelines. Richard glanced at the time stamp at the top of his phone and noticed that he'd been waiting for over thirty minutes.

"Let me call this bitch and see what's taking her so long," he said. Richard dialed her number and began speaking as soon as someone picked up.

"Hey, what's good? We still gon' do this or what?"

The answer he received chilled him to the bone.

$$$

"I'll show this muthafucka," Melissa said vengefully as she strutted out of Victoria's Secret. She couldn't wait to see the look on Wayne's face when he found out that she'd screwed Richard. Truthfully, she was hoping that her plan would cause her lover to see what he was missing and come to his senses. Once she got inside of her car, she opened her bag and examined the items that she'd just purchased. Melissa nodded her head approvingly at the red, sheer negligee and sweet smelling Angel Gold perfume inside of the bag. Since her only credit card was maxed out, Melissa was forced to use cash, which left her pretty much broke. She opened her purse and saw that she only had one lonely ten dollar bill left.

"Damn! Now I gotta go to the fuckin' bank," she complained. She was halfway to the bank when her cell phone rang.

"Hello," she answered sexily. "I'll be there in ten minutes," she responded, before ending the call. She knew that it would probably take her closer to twenty minutes to get home, but she figured a little anticipation wouldn't kill him. After hanging up from Richard, Melissa called her sister Tori. Tori was the assistant manager at Trustwell Bank. She cashed the paychecks of the police officers who didn't have direct deposit, but for her sister, she went that extra mile. As soon as her sister answered the phone, Melissa started blabbing.

"Hey, girl! Listen; I need you to go into my account and take out a hundred…"

"I can't talk right now," Tori said, cutting her off.

"I'm not asking yo' ass to talk; I'm asking you to bring a hundred dollars to the back…"

"I said I can't talk!" Melissa held her cell phone away from her ear and looked at it.

"The fuck wrong with you, bitch?"

"Melissa, I really have to go! Just make sure you lock up when you leave." Melissa quickly hung up and dialed 911. She and Tori had developed a code phrase just in case Melissa happened to call her in the middle of a robbery.

"911, what is your emergency?"

"Yes, this is Officer Melissa Watkins from the fourth district! I've just received confirmation that Trustwell Bank is currently being robbed! I need all surrounding patrol cars dispatched there immediately!"

Melissa ended the call and hit the gas. To keep the element of surprise on her side, she decided to use the back door key her sister had given her to enter the bank. Her car screeched to a halt three blocks down. Melissa jumped out of her car and bolted toward the rear of the bank. With every step she took, she was increasingly pissed thinking about how her plans were getting derailed by a fucking low-life criminal. After unlocking the door, Melissa pulled out her service weapon.

Maybe I can take this asshole down in time to still get me some dick later on, Melissa thought as she slowly opened the door.

$$$

The fur ball on top of the Santa Claus hat Butch was wearing flopped to the side as he cocked his head. Instinctively, the woman had answered her cell phone when it went off. It was from sheer habit. At least, that was the lie that she'd told him.

"You think I'm stupid, bitch?" he asked. When she didn't answer him in what he felt was a timely manner, Butch kicked her in the stomach. The woman fell to her knees in pain.

"I asked you a question, hoe! You think I'm stupid?"

Unable to answer his question with the wind knocked out of her, the woman silently shook her head. Butch had been listening closely to every word that was said. He replayed the conversation between her and whomever she was talking to back in his mind. One sentence stood out to him.

"Y'all got a back door to this place?" he asked, already knowing the answer. The woman weighed her options carefully. If she lied and got caught, it would not only put her sister in danger, but it would also put her in more danger than she was already in. Since her sister was a trained cop and she wasn't, she decided to play it safe. With trembling hands, she pointed in the direction of the rear exit.

"I see you're not a totally dumb bitch after all! Here, make ya'self useful," he said, pushing the bag of money into her arms. "Lead Santa Claus to the North Pole, bitch! And you better hope it ain't one of them exploding dye packs in here 'cause if it is, yo' head is gonna explode right along with this fake ass money!"

With Butch's pistol pointed directly at the back of her head, Tori slowly walked down the corridor and to the rear door. Just as they got there, it opened.

"Freeze!" Melissa shouted, raising her gun.

"Nah, bitch, you freeze!" Butch cocked his gun and placed the end of the barrel to Tori's temple.

"God, no, please!" Tori shouted.

"Shut up, bitch! And you, drop that damn heat!"

"Okay! Just calm down."

Melissa knew that she had no wins in this situation. All she could hope for was that her back up got there in time to change the odds.

Melissa put her gun on the floor and held up her hands. Butch smirked. He knew that there was a good chance that Melissa had already called the robbery in and it would just be a matter of time before he was surrounded. There was no way he was going to let that shit happen. Without even blinking, he fired a single round into Melissa's forehead. Tori tried to scream but was quickly silenced when Butch slammed the butt of his gun into the back of her skull. Tori was unconscious before she hit the floor. Butch sprinted out of the door and looked around. When he spotted a car, he assumed correctly that it was Melissa's. He reached down into the dead woman's pocket and took her keys. A large smile crossed his face as he grabbed the bag of cash and sprinted toward her car. As soon as he jumped in, Melissa's cell phone, which she'd left on the seat began to ring. For shits and giggles, he clicked the answer button.

"I don't know what the fuck you gon' do, nigga, but that bitch ain't gon' do shit but die!"

Butch laughed maniacally as he ended the call. After starting the car, he peeled off down a back alley. Butch hung a right and headed for the freeway. Before he could get far, however, the sound of police sirens attacked his ears.

"Fuck!" Butch yelled, as he swerved through traffic. He might have gotten away had he not plowed into the back of a garbage truck he didn't see.

$$$

The muscles in Butch's forearms bulged as he balled up his fists tightly. He would give anything to be able to wrap his hands around the judge's neck right now. Even though he knew what kind of time he was facing for aggravated robbery and capital murder, it still angered him that the judge threw the book at him.

"Twenty-five to life," the judge announced, triumphantly. Led by Detective Wayne Morris, every cop who'd attended the trial jumped up and cheered.

Some of them didn't even like Melissa, but that didn't matter. She was still one of theirs and a lowlife thug had murdered her. For fear of police retaliation, Butch had informed his lawyer to tell Hershey to stay away. She didn't like it, but the lawyer convinced her that it was the right thing to do. As Butch listened to the cheers for his impending imprisonment, a sneer adorned his lips. As a defiant gesture, he turned and looked every one of the pigs in the eye. When his gaze fell on Detective Morris, the two of them locked eyes for what seemed like an eternity. The detective broke the staring contest by turning his line of sight toward the judge. The two of them nodded and exchanged smiles. The solidarity demonstration enraged Butch. Right then and there, he was convinced that they were in cahoots to give him the maximum sentence. Butch swore to himself that he would get even with them both. Out of the corner of his eye, Butch saw his lawyer take a deep breath and shrug as if to say, *oh, well*. That was a big mistake. Already feeling that he'd gotten fucked on the sentence, Butch's mind started playing tricks on him.

"The fuck you shaking yo' head fo', cracka? You in cahoots with these muthafuckas or something?"

Before the slim, gray-haired attorney could utter a response, Butch head butted him in the nose, breaking it instantly. The man fell to the floor in pain. He was barely on the floor five seconds before Butch started stomping him. After the third kick, every police officer in the room converged on him like flies on shit. They beat Butch something terrible. Had it not been for the judge commanding them to stop, they would have surely killed him. As Butch passed out, there was only one thing on his mind. Payback.

One Month Later

Under the watchful eyes of the prison guard, Butch sat across from Hershey, lamenting the fact that he may never see her again. Although his conviction was going through the appeals process, he knew that there wasn't a snowball's chance in hell that the verdict would be overturned. Even though they'd been granted conjugal visits on occasion, it wasn't the same. He couldn't touch her whenever he wanted. He missed her intimacy. He would give anything to be able to sleep in the same bed with her at night. He stared across the table at her lustfully. He'd been doing that from the moment she'd arrived. He drank in her body. He desperately wanted to touch her, but such actions were forbidden.

"Damn, I miss you, baby," he confessed, sadly. She, too, was sad. Tears sat in the corners of her eyes, just a blink away from falling.

"I miss you, too," she said, reaching across the table to touch his hand.

"No touching," a stern voice yelled from across the room.

"Bitch ass nigga," Butch mumbled. Hearing the guard suddenly put him back in payback mode.

"Listen, I'm going to need you to do something for me," he whispered. When he was sure that he had her undivided attention, he continued.

"You love me, baby?"

"You damned right I do."

"You still my ride-or-die bitch?"

"You damned skippy."

"When a muthafucka hurt me, they're hurting us, right?"

"You better believe it, baby."

"Okay. Here's what I need you to do," he whispered even lower. Hershey listened intently as Butch laid out his instructions. When he was done, he looked at her and saw concern in her eyes.

"You good with that?" He asked to be sure. After all, he was asking her to commit a felony.

"Yes, but are you good with it? I mean, are you sure you want me to do that?" Truth be told, Butch wasn't sure. He hated even thinking about what he was asking her to do, but the ends justified the means.

"Nah, I don't want you to, but it's necessary. Besides, there's a part two to my plan." Hershey smiled. That was music to her ears.

$$$

Detective Morris sat on a bar stool nursing his third shot of Patron. He'd been in a rut ever since Melissa's funeral. Although his fellow officers had tried to convince him that her death wasn't his fault, Wayne still blamed himself.

If only I hadn't dismissed her so harshly, she may still be alive, he thought.

"Oh, my God," a young lady sitting next to him said, while covering her mouth. Wayne was so absorbed in his own thoughts that he didn't realize someone had sat next to him. When he turned his head and looked at her, he saw that she was staring at the television that hung above the bar. He turned and looked at the same screen and was shocked to see a picture of the judge who had sentenced Melissa's killer.

"Hey, Randy, turn that up!" The bartender grabbed the remote and clicked the volume button a few times.

We repeat the breaking news. Judge Tracker was found dead on his bedroom floor this afternoon. His security cameras picked up this woman on as she left his residence.

Wayne squinted his eyes and looked closely at the attractive, African American woman. She was wearing a wig and sunglasses to disguise her appearance. He wanted to dive headfirst into the case but was powerless to do so. His captain was adamant that he take some time off in light of the situation.

"Wow, that's a damn shame. If a judge can get got, I damn sure ain't safe in this fuckin' city. I gotta get the hell outta Cleveland," the woman sitting next to Wayne said.

"Yeah, Cleveland is pretty fucked up nowadays, pretty lady." Wayne hadn't meant to add 'pretty lady' to the end of his comment, but he couldn't help but notice the obvious. The woman was gorgeous.

"Let me get another one, Randy," Wayne slurred, before getting up and going to the bathroom. The liquor was starting to take effect. He felt bad for the judge and wondered if Butch had anything to do with what happened. He was hoping that his death was from natural causes, but his gut told him otherwise. He got back to the bar just in time to hear the woman rendering her thoughts on cops.

"The police force ain't shit in this city! They could give two shits about our black asses!"

The bartender tried to shut her up before it was too late, but was unsuccessful.

"Sorry you feel that way," he said. Wayne looked at her tight frame and became aroused. Instantly, he thought about taking her home and bouncing her up and down on his lap. In addition to feeling guilty about Melissa, Wayne was also feeling extremely horny. He needed to release bad and jacking off wasn't cutting it. He needed to bust a nut, either by penetrating a woman or getting a blowjob from one.

"I just happen to be one of Cleveland's finest." The woman looked at the bartender who simply nodded.

"Oh. I guess I should apologize. Sorry. I'm just tired of seeing or hearing about good people getting killed in these streets. Accept my apology?"

"Nope. Not unless you let me buy you a drink," Wayne offered. "What's your name?"

"Sandra, and thanks."

"Give the lady whatever she's drinking." Just then, a dark-skinned woman walked into the bar and stood directly behind Wayne. It was a good twenty seconds before anyone knew she was there.

"May I help you, ma'am?" the bartender asked. Wayne and Sandra both turned around and looked at the woman. She stared at Wayne a few more seconds before speaking.

31

"No, I got what I came here for," she said, before turning around and heading for the exit.

"Who the fuck was that bitch, your wife or something?" Sandra asked.

"Nah, I ain't ever seen her before."

Sandra shrugged and downed the rest of her drink. She then turned to Wayne.

"Look, I'm too old for games. Are you going to ask me back to your place or not?"

Wayne nearly spit out the rest of his drink. Her question caused his dick to harden immediately. He took out his wallet, paid their tab, and pretty much dragged her out of the door. Meanwhile, a vengeful set of eyes watched as Wayne pulled off. The mysterious woman from the bar tailed him from a three car distance. When he pulled into his driveway, she committed the address to memory and kept going. Pay back was coming soon.

$$$

After bringing herself to an unfulfilling, yet much needed orgasm, Hershey sat on the side of the bed staring at the floor. Every thought she had was of Butch and how she would give anything to be with him again. He mattered to her. He was the only thing that mattered to her.

Most women would have had a severe problem completing the task that he'd asked her to do, but not Hershey. Not only was she a ride-or-die-bitch, she was a jump in front of a bullet for her man type of bitch. Feeling the sudden urge to drink, Hershey got up and walked toward her kitchen.

The light from the open refrigerator hit her naked body and cast a seductive shadow on the wall. She took out a bottle of beer and turned it up. Hershey looked sexy as hell standing there naked, chugging a bottle of beer. After quenching her thirst, Hershey walked into the living room and stood in front of her Christmas tree.

She didn't know what Butch's plan was, but she hoped that it meant he would be home for Christmas. The date was December 23rd. It had been three weeks since he'd given her his instructions. She was just getting ready to head back to her bedroom when she felt a hand snake around her neck.

"Don't fucking move, bitch." Hershey froze. Her heart nearly burst through her chest. "Do you know the penalty for killing a fucking judge?"

Hershey took a deep breath. She didn't want to anger the intruder, so she figured she better answer.

"Yeah, I know the penalty, but the muthafucka deserved it!" The intruder leaned down and whispered into her ear.

"You damned right he did, baby."

A large smile popped onto Hershey's face. She was so alarmed by the intruder that it had taken her a minute to catch the voice. She spun around on him so fast, their heads almost collided.

"Butch! Oh, my God, baby, you're home! How did you get out?"

Butch went on to tell Hershey about Hector, a Mexican he met while in prison. Hector was the nephew of a drug lord in Mexico named Jose Rivera.

He had been working on a plan to break out of prison for the past two months. When he did get out, he was going to flee to Mexico and work in his uncle's organization making fifty thousand dollars a week. Butch's eyes lit up. He would have to rob three banks to make that kind of bread. He slyly asked if he thought his uncle could use another soldier in his army.

"I'm sure he can. One word from me and you're in there like hot pussy," Hector had told him. "But for me to do that, it's going to cost you." Butch had already figured that. He'd learned a long time ago that nothing in this life was free.

"How much, amigo?"

"Five grand."

"You got a deal."

The two of them shook hands to seal the deal.

"Oh, there is just one more thing, my friend. My uncle has one condition that anyone who works for him has to follow."

Butch listened in stunned silence as Hector laid it out for him. It was the dumbest shit he'd ever heard in his life. It also meant that he had a major decision to make.

"Did you do what I asked you to do?"

"Of course, baby. I told you I'd do anything for you." Butch felt like shit. He quickly brushed his feeling to the side and thought about the big picture.

"Let's go to bed. I've been dreaming about digging into that wet pussy for two months now."

As soon as they entered the bedroom, the two of them went at it like wild animals. Lewd sex acts, dirty talk, and earth shattering orgasms filled the night and part of the next day. Then, on Christmas morning, it would be time to put the finishing touches on his master plan.

CJ Hudson

Christmas Day

It had been barely a month since they'd met in the bar, but Detective Wayne Morris and Sandra had really hit it off. They'd been together every day with the exception of Christmas Eve. Detective Morris hadn't been this happy in quite some time. He would often look in the mirror at himself and smile. He couldn't believe that he'd fallen for a woman he'd met in a bar while trying to drown himself in a mixture of liquor and his own guilt. Although he hated to admit it, Detective Morris had become smitten with Sandra. It wasn't just her cloud nine sex game and volcano fire head that drew him into her web, although those things helped. She was much more interesting than any woman he'd ever met, including Melissa. He hadn't forgotten about Melissa, but he was finally getting over his guilt about her death.

Although he hadn't put up a Christmas tree, Detective Morris was overcome with the holiday spirit. He'd been playing the CD, *a Motown Christmas,* all morning. He was slightly disappointed because he couldn't get Sandra to spend the night with him. She'd told him that her mother was sick and that she didn't want her to be alone. He understood but was still disappointed. Sandra promised that she would come over and spend Christmas morning with him and he was looking forward to it. She even told him that she had a special Christmas present for him. Detective Morris had become so infatuated with Sandra that he pried open his wallet and bought her a very expensive pair of diamond earrings. In all, the gift set him back fifteen hundred dollars, but in his opinion, she was well worth it. Detective Morris nearly sprained his ankle when he heard his doorbell ring and jumped up to answer it. When he opened the door, he nearly fainted at the sight of her. In his eyes, Sandra got more and more beautiful every time he saw her.

It had only been a day and a half since he'd last saw her, but to him, it felt like two months. She'd put the sex on him so good then, that it was a major task just for him to think of anything else except her.

"I missed you," he said, smiling from ear to ear.

"Oh yeah? What did you miss about me?"

"Everything."

Detective Morris grabbed her hand and pulled her inside. After closing and locking the door behind her, he spun around and cupped her face in his hands. He leaned down and kissed her passionately.

"I've got something for you," he said, leading her over to the couch. When they got there, he motioned for her to have a seat. When she did, he reached down and picked up a black, velvet box sitting on the table.

"Here, baby. Merry Christmas." When Sandra opened the box, her face lit up. Her smile warmed Detective Morris' heart.

"Thank you, baby," she said, hugging him tightly. "Now, it's time for your gift. I'll be right back," she said, as she got up and walked toward the door. Detective Morris waited patiently for her get back. His manhood hardened as he thought about lying her down in his bed and making sweet love to her. His daydream soon turned into a nightmare when he heard Sandra scream. Instinctively, he jumped up off of the couch and rushed toward the sound of her voice. His heart nearly stopped when he saw her being held from behind at gunpoint.

"'Sup, bitch ass nigga? Remember me?" Detective Morris frowned. He would never forget the face of the man who'd killed his fellow police officer and former lover. And if he didn't think fast, he was about to lose his current lover.

"Yeah, I remember you, scumbag. You okay, baby?"

"Muthafucka, ain't nothing wrong with this bitch!" Butch yelled, as he pushed Sandra in his direction. Morris caught her just as she fell. Enraged, he took a step toward Butch.

"Nigga, I wish you would." Butch cocked his gun, walked up to Morris, and slapped him across the face. The detective stumbled, but he didn't fall. He wasn't going to give Butch the satisfaction.

"Oh, you a tough muthafucka, huh? Move, muthafucka! You, too, bitch," he said, ushering them toward the living room. As soon as they got there, Butch slapped Morris upside the head again. This time, the detective did fall. Sandra rushed to his side to make sure that he was okay.

"Leave him alone, you bastard!" she cried. Butch let out a roaring laugh.

"You okay?" Sandra asked. When she got close enough, Morris whispered in her ear.

"Baby, I'm going to try to distract him. When I do, I want you to reach in between my sofa, take out my spare gun, and blow his fuckin' brains out." Before Sandra even had a chance to protest, Morris pretended to go into cardiac arrest.

"Nigga, what the fuck wrong with you? I know damned well you ain't about to die on me! Nah, fuck that! I want the pleasure of killing yo' ass!"

Butch walked over to Morris and snatched him up by the collar. Morris was clutching his chest, giving an Oscar worthy performance. He slumped down to the floor, making it hard for Butch to hold him up.

"Muthafucka, get up!"

When Butch tried to use his other hand for extra strength, Morris made his move. Grabbing the gun with both hands, he pushed it up toward the ceiling. The tussle continued as the two of them fell to the floor. Butch was surprised at the detective's strength. The two men were pretty even in size, but Butch had an edge that Morris didn't and never would have.

A strong desire not to go back to prison. Just thinking about being a rat trapped inside Amerikkka's cage was enough to give Butch the added strength to overpower the detective. He stunned Morris by biting him on the bridge of the nose. Morris screamed in pain. He was down, but not out. Morris knew that if he didn't win this battle, not only was he a dead man, Sandra would most certainly be killed as well. In a last ditch effort to save their two lives, he grabbed Butch's nuts and yanked as hard as he could. Butch screamed to the high heavens. He'd never felt so much pain in his life. Sensing the opportunity to gain the upper hand for good, Morris yanked again. The second yank sapped Butch's strength and forced him to release the gun. When he looked back, Sandra was standing there holding the gun that was hidden in the couch. Her hand was shaking as she pointed it at Butch. Morris slowly got up and staggered toward the couch. It took him a full minute to recover from the fight.

"I hope you liked prison, asshole, because you're about to go right back. Baby, cover this asshole."

Morris then laid Butch's gun on the table and picked up his cell phone. He was just about to call for backup when he felt cold hard steel press against his temple.

"Put it down." Morris froze. Something was terribly wrong here. He had to be imagining this.

"Sandra…what?"

"Put it down, muthafucka!" She yelled, pressing the gun harder into his temple. Slowly, Morris let his phone fall to his side. He couldn't believe what was happening. The woman he was in love with was betraying him and he had no idea why. He looked over at Butch, who now had a shit eating grin on his face. Sandra, AKA Hershey, picked up Butch's gun and went to stand by his side. She'd played her part to perfection.

It involved quite a bit of sacrifice on her part, as she had to sleep with him to gain his full trust; but, it was worth it if it would help her lover get even with Morris. Morris looked at her and saw a completely different woman than the one he'd been sleeping with. Her eyes were no longer loving, but hard and cold. It had all been a magnificent ruse. An elaborate scheme to get Morris to drop his guard so that it would be easier for Butch to get his revenge.

"I would waste time telling you how good this shit is going to feel, but I got shit to do," Butch said before shooting Morris in the groin. "That was for fuckin' my bitch while I was locked up, nigga! And this is for getting me locked up in the first place!"

"No, baby, let me," Hershey said, as she shot Morris in the forehead with his own gun. Butch walked over and spat on Morris' corpse. His plan of revenge was now complete.

"Let's get the fuck outta here, baby."

Butch and Hershey made hurried steps to the front door. As soon as Butch opened it, he was staring down the barrel of a .38 special. Instinctively, he jumped back. Tori walked in and slammed the door behind her.

"Who the fuck are…" Before she even completed the question, Hershey realized where she had seen the woman before. "Wait a minute. You're that bitch that came to the bar when I first started working that nigga over," she said, pointing at Morris.

"Good memory," she said, pointing her gun at Butch. The instinct to protect her man outweighed any fear that Hershey was feeling. She slyly moved in between Butch and Tori.

"Ah, ain't that sweet? Move the fuck out of the way, dumb bitch!"

Tori came to the detective's house with the sole intent of getting revenge for her sister.

She had no idea that Butch had broken out of jail, but since he was here, she was going to kill him, too. Although she knew that Butch, and not Morris, had pulled the trigger, she blamed them both for her sister's death.

"You don't remember me, do you, asshole?"

Butch narrowed his gaze on her face. Then, like a tidal wave, her face rushed back to his memory. It was the woman from the bank.

41

"Yeah, I remember you. You that bitch from the bank. How's that bump on the head I gave you?" he smirked.

"Watch ya' mouth, muthafucka! I came here to get even with that punk ass cop over there, but imagine my surprise when I see this bitch come in here and you follow her a few minutes later. I guess good things do happen on Christmas," Tori said.

Tears were now streaming down her cheeks. She may have been sad, but her eyes also said that she was serious about what she was there to do. She had a crazed look in her eyes and when Butch looked into them, he knew that she wasn't just issuing idle threats. If he didn't do something and do it soon, he would never make it to Mexico. Without warning, he shoved Hershey in the back, causing her to fall into Tori. Inadvertently, Tori's gun went off. The bullet entered Hershey's body and crashed into one of her ribs, smashing through it and lodging in one of her organs. Hershey fell to the floor, grabbing her side. Tori was momentarily stunned. She couldn't believe what Butch had just done. Her hesitation was just enough time for Butch to pull his gun and fire two shots into her face. Butch then looked down at Hershey, who was now struggling to breathe. The shock and hurt in her eyes broke Butch's heart. She was his ride-or-die, his partner in crime, his lover, and his best friend. When she met him, it had never, in a million years, occurred to her that the day would come when he would make her the sacrificial lamb.

As much as Butch loved and cared for Hershey, he just couldn't give up the chance to be in Jose's organization. Jose's rule was a simple one. No outside bitches. If one of his workers wanted to fuck, they would fuck one of the many women in his harem. Every single one of them knew that their only job was to please the workers. No feelings would ever be caught by them. Jose felt that women with feelings were dangerous to his organization, so he forbade his workers to bring in their own women.

"I'm so sorry, baby. Merry Christmas," Butch said, as he shot Hershey in the head. Tears fell from his face as he turned and walked toward his car. Feeling like shit, he called Hector and told him that he was on his way.

THE END

"When thoughts become things, the evil manifested bares all secrets."

–E. Raye Turonek

The Beginning

The Mead moon shined brightly, that foggy night in Metamora Township. A ray of light combed the cornfields in search of its operatives miscreant. Soon the beams of illumination would be upon him, he feared. The thirteen years old, John Henry Butcher ran as fast as he possibly could, with no actual destination in mind. The beads of sweat running down his forehead drenched his face. The sweat had saturated his plaid shirt making it visible at his pits.

A deep raspy voice roared from inside of him, "Woo Whoooo! Run, Henry… Run" John Henry paused, kneeling on ryegrass and dead corn stalk, panting yet at the same time gasping for what little breath he could catch. "Oh no, not your asthma again… Poor Henry," the voice teased. "Let me take a stab at it," it demanded, boring even further into his psyche.

John Henry used his hands to cover both ears as if that would purge the voice from his mind. "Shut up! Please, just shut up," he pleaded, wincing from the arrant intensity of its voice.

John Henry questioned why he was running in the first place. A swift glance at his bloody hands jogged his memory. He could hear the dogs barking. *They're getting closer*, he thought.

Where would John Henry hide?

"They're going to catch you, Henry Butcher! You'll pay for what you've done," Auty Rae took her turn, boasting from her post, awaiting her turn to take over. "You should have listened to me, boy."

Suddenly, a tap on the shoulder sent a then lucid John Henry Butcher reeling into spasms. He flopped wildly from the plastic pastel common room chair onto the white, immaculate, hard linoleum flooring.

Three additional male orderlies hurried over to assist. "Quick, get Dr. Kanya," one of the orderlies instructed his counterpart as he held John Henry down with the aid of two others.

The other patients quickly backed away, huddling in pairs with their hands perched firmly at their lips, making the widespread chatter inaudible.

A loud buzz sounded, followed by a click just before Dr. Visha Kanya rushed in through the security door. Dr. Kanya was a beautiful Indian American woman in her mid-thirties. She'd spent several years caring for Henry. They used to be the best of friends during their early years... Sweethearts since elementary school in fact.

"Keep the patient restrained. It'll be okay, John Henry. Calm down," she instructed, looking deep into his bright hazel eyes. When kissed by the sun they seemed golden, reminding her of the time they spent playing in the cornfields as adolescents. It was hard for her to see him so broken, but still, she was determined to stick by John Henry's side.

48

Dr. Kanya pulled a syringe from her lab coat pocket. "I'm administering five milligrams of midazolam."

One of the orderlies tugged at the waist belt of John Henry's pants. "Gently now," Dr. Kanya instructed with a warning note in her voice. She knelt beside him, then plunged the syringe into John Henry's left buttocks. The serum had made its way through his body rendering him compliant in seconds. His arms relaxed, his chest folded inward as his eyes fixed themselves on Dr. Kanya's. Her deep brown eyes always seemed to comfort him. He trusted her. After all, he was the single reason she'd decided to become a psychiatric doctor.

"I'm here, John Henry. It's okay, now," she assured him as her petite hand lightly caressed his shoulder.

"Please escort the patient to his room. He needs to rest now." The orderlies carefully lifted John Henry from the floor, escorting him from the common room.

Dr. Kanya stood but waited, collecting herself so that her emotions wouldn't surface. She lowered her head, causing her brown bobbed hair to hide the sides of her face.

Once she'd taken in a deep breath then exhaled, slowly gathering herself, she used her finger to tuck her hair behind her ear exposing only the right side of her face. She refused to let the other patients see her unhinged.

The loud buzz from the security door seemed to rush Dr. Kanya over, then out of the room. The other patients calmed as the click of her heels faded from earshot. 10:45 p.m. It was almost time for "lights out."

Chapter I

Early Christmas Eve, John Henry lay awake in his twin sized bed, covered up to his neck - a prisoner to his insomnia. With his body completely wrapped, he was able to capture the warmth his pewter-colored blanket provided him. The Ambien induced nightmare from the previous night still lingered in John Henry's psyche. He could hear the nurse's shoes squeaking across the linoleum floor, down the hallway as she checked to make sure every patient was nestled securely in their quarters. He longed to hear the click of Dr. Kanya's three-inch heels.

Until then, he'd wallow in the thoughts of the past. Memories of them as children. Before the accident, before he was confined to juvenile detention, before Visha Kanya married his older, more sane brother, Jack Jacob Butcher.

Jack was John Henry's exact opposite. Jack had thick, short dark hair whereas John had thin, shoulder length, sandy blonde locks. Jack's dark brown eyes could command an entire room, whereas John's vulnerability was plainly seen through his own. Jack's deep olive complexion perfectly complimented his chiseled physique. John Henry's milky pale skin showcased a tall, large build with no real muscle tone, an effect of the medications, moreover lack of exercise.

John's descent began at Jack rise. Visha Kanya had always been the object of their affections. Although Visha liked them both, she had a special place in her heart for John. His characteristics were unmatched. He was kind with a disposition that showed a readiness to help the weak. Jack, being the older more dominate sibling, was consumed with jealousy. He exuded the

50

"me first" temperament. Still, he was cunning which usually landed him on top.

***

At thirteen years of age John Henry was committed to St. Mary's, the only mental asylum in Lapeer County which housed the towns mentally challenged. With the charges reduced to manslaughter, he was ultimately convicted. Sentenced to eighteen years detainment, six in juvenile detention to be followed by twelve at St. Mary's Psychiatric Hospital.

It all happened so fast - events that would imprison John for the remainder of his adolescence, dragging down with it the beginning of his life as an adult.

One day, Jack, John, and Visha were playing around outside at the paper mill. They would usually play tag or hide-n-seek, but when they were feeling particularly brave, they'd climb the lumber piles, which towered well over fifteen feet high. July 27, 1995, was the day Jack Jacob Butcher decided to teach his little brother John who's boss.

"Hey, guys, who's up for climbing the lumber stacks? Last one up looses and has to face the music!"

John looked confused. "Music? What mu…" Before he could finish his query, Visha and Jack had already darted off toward the tallest lumber pile they could find. Visha was first. Her Chuck Taylors kicked up dust like no other. Jack trailed close behind. He could have easily gotten in front of Visha but had ulterior motives which prompted him to lag behind.

"Last one up is a rotten egg," Visha playfully reminded them as she trotted backward, before turning back around, taking off into a full sprint.

Once her right foot caught the first log, she pulled herself up with ease. There was no stopping her.

Jack and John were just about neck and neck as they climbed the lumber stack. He waited for Visha to reach the top, then seized his opportunity. Jack stomped down on John Henry's foot. The disbelief in his eyes during his descent brought Jack a feeling of satisfaction that would carry him confidently through the years. He'd damaged John Henry for life. Once John hit the ground, a few logs had fallen on top of him. The damage to his frontal lobe changed him forever. The kind, chivalrous John became withdrawn, apprehensive, even aggressive at times.

Visha was John Henry's Achilles' heel. From that point forward, anyone who messed with her would suffer his wrath.

***

6:30 a.m. Still, John heard no high-heels clicking down the hall toward his room. He turned his head to look out of the window. There was a whiteout. He couldn't see past the snowfall that morning. *I hope Visha is okay*, he thought. He knew how much she hated driving in the snow but secretly hoped it wouldn't keep her from coming in to work that day. Only one more day, till he'd be rid of St. Mary's for good.

John Henry Butcher was going home for Christmas.

He was more than eager to be free yet nervous about being able to hold himself together. Had he forgotten to take his medication just once, it could all come crashing down. The others would most certainly be waiting to take over. Auty Rae Butcher and Sylus Ransford Butcher, that's what they called themselves. Those who'd witnessed their manifestation feared John's alters.

52

That is, all except Jack; he seemed to fear nothing, especially his feeble-minded younger brother. John harbored a particular hatred for Jack Jacob. The mere mention of his name would curl John's upper lip in disdain.

John had to keep his temper under control if he wished to remain free once released. So, he was determined to do the best he could to function as a productive citizen.

7:00 a.m., It was time to drag his restless body out of bed, brush his teeth then prepare himself for breakfast. Not only was it Christmas Eve, but that day also happened to be maple cakes Monday. Most of the patients were looking forward to their morning meal. So, they all lined up in the hallway to be counted, then lead down to the cafeteria.

Betty, a sixty-year-old German nurse that worked midnights, was exhausted by that time of the morning. Her shift was to end at 8 a.m. and not a minute later as far as she was concerned. Betty led them down the hall but didn't utter a word. She walked, then they followed without testing her patience.

A festive Christmas decor lined the walls, near the ceilings, all the way to their destination. The red, gold and blue lights seemed to lift the patients' spirits. While traveling the length of the hallway, the majority of them shuffled along with their chins aloft in awe at the beautiful colors. The cafeteria had a large, upside down Christmas tree, right in the center of the room. Had it been a couple of feet more in length it would touch the floor. The circular pile of empty gift boxes that sat atop the gold felt tree skirt almost made them feel as if they'd actually open presents, as a family, from one to another on Christmas morning. Christmas Day was almost upon them.

At breakfast, the nurses were very careful as they checked each of the patient's wristbands, to ensure they were doling out the correct medication. One by one the nurses watched each resident swallow their morning dose of meds.

John couldn't wait for the medicine to kick in so that the malnourished, anxiety-ridden motor mouth sitting next to him would finally calm down. Oliver was his name. He sat next to John every day. At breakfast, lunch, dinner, even during community group, he was there beside him, jittery and as red as a beet. The entire time Oliver would ramble on in great detail the many things that brought on his anxiety. Of course, none of the medicine was strong enough to combat his worries.

"Oh no, I hope they didn't put any pepper on my eggs. I hate pepper. I'd much rather have salt. Salt is good. As long as it's sea salt… Sea salt is best…. I can't have Iodized salt. It's the processing. The processing eliminates minerals. And the added additive that prevents clumping will kill me. I told them it'd kill me. They want to kill me…"

"I really think they are trying to…," he whispered, leaning in close to John before turning his volume back up, "They're trying to kill us all!"

"They'll kill us all," Oliver, hollered out in distress."

"Cue the orderlies," John mumbled in an exasperated tone. He, unlike Oliver, had allowed his medicine to take hold.

Two orderlies rushed in, the first a tall bald African American fellow by the name of William. Everyone called him Willie instead. Willie was in his mid-thirties; in fact, he'd attended school with John Henry, Visha and Jack Jacob.

Pete with the salt and pepper hair wasn't far behind. He was an older gentleman. You know the kind that has to use the restroom every time he goes into the supermarket…

Pete was only in his fifties, but they were all waiting for him to retire. Although he was a bit rough with the patients, you could say he would only beat his chest to assert his authority around once a day, no matter how little it was.

They each picked an arm snatching Oliver up from his seat, post haste. The armless, green, plastic stack chair with the metal legs made a loud bang when it hit the floor.

That got Annie all upset. Annie was beautiful, even in her early forties. She had long blonde hair with hazel eyes; the most honest you'd ever see.

Annie suffered from a type of anxiety that caused excessive worrying. She stood, "Oh no, they're going to hurt him… I know it! They're really going to hurt him this time. I'm sure of it!"

"They will," she proclaimed as her bulging eyes seemed to glaze over.

"Will you do nothing, John Henry?!" With a quick reluctant jolt of her arms, Annie raised her hands to her lips to quiet her pleas. She cried out in a low moan as her head began to shake, "No… No… I'm sure of it. They're going to hurt him. Pete will!"

"Quiet Annie, or you'll be next," a low lull rumbled out from behind her.

Annie straightened up, "Oh no… I'm next… I'm sure of it," she whispered with worried eyes before inching slowly back down into her seat.

Once seated, Annie lowered her hands to her lap, then clenched her mouth closed using her teeth to bite down on her lips.

By the time Willie and Pete escorted Oliver out of the cafeteria, into the comfort of a Seroquel induced coma, the residents had calmed themselves all on their own. Most finished their pancakes then washed them down with a watered down cup of coffee. Very few opted for orange juice, being that they were attempting to chase a caffeine high.

9:00 a.m. Time for group therapy. Group therapy or community group, which was what the residents called it, was split into groups of five. John Henry's group consisted of himself, Oliver, Annie, Macy, and Gregory.

Of course, Oliver wasn't present that day.

Annie sat quietly still fearing she'd be next. John Henry stared at the entrance waiting for Visha to walk through the security door. Finally, the click of her heels were heard coming up the hallway, nearing the room where group discussion would be held. Where John Henry waited patiently...

"Here she comes," Gregory announced. "Coming to pick our brains, invade our memories," he complained. "Huh," Gregory huffed. "As if she has the right..."

John Henry didn't utter a word but cut his eyes toward Gregory before completely turning his head that way. The stare down John bestowed was enough to shut him up for the time being.

Gregory, in his early forties, was skinny and pale. Due to his brown tarnished teeth along with a wrinkled profile, his blonde hair and blue eyes did nothing to compliment his looks. He suffered from depression. After several attempts at taking his own life, he was finally committed to St.

56

Mary's. Gregory was a high school jock who'd dabbled in prescription drugs which ultimately cost him his football scholarship. Everything went downhill from there. His longtime girlfriend broke up with him, once she'd realized her meal ticket was no longer.

Feeling he had nothing left he allowed the drugs to take over. That's when the attempts at suicide began.

His love/hate relationship with Dr. Kanya was no secret amongst the residents and staff. No one worried too much though. They all knew Dr. Kanya was off limits. John Henry made sure of that.

The security door buzzed as Dr. Kanya entered the room. Everyone remained quiet until she was seated amongst the group's circle, right next to John Henry, of course. Dr. Kanya crossed her legs, placing her clipboard on her lap.

"Hello, everyone! How's everyone doing today? I've heard you all had an eventful breakfast."

No one said a word, so Dr. Kanya turned to Annie.

"Annie, would you like to talk about what you witnessed at breakfast?"

Annie shook her head. "No," she answered with worried eyes.

"It's okay. I assure you, no one is in any trouble," Dr. Kanya replied.

"Then where is Oliver?" Annie rebuffed. Dr. Kanya looked to Annie with a quizzical expression. "Well…. Where is he? Did PETE hurt him?"

"Annie. Oliver is doing just fine. I promise."

Annie relaxed. She crossed her legs, then let her hands rest in her lap, mirroring Dr. Kanya. Not only did she trust Dr. Kanya, Annie admired her as well.

Dr. Kanya had caught Macy's look of skepticism. "Macy… What about you? Have you anything to add."

"I didn't see nothing, so I ain't saying nothing," Macy rebuffed.

Macy, an eighteen-year-old African American girl, was committed to St. Mary's a few months prior. She kept her natural hair braided in cornrows that stretched down the center of her back.

Although Macy was what you would call a beautiful brown eyed girl, she had a hard exterior that was seemingly unpenetrable. The sexual abuse she'd suffered at the hands of her uncle proved detrimental to her mental state. At the point of anger, she'd black out, unable to remember the events that took place. Her parents reluctantly had her committed hoping she could be cured of her condition.

During one of her episodes, Macy seriously injured two fifteen-year-old boys. Their crime was teasing her homosexual younger brother. If there was one thing Macy refused to tolerate, it was the bullying of her younger brother. Even though she was just three years his prior, Macy felt it was her duty to protect him. She protected him the way she felt she should have been, yet never was.

"Macy… I completely understand. And that is your right," Dr. Kanya politely replied.

"What I would like to discuss is someone stealing my book. I don't mess with anyone's personal belongings, so I'd appreciate the same in return."

"What's the name of your book, Macy?"

"Compelled To Murder," Macy replied in the driest of tones.

"Macy... Do you think you should be reading a book that depicts such violence?" Dr. Kanya asked.

"It's a book. Fiction. Besides the things I've done were done before the reading of the book. Therefore, I really don't think it makes a difference."

"This is true. Okay, Macy... we'll keep an eye out for your book."

"I hope you'll find out who has it before I do. I don't appreciate being stolen from," Macy warned.

Annie's eyes filled with tears, "Oh, no..."

Only a few seconds had gone by, by the time she'd broken down completely. "I'm so sorry, Macy! I just wanted to read it. I was going to put it back. I swear. Please, don't hurt me!" Annie's voice trembled.

Macy looked Annie directly in the eyes, "I would never hurt you, Annie. You hear me. Never... Now stop crying, and get my book back to me... After you finish reading it, of course." Macy smiled, prompting a sniffling Annie to smile back.

"Look who's not so mean after all. I think we may have found Macy's soft spot," Dr. Kanya proudly proclaimed.

"Well, now that we've gotten that out of the way, are you guys ready for a group exercise?"

Everyone in the group, with the exception of John Henry, moaned expressing an unwillingness to participate.

"Aww... Come on, guys. It'll be quick and painless. I'd like everyone to open their notebooks, then write down a negative thought or dream you've recently struggled with. Everyone will take a turn reading theirs aloud; then we'll destroy the paper along with the negativity. Let's get started!"

Each one of them opened their notebook, then began to write.

Dr. Kanya let about five minutes pass, while she jotted down notes on her clipboard, before choosing who'd go first.

"Gregory, I'd like you to go first."

"Pick someone else," he responded without haste.

"Come on... You can do it," she urged him on.

"Very well then... In my dreams, I'm not alone. You're there with me, Visha," Gregory admitted. As Gregory continued to ramble on about how he and Dr. Kanya lived together through wedlock, in the kingdom of hell, John Henry lowered his head, taken away by his sub-conscience.

His body had begun to run hot from the inside. The light on the wobbling ceiling fan flickered. John could hear the slow playing of the piano in the background. It was Sylus's music, Beethoven's Moonlight Sonata. He'd waited there for his entrance key to drop.

Finally, Sylus Ransford Butcher crept from the darkest corner of the room. The bald entity stood at least ten feet high. His eyeballs were black, his skin; cold and pale. With his long right arm outstretched, Sylus slowly dragged his filthy monstrous hand across a wall in the room. He wore a plaid shirt and blood-stained overalls. The long metal pitchfork he pulled along his side had five points and stood as tall as his person. A rusted chain was attached to the pitchfork. At the end of that chain was a metal collar, which was clamped around the neck of an adolescent boy, Myron.

Myron was only fifteen when John Henry had taken his life by way of strangulation. Well, John Henry in the physical form, anyway. His soul belonged to Sylus. Myron too was bald, cold and pale. His pupils were pitch black. His naked frame was frail. You could see plainly his spine protruding from his back. The bones stuck out almost as much as Sylus's horns did from under the skin of his skull. Myron was always there with Sylus, quiet… never to utter a word. He stood behind Sylus where ever he'd surface, trembling in his white, mud saturated underwear. The rusted thick metal collar latched tight around his neck which made it impossible for him to lower his head. His eyelids were no longer. Therefore, his black pupils were never hidden. He stared at John Henry void of emotion as he walked along, behind Sylus.

Sylus made his way over to where Gregory sat, in the realm of reality still rattling off his dream, then knelt alongside him. He took in a big whiff of his stench. "You can smell his soul, John Henry. It is evil. He must come with us. It is his destiny," Sylus demanded.

"Stop!" Everything in the room had frozen still. Even Sylus. The sound from the piano faded into nothing. Auty lowered her hand. Her stone grey eyes seemed piercing to John Henry.

At that moment, it was all he could give his attention to. "John Henry, you must be smart. There is no need to behave so brutally."

Auty Rae Butcher wore a long grey dress that touched her ankles, but it was covered in most part by the white apron that tied around her neck and waist. The white bonnet atop her head covered the front of her long, auburn hair, which traveled down her back just past her butt. She was barefoot. Like her short fingernails, her toenails were thick and black. Although her feet were soiled, they never touched the ground. She seemed to float there, an inch from the floor.

"Release me, witch! Release me at once," Sylus roared in a deep rumbling voice.

Auty raised her finger to her lips. "Hush now, Sylus. I have not allowed you to speak," she instructed with a calm, tender, steady voice.

Sylus's cleft lip twitched as he snarled at Auty through the holes of his absent nose. His sharp pointy tarnished teeth grinned together once he'd attempted to try to release the hold Auty had imposed on him.

"Don't listen to him, John Henry. Sylus can only take you so far. True power is not garnered by standing with the greats. It is bestowed while sitting amongst the broken. These souls are yours for the taking. They are not for Sylus. When will you choose to absorb their power? Let me show you, John Henry." Auty propositioned with glowing eyes.

Auty Rae snapped her fingers, waking John from his dreamlike state.

With his consciousness restored, the lights flickered no more. His body had cooled to its usual temperature. He raised his head, staring directly at

Gregory. Gregory had noticed John's glare instantly, which caused him to stutter.

Dr. Kanya had taken notice to it as well, "John Henry, are you okay?" She inquired, touching her hand to his forehead. The cold sweat she felt alarmed her, although she gave no inkling of worry to the others.

"I'm fine, Visha," John Henry answered in a dull, steady voice, still glaring at Gregory, who'd shut up by that time.

Calling her by her first name asserted a kind of kinship to her that only he possessed. It let them all know how much he adored her.

"John, I think it's best you lay down. I'd like everyone else to wait here so that we can continue, once I return," Dr. Kanya stood. "Come now, John Henry," Visha instructed with her hand reached out for him. John rose from his chair, grabbed Dr. Kanya's hand then allowed her to lead him out through the buzzing security door.

Macy's eyebrows wrinkled. "What the fuck was that?"

"Ahhh, it's nothing. He's nothing," Gregory boasted.

"HA! It didn't seem like nothing to me. And when did you develop a stuttering problem, Gregory? Today, I guess… huh? Huh… He's nothing alright. Nothing you want to mess with."

"Shut up, little girl! Before I give you something to worry about."

"Don't fight. Pleeeease," Annie pleaded.

"Boy, bye; ain't nobody worried about you! Calm down, Annie. He's a coward at best. We just saw that with our own eyes," she teased, starring Gregory down.

63

"AHHHHH!!!" Gregory yelled as he leaped up from his chair, lunging it across the room, sending it crashing into the wall behind him. He panted, staring at Annie and Macy with wild eyes, but only for a second before Pete had eagerly rushed in tackling him to the floor.

"That's it, buddy. It's night-night time for you," Pete announced.

Willie rushed in afterward, helping Pete to lift Gregory from the floor.

"Come on, Gregory. Stop showing off. What did I tell you? Cool and collected gets the ladies, not hot and bothered." Willie shook his head in disappointment as they led a disgruntled Gregory from the room.

***

2:00 p.m. Later that day visitation hour had come. John Henry rarely received a visit from loved ones. Although his mother still loved him, his father, Joseph Lyle Butcher, made certain he kept her busy enough to miss daily visiting hours. Joseph Lyle Butcher was dying of colon cancer. He hadn't much longer to live. So his mother, Verna Mae Butcher, stayed home doting on him most days. Besides, anytime she'd make time to visit by calling Jack Jacob over to keep an eye on his father, Jack would go on and on about how terrible a person John Henry was, ultimately convincing her to stay home. She'd allowed her husband and older son to alienate John Henry almost entirely from her life.

"Visha has it all under control," Jack would always say.

So, John Henry's visiting hour mostly consisted of him lying in bed while Visha sat at his bedside reading to him a book of his choice, which was usually something that contained a lot of romance with a smidgen of erotica. He liked it better that way instead.

John Henry had no desire to see the disappointment in his mother's eyes. Verna's disapproving glare was something she couldn't hide.

Dr. Visha Kanya enjoyed reading to John Henry. It kept him calm. Moreover, he felt comforted by her presence. That day as Visha read to him, she'd begun to cry. "Why the tears, Visha? Is it the story? Would you rather me choose another?" John Henry inquired.

"No, John Henry. It's not the story. But, these are my problems not your own. I'm supposed to be here to comfort you, not for you to comfort me. Besides, I'll be fine. I always am."

Willie walked past John Henry's room but backed up to take a peek in through the small window.

"Now, look at these two," he whispered to himself, as he shook his head with disapproval. "Christmas at the Butcher house should be pretty interesting this year. Wish I could be there to see Jack's face when his not so darling little brother walks through the door."

Whatever Dr. Kanya was saying to John seemed to put a frown on his face. His eyes had even begun to water. His look of adoration had turned to pity.

"What are you up to?" Pete blurted as he'd snuck up behind Willie.

Willie just about jumped out of his skin, he was so startled. He turned around without haste, "What the hell?! Don't you ever sneak up on me like that, Pete."

"Awww..." he exaggerated with his lips perched outward. "Did I scare the big ole baby?" Pete teased.

"I'm not scared of anything. Especially your old behind. Why are you here breathing your heated ass breath down my neck anyway, Dr. Strange? Aren't you supposed to be in the television room getting things ready for today's movie?"

"I am. But, I need some help with the wires. Come on. Show me how its done, my brother from another mother." Pete threw his arm around Willie's shoulder as they'd begun to walk up the hall.

"Oh, now I'm your brother? I go from a big ole baby to your brother real fast when you need something." Willie playfully furnished Pete a quick not so hard punch in his side, causing Pete to flinch then run ahead a few paces. "Come on, man. Cut it out. You know I'm getting old."

"Yeah, yeah… Lead the way, grandpa," he joked.

After Dr. Kanya had finished her story, she got up leaving a sleeping John to his dreams.

Not more than fifteen minutes later, his feet had begun to twitch. His head moved back and forth across the sweat drenched pillow. John Henry's nightmares were invading his afternoon nap.

It was the memories of Myron that had come from the past to grace its presence. He imagined Myron on top of Visha just as he was the day of his death.

He'd force himself on Visha, wearing only his tighty whities and a red V-neck t-shirt with his blue jean shorts hanging around his ankles. She laid pinned down on top of the hay pile, screaming at the top of her lungs when John Henry found them. With no hesitation, John Henry snatched him up by

66

the neck, tossing him across the old barn into a horse's stall. He seemed to have the strength of ten men.

Visha sat up fixing the buttons on her ripped plaid rayon top. "Stay, there," John Henry instructed. John walked into the horse stable closing the door behind him. "I'm sorry, man. Come on. I was just kidding around," Myron pleaded.

He didn't utter a word as he lifted Myron into the air by his neck.

John stood no taller than 5' 8" yet his own shadow depicted on the wall of the barn towered over them both. Myron dangled there, pulling at John's hands in an attempt to free his tight grasp from his throat. His face burned red as the veins protruded at the top of his forehead. No punches nor kicks had any effect on John Henry. He strangled Myron until the blood ran from his eyes. "Now you cry," John Henry demanded. Once Myron's body was limp, John Henry tossed him onto the hay pile.

"John Henry," Visha called out to him, waking him from his trancelike state. Her voice ended the trip down nightmare alley abruptly.

John Henry awoke in a cold sweat. His blond hair was drenched. He panted with hard steady breaths. "It's going to happen again, John Henry," Auty Rae whispered, under the cover of darkness from the corner of his room. "Look not to me for the answer, John Henry. There it lies." Auty eliminated a section of the floor underneath the chair where Dr. Kanya previously sat. A full syringe. There for the taking. "What will you do, John Henry?"

John calmed yet did not utter a word. He got up from his twin sized bed, grabbed the syringe then placed it in the pocket of his jeans.

"Careful now, John Henry. It's deadly," Auty warned.

Chapter II

7:00 p.m. It was quiet that night during dinner. It seemed as if everyone's medication was doing its job ensuring the tranquility of the evening.

With his head hovering over a plate of pepperoni pizza, Gregory sat sulking over the day's events. He used both arms as a barrier encircling his plate, feeling secure in the fact that he'd conveyed the message of his intent, which was to be left alone. That was until he'd realized John Henry was standing there across from him on the opposite side of the table. A nervous feeling had begun to boil up from the pit of his belly, yet he refused to show even an inkling of uneasiness.

Once John had taken his seat, Gregory exuded a noticeable amount of aggravation tossing the pizza down onto his plate, before straightening his posture only to challenge John Henry's purposeful glare.

After what felt like ten of the longest seconds he'd experienced in history, Gregory faltered, letting out a quick, nervous chuckle before attempting to reason his way through it. "You and I aren't so different, John. Ya, know, I get it," he admitted, taking a bite of his pizza while nodding his head in accord, "You're territorial. Dually noted... Let's just agree that this was all some big misunderstanding."

Still, John Henry's purposeful glare had yet to wane, leaving Gregory at an impasse.

"Great... It's good we got that all sorted out. Wouldn't want any bad blood between us, right? Besides, you're getting out of here tomorrow. No need to complicate things," he reminded John Henry, before snatching up his plate, as he'd gotten up from the table.

Although John Henry had maintained his silence as Gregory weaseled his way to a more comfortable area to finish his dinner, it was partly due to the truth he'd found in Gregory's last words. John had no desire to complicate things.

What if Auty were just trying to trick him into keeping himself locked up there for the rest of his life, he questioned. There, where his demons were free to torture him as he lay in confinement. John Henry had grown tired of living as a prisoner. His mind would never truly be free of his alters but at least he'd be able to move physically, without restraint. Come hell or high water, John Henry was going home for Christmas, and nothing was going to stop him.

3:00 a.m. Early that restless morning John Henry laid awake in bed curled up on his right side with only the light of the waning moon, which shined in through his slender rectangular window, to illuminate his quarters. The dead silence felt eerie. He'd not heard the squeaking of Betty's thick rubber soles coming up the hall.

Out of nowhere, a distinct CLICK. John Henry sat up, slowly tossing the blanket off of him, before letting his bare feet touch the cold linoleum flooring. He made his way over to the door, then peeked through the glass before turning the knob. It was open. Not even attempting to fight his curiosity John Henry opened the door, then crept up the dimly lit hallway, headed straight toward Visha's office. *I hope she's still here,* he thought.

Suddenly, the sound of the piano had begun to play in his psyche, Moonlight Sonata. Again, John's body burned from the inside. He leaned against the wall, before eventually succumbing to the dizziness he'd felt, sliding down onto the floor. His forehead was riddled with beads of sweat. Sylus was coming whether he liked it or not.

His monstrous shadow could be seen along the wall coming up the hallway toward John. John lowered his head, squeezing his eyes shut. "I'm okay," he told himself. "Pull it together, John."

When John opened his eyes, Sylus's elongated body had contorted itself in such a way that he was face to face with John yet still standing. He grabbed John up by the front of his linen button up pajama shirt lifting him into the air until he stood upright.

"Give me what I want, Johnny boy. Give me what I ask, and I'll leave you alone. Cross my blackened heart," he whispered, before vomiting a violent stream of blood straight across into John's face. He gagged as the blood flooded his eyes, nostrils, mouth, even John's hair was drenched once the blood had finished streaming. Finally, Sylus released his grip, letting John's body drop to the floor, then backed away allowing John sight of Myron, who's pointing finger illuminated the way. His black eyeballs perforated John's cranium, seemingly boring a hole until he'd relented, eventually getting up to follow the path presented.

John inched his way up the hall until another CLICK was heard on his right. He stopped, then peaked in through the glass on the door. There was someone in bed, nestled there comfortably. John turned back, changing his mind, only to be met with Sylus's pitchfork at the base of his abdomen. At that point he'd surmised, there was no way out of this nightmare. John Henry was to enact the will of Sylus.

71

He twisted the knob, but only opened the door just enough to creep inside.

There Gregory slept peacefully. He didn't move a muscle as John peeled the top sheet back from his body. John Henry stood at Gregory's bedside staring at him as he wound the linen sheet in his hands. "Go on... Give him to me." Sylus nudged him forward with a poke of the pitchfork at his spine.

John Henry knew what he had to do. Still, something in the back of his mind warned him against committing the heinous act. "Now!" Sylus demanded with his mouth perched at John's left ear.

John laid the thinly wound linen sheet across Gregory's neck, before sliding his body underneath the twin sized bed. Grabbing both sides of the sheet in each hand, John pulled tighter, lifting his upper body from the ground. The bed started to shake violently, and even though John could not see his victim, Sylus hovered there above a then lucid Gregory as he struggled to free the grasp on his neck the wrapped sheet harbored. His beady, bloodshot eyes bulged. The more his breath waned, the more visible Sylus had become to him.

Gregory's hands jerked from his neck to his chest as he'd clutched his heart. He was being strangled yet having a heart attack at the same time. The saliva bubbled up spilling from the corners of his mouth, down the sides of his cheeks, then into his ears. Gregory winced from the pain but for only for a few seconds before death took hold.

Sylus unveiled a slowly broadening grin of delight that showcased the many layers of sharp teeth rooted in his blackened mouth as the pungent stench of death penetrated the atmosphere, yet his eyes still maintained their soulless inky character. After years of starvation, John Henry had once again fed the beast inside.

John Henry rolled from underneath the bed, stood, then walked away as if nothing had even occurred. He opened the door, but as he stepped into the hallway, he saw Oliver rushing up the hall, then quickly turning the corner. "If the chatter box knows, you'll never make it out of here, John Henry. Now, what do you plan to do about that?" Sylus whispered, ushering him onward. He wanted more. John bolted in Oliver's direction. Once he'd caught up with him, Oliver was hiding, crouched down low in a dark corner of the tv room.

Not even the Christmas bulbs that lined the ceiling could shine down on him. His heart pounded harder; the closer John Henry came in proximity to his location. Oliver whispered but agitation coupled with the unfeigned fear he felt had rendered him incapable of completely quieting himself. "Oh my God, he's going to kill me," he reckoned, crawling across the floor underneath the tables.

"Come on out, Oliver. What are you doing in here all by yourself?"

"I'm not going to hurt you," John softened his tone, peeking under the table at him.

"Is that what you told Gregory?" Oliver daringly rebuffed.

"Now Oliver… Why'd you have to go and say something like that?"

John Henry bolted into the darkness toward Oliver. Oliver panicked, crawling underneath a neighboring table. John followed, crawling across the floor on his hands and knees.

"Please, John Henry. What did I ever do to you?"

John smashed his left hand to Oliver's lips covering his mouth entirely, "shhhhh." Although the sound from his mouth had been suppressed, Oliver's tear fear-filled eyes screamed for mercy.

"You know what they say, Oliver. Thoughts become things."

John Henry's right hand wheeled the syringe, impaling it into the side of Oliver's scrawny neck once, twice, then a third time, before emptying its deadly contents into his veins.

Oliver's head slumped. His body leaned to one side, allowing John's arms to slide from his grip as he fell over onto the floor.

John crawled from under the table, with a firm grasp on Oliver's left arm.

He trekked onward lethargically through the television room, then back down the hall. Oliver's limp corpse slid across the linoleum floor like a wet mop.

John paused. He'd reached Gregory's room, peeking inside once more before turning the knob, then entering as if it were his own. John Henry dragged Oliver's dead body inside with him, allowing his bare feet to be the last thing smashed in the sturdy door's grip. A swift tug on Oliver's arm allowed the door to latch closed.

Chapter III

The final act – Christmas day

6:00 a.m. Annie sat, reading Compelled to Murder when the cumbersome wave of sadness had surmounted. She'd closed the book placing it on her blanket, then got up from her bed only to stare out of the small rectangular window that gave view to the outside atrium.

Although the snowfall was heavy that Christmas morning, the lights from the police squad car and EMS cut through the whiteout, alarming every patient that dared peer out of their window that danger was afoot.

In the hallway, Betty stood near Gregory's room alongside Willie, giving her account of what she thought to be true, as two uniformed detectives walked back and forth from the hallway, then into Gregory's room gathering what evidence they could.

"He murdered poor Oliver, then hung himself. They'd found him on his knees with a sheet tied from the bed railing to his neck. Looks like he just leaned forward until he'd strangled himself to death. I knew those beds being bolted down to the floor would become an issue," Betty admitted, shaking her head in dismay. "I don't think I've ever heard of anyone strangling themselves that way," she recalled before pausing to contemplate the revelation.

Willie winced at the thought, "Wouldn't it be a natural impulse to stop. Ya know, self-preservation?"

Inside, the male officer squatted near Gregory's kneeling corpse, then used his gloved right hand to guide a Q-tip, swiping under the base of Gregory's ear. The officer brought it in close to his eyes.

Why on earth would it be damp behind his ear if he were leaning forward, he asked himself.

The female officer walked over to assist, "What cha got there?"

"He's wet behind the ears," the male officer pointed out, lifting the cue-tip so that she could see.

"Is that not odd?" he asked, while meticulously examining the side of his head.

"Well, if there were a struggle that ensued between the two deceased where Gregory was somehow hit in the ear, causing the eardrum to rupture or detach, that would be a plausible explanation for the fluid secretion. Either way, we should bag it as evidence," the female officer concluded, as she opened a Ziplock bag for the male officer to place the Q-tip there securely.

6:30 a.m. John Henry had awoken in a panic. He sat up, first examining his shirt. There were no blood stains visible. Then his hands, still no blood. John ran his fingers through his hair. It was dry but soft, more importantly, free of blood. He turned quickly to check his pillow. It was white. No stains there. Maybe he'd dreamt it all. Maybe Sylus hadn't vomited the torrent stream of blood upon him. He was safe in his bed. He hadn't killed Oliver nor had he strangled Gregory. It was just a nightmare, he'd concluded, furnishing him the peace of mind needed to breathe easy. A sigh of relief washed over him. John Henry peeled back the blanket, then climbed out of bed. It was Christmas Day; he relished in the thought of its arrival. He remained silent, yet nothing but delight was portrayed in his eyes. They were beaming. Freedom was upon him.

It was almost time for breakfast. John Henry couldn't wait to have his last breakfast there at St. Mary's before going home to start his new beginning. What excited him, even more, was that Visha would be by his side. She was off that day but would be picking John Henry up to take him home once released. They had until noon to have his discharge papers completed.

John Henry walked over to the door, then turned the knob. It wouldn't budge.

"Why is the door locked?" he mumbled, before looking out the small glass window. He could see Betty and Willie huddled together up the hallway near Gregory's room. When the male officer darted past John's door, a feeling of doom crashed into him like a tidal wave. It wasn't just a nightmare. John Henry was horrified by the events that had taken place just hours ago. Terrified he'd remain there locked up. Devastated by the thought that he'd never be free. Mortified that Sylus would eventually have his way. John Henry turned his back, leaned against the door then slid down onto the floor in a seated position. He lifted his knees to his chest, resting his head upon them. "What have I done?"

The male officer approached Betty and Willie, "We understand the other patients have to have their breakfast and medication. It's not our intent to delay your Christmas Day, but we need to talk to the other staff that was on duty last night. I'm really having a hard time understanding a few things. Why were these doors unlocked? How on earth did Gregory get his hands on a syringe filled with a lethal drug?

Betty and Willie shot one another a nervous glance. They were both on duty that night yet neither of them had heard a peep.

"This matter is far from being solved. But we'll remove the bodies, then tape off the scene, so that things can progress as usual.

This room is not to be cleaned nor entered unless it's by a member of the police department, until further notice."

Another hour had passed by the time they'd unlocked the other patient's doors, ushering them into the hallways to be led down to the cafeteria for breakfast.

That morning Annie and Macy sat at the same table as John, figuring if they put their heads together they could figure out exactly what had gone on the previous night. John remained quiet while listening to the two chat amongst one another.

"The authorities were here. Did you see, Macy?" Annie whispered.

"By the looks of things, we all saw them," Macy answered, looking around at the other patients immersed in nervous chatter.

"Oh gosh, I hope nothing bad happened to Oliver."

"Haven't you noticed. Gregory is missing, too," Macy pointed out before turning her attention to John. "Hey… Have you seen either one of them?"

John hadn't heard a word she said. Lost in a daydream, he seemed unable to free his mind from the memories of what he'd done. What Sylus had made him do…

Macy waved her hand into John's view. "Hello… Anybody home?"

Still, he remained silent. In unison, the ladies looked at one another with an equal amount of concern.

Then, out of nowhere, the security door buzzed turning everyone's attention to the door.

In came Dr. Visha Kanya. They'd missed the clicking of her high heels, usually alerting them of her presence.

That day she'd worn her Bearpaw boots and black leggings, along with an ugly Christmas sweater, which was a Butcher family tradition. Visha headed directly for John Henry. She had already spoken with the staff who'd filled her in on the events that had taken place. So, she intended to get John Henry out of there as soon as possible. "John Henry.... John Henry look at me." Visha lightly touched underneath his chin, turning his eyes on her.

"It's Christmas Day, John Henry. Look," she softly spoke, while pointing at her sweater.

"You look beautiful, Visha," he responded with a hushed tone.

She smiled, "Thank you," then proceeded to whisper in his ear, "I got you one, too."

John's eyes beamed with desperation, "I can go?"

"I've taken care of everything. I have your new prescriptions filled, and your bags packed. We're leaving this place. It's time to take you home," she answered.

"Home," he replied.

"Yes, of course. Everyone comes home for Christmas, John Henry."

"It's finally time." Visha held out her hand, "with the snow coming down we've got about an hour drive ahead of us."

John stood without further hesitation then walked out of the cafeteria lead by Visha's hand.

When he put his duffle bag into the hatchback of Visha's Jeep Wrangler, John shut the door but paused there for a moment taking one last look at St. Mary's. John took in a deep breath before closing his eyes, then exhaled releasing the painful memories he'd made there. Visha rubbed her hand across his back. Although her touch was tender, he could still feel it through the navy blue Carhartt coat she'd purchased. He felt safe with her moreover comforted in knowing she'd never abandon him.

"No more St. Mary's. No more locked doors. No more scheduled visits. You're free now, John."

John opened his eyes, "Let's get outta here."

The pair got into the vehicle then headed off on their journey. Visha intended to keep him calm, so she turned the radio to the classical music station.

Everything looked so new to him. He gazed out of the passenger side window, taking in every bit of nature he'd laid his eyes upon. After a few moments, John found himself thanking the clouds for the shade they provided from the sun, for the water they brought back to the earth, the warmth they trapped during the day, keeping them cozy during the night. He was thankful to be there.

The snow came down harder as they traveled north up the two-lane highway. Visha turned the windshield wipers to high speed. "It's really starting to come down. I hope we make it into town before they start closing the roads."

Visha's phone chimed before John had a chance to respond. She touched the car phone button to answer. "Hello!"

"Hey, babe. Are you on your way back yet? It's coming down pretty good out there." It was Jack Jacob.

John's upper lip immediately curled in disdain at the sound of his voice.

"It's terrible out, but we are making our way there now."

"Would you mind stopping to get some wood from the gas station. I really don't feel like going all the way out to the shed."

"If you feel that it's necessary I'll stop and pick some up."

"Awesome, babe! I'll see you soon." CLICK. Jack Jacob disconnected the call before she'd even gotten the opportunity to say goodbye.

"His concern knows no bounds," John Henry responded still staring out of his window.

Visha nodded in agreement with his sarcastic comment. "Well… you know your brother. Ever the gentleman."

John pointed up ahead. "There's a gas station up on the right. The lights are on. They must be open."

Visha pulled in, parking right in front of the doors. She grabbed a twenty dollar bill from a compartment on the dashboard. "I'll be right back."

"I really don't want you out in this storm. I'll go inside to pay for the wood."

Visha didn't put up a fight. She handed the twenty dollars over to John, then smiled as he got out of the Jeep. *He really is a great guy,* she thought.

The cashier looked to be in her early twenties. She had long curly red hair with a face full of freckles. She'd started eyeballing John the minute he walked through the door. She stood chewing her gum while twisting a lock of her hair. "Hey there, handsome. How can I help you?"

"I need some firewood. The piles you have out front. Is that what you have left? I need about three bundles."

"Yes, that's what we've got left. On the count of the storm, they've been selling awful fast. It's gonna be five bucks a bundle. So, that would cost you an even fifteen bucks. I won't tax you on the count of your good looks."

"Well... I appreciate that." John handed over the money.

"I've never seen you before. You from around here?" She tried to make small talk while getting his change in hopes that he'd ask for her number.

"I live about thirty minutes from here."

"Maybe, I'll see you around," she winked while handing over the change along with her telephone number she'd managed to quickly scribble on a small piece of paper.

Just as John had gotten ready to take the change, Visha's hand came forward grabbing the five dollars along with the piece of paper. They hadn't even noticed her walk into the gas station.

"He won't be needing this though," she announced handing the paper back to the cashier. "We should really be getting home, John."

They walked off leaving the cashier there with a sour look on her face.

John grabbed the bundles of firewood, piled them into the hatch then climbed back into the Jeep. "What was that all about?"

Visha started the Jeep. "You haven't even gotten settled yet. I just don't think it's a good idea to further complicate things by getting involved with someone so soon. She has no idea how to handle you, John Henry."

John turned toward the passenger window to hide the grin on his face. "I think you're the only one who does," he admitted.

Visha switched the Jeep into drive. "That's what best friends are for," she responded before pulling off.

It wasn't long before they'd made it to the big farm house where he'd grown up. John's heart pounded so hard he could feel the thumping in his chest. He hadn't seen his parents in years. He didn't know what he'd say to them. He didn't know if he even wanted to say anything to them.

They'd practically abandoned him. It was as if Jack Jacob was their only child. The long, snow-covered dirt road up to the house had finally come to an end. John sat quietly staring through the living room window. He could see his mother fiddling with the lights on the Christmas tree. The apron that covered her dress was stained with gravy and other tasty vittles she'd already begun preparing for Christmas dinner. She had her hair up in a tight bun as she'd always worn it. Only now the color had changed from blonde to gray. John hadn't seen her in over a decade. He didn't realize how old his parents had gotten.

"Don't be nervous. Everything is going to be just fine," Visha assured him with a tender rub on his shoulder.

John's mother, Verna, stood next to his father, Joseph, as they walked through the front door. An obvious awkwardness filled the air. He didn't know whether he should hug them or not but as he moved toward his parents Joseph Lyle spoke. His stern voice trembled, "Your brother has made up the spare room over the garage for you. You're going to have to work for what you get here. This isn't a charity house. You've made your bed so; you'll have to lie in it. By blood, you are still my son, therefore, it's my duty to make sure that you have a decent start in life. I'll give you six months to get a job and get on your feet. After that, I owe you nothing."

Verna lowered her head in shame. Not because of what John had done but because of the way she was allowing her son to be treated. Verna wouldn't dare disobey her husband so; she cowered there neglecting to speak up as usual.

"I understand," John replied. When his father spoke all he could see was his brother. Although his father was old and gray, he and Jack looked just alike.

"Go on now, John Henry. Put your bags up and get settled in. Visha and your mother will finish dinner."

"Yes, sir." John turned, walking back out of the front door straight to the garage. He shuffled through the snow, then up the stairs to get to the one bedroom apartment over the garage.

Once John had gotten inside, he dropped his duffle bag onto the bedroom floor, then covered the mattress with the folded sheets Jack had left for him. John couldn't wait to lay in a bed larger than the twin sized cots they had at St. Mary's. He'd gotten the feeling his father wasn't happy about his presence there, so; he'd opted for taking a short nap before dinner as opposed to heading back to the house.

A couple of hours had gone by before John had awoken. He'd gotten up staring out of the window at the winding dirt road he'd traveled on his bike as a child. Yet, in an instant, the beautiful memory was tarnished by the torture he'd dealt with there as the younger brother. He reminisced over the time Jack taught him to ride his bike without training wheels. He recalled falling off of the bike, skinning his knee. Jack walked over, then held him down, picking out each pebble ingrained into the bruised skin of his bloody shin. "Quit your crying, you big baby," Jack teased. John Henry was only five years old at the time. He remembered Jack kicking him in the chest when he wouldn't get up from the ground. The memory brought tears to John's eyes.

Just then, the sound of a loud engine roared up the dirt road. It was Jack Jacob. His brand new white pickup truck with the huge all-terrain tires cut through the snow like butter.

John's pits began to sweat. His heart raced. John felt a headache coming on as he'd put his hand to his forehead rubbing across it. "My medicine," he mumbled to himself.

Jack Jacob hopped out of his truck, then headed straight up to the apartment above the garage. John stood there still staring out of the window when Jack rushed inside. "So... little brother, what do you plan to do with your life now? I think this looks to be a good start for ya. How old are you now? Over thirty, right? You have no car, but at least you can count on the studio apartment above our parent's garage."

Jack continued to ramble on, "Geez, it's like a cave in here." He stepped closer, switching on the lamp that sat atop the old oak dresser illuminating an infuriated John Henry. He charged at Jack catching him off guard. John used every bit of strength he had pushing Jack back out of the door. A wide-eyed Jack staggered backward tumbling down the stairs. John stood at the top of the stairs with the wildest look in his eyes. Jack got up then darted toward the back of the house where he figured his mother would see him through the sliding glass doors. He couldn't wait for her to see John in the act of violence so that he could send him back to St. Mary's. Jack saw Visha cooking as he ran toward the sliding glass door. He pounded on the glass. A Visha startled quickly turned walking over to the door with a look of concern. Jack pulled at the door. "Visha! Open the door! Hurry up!"

Visha's look of concern vanished into a stare that was as cold as ice. She pulled a picture from the pocket of her apron. It was a photo of Jack in a passionate embrace with another woman. A nurse he'd been carrying on an affair with for years, right under Visha's nose.

Jack couldn't believe his eyes. How did she find out? "Babe, I can explain. Open the door." A sinister smirk of hatred was all Visha left him with before she closed the curtain on the entire scene, then turned the classical music up on the radio.

Jack turned around just as John wheeled the ax down at him. He'd managed to dodge the incoming blow, taking off into the darkness. But, John was close behind giving chase.

Back at the house, Visha poured three drinks. One for her, her mother-in-law and the last for her dear father-in-law. Visha added a little something extra to her in-law's glasses of eggnog.

"It won't take much," Auty whispered, standing beside her.

Visha quickly turned to look around the room. She heard the voice but didn't see anyone there. She shuttered from the eerie feeling she felt but continued with her plan. Visha placed the mugs of eggnog on a tray then headed out of the kitchen.

Jack Jacob ran as fast as he possibly could but slipped on wet snow triggering a stumble forward. Just as he'd braced his hands in preparation of the incoming fall, Jack managed to pick up speed, taking off into the darkness. He'd made it to an old well out back before John could get him in his sights. Jack pushed the top back, leaving it open just enough for him to slip through. He sat on the edge, swinging his legs around so that they hung down inside the well, then gripped the edge with both hands. Jack slid inside allowing his body to dangle there secured by only the strength in his arms.

As John trudged through the snow, he saw Myron on his left showing the way with a pointing finger.

Jack could hear John's purposeful footsteps as he passed by. Once they'd faded from earshot, he moved one of his hands to grip the wooden top on the well.

Jack struggled to lift his legs but was finally able to get one up along the edge. That gave him the leverage he needed to pull himself out, escaping the self-inflicted imprisonment.

"Jack! Come on out, Jack. It's just your little brother. You're not afraid, are you? Nahhh... not you. Not big bad Jack!" he hollered out, every breath he released being chilled by the frigid air.

Unable to resist his taunts, Jack popped up from behind him. "Let's go mother fucker. I ain't afraid of you," he boasted. John turned, swinging the ax. But, it was dark, which made it difficult for John to see the wooden top from well Jack wheeled down on him. Just as the wooden handle of the ax made contact with the side of Jack's body, the wood top hit John on his shoulder before falling to the ground. Jack grabbed hold to the handle, initiating a struggle. Both brothers tugged mercilessly to gain full control of the weapon, but in the end, John was the victor flinging Jack across the snow onto the ground while he tried to hold on as if his life depended on it. But, to no avail.

John bolted toward Jack. He shuffled his hands and feet taking him backward through the snow.

Just as Jack turned to get up, his eyes bulged, shocked at the sight of the metal stake in the ground, used for pitching, so close to his face. John stomped his foot down hard on the back of Jack's head, forcing the metal stake through his throat then out the back of his neck. The blood painted the snow underneath him soaking in slowly changing white to red. Jack's legs twitched while he choked on his last breath.

The next morning when Verna awoke in her bed, she couldn't seem to remember a thing. She looked over to her left at her husband. "Joseph… Joseph, honey…" she nudged him. He was as stiff as a board. His skin felt cold to the touch.

Verna gasped bringing her hands to cover her mouth. Joseph Lyle Butcher was dead.

Visha had given him the lethal dose yet spared her mother-in-law. The note she'd written in Verna Mae's handwriting would tell a story of Romeo and Juliet. Joseph was dying of colon cancer so; it was Verna's intent for them to die together, of course. At least that's how it would appear if need be. Besides, no one would ever find Jack's rotting corpse in the old well John dumped him in.

As their story had ended, John and Visha's was finally beginning.

AN ENDING PRECEDING IT'S BEGINNING

Release

Date

It's cold as fuck in here," one inmate yelled, as he wrapped himself in a blanket. The furnace had gone out in the housing unit and the maintenance man said he was waiting on a part to repair it. All of the inmates in the unit had on double layers of clothes. Ed bundled up with his winter coat and skull cap on as he watched TV in the day room.

It was December 13th and that meant Jack Frost was taking no prisoners in the Midwest. Not even in prison. The cold air outside the Ohio correctional facility was sharper than a samurai sword. All that attempted to walk across the yard felt its wrath. Several inmates that were caught doing minor offenses shoveled the walkway as 'extra duties punishment'. The officer that was detailed to supervise them was being punished just as much as they were.

Back in the housing unit, some were doing calisthenics to keep warm. Some guys just stayed in their beds under the covers. A few of the white guys played cards like it was a nice summer day in their t-shirts, shorts, and flip-flops.

"Mail call," the C.O. said loudly. Even she had on her winter coat, gloves and scarf. Many of the inmates ran to the podium, eagerly awaiting hearing their names called. "Johnson, Lloyd, Hendrix, and Hamilton," the officer passed out envelopes. The men signed the paper to receive their mail and opened them like it was their birthdays.

Some had early Christmas cards, others had letters from their kids, wives, and girlfriends. The officer passed out thirty envelopes. The crowd around her started to thin out as each person went about their way to read the mail. There was one letter left in her hand; four inmates stood, hoping it was for them.

"Last, but not least, Edward Wilson," the C.O. said. All of the inmates around her pouted and huffed as they walked away, disappointed. Ed sat on the other end of the day room, not paying any attention to the mail call. He usually didn't get any mail, so he never went over to the podium.

"Yo, Ed," one of the inmates yelled to get his attention. Ed turned around with an irritated look on his face. The inmate that called his name pointed in the direction of the officer handing out mail. She held the envelope in the air and waved him over to her. Ed pointed at himself. He couldn't believe it was for him. All kinds of thoughts went through his head as he walked over to get his mail.

Ed wondered if he was getting a *Dear John* letter from his girlfriend. He thought maybe something had happened to one of his parents. He could think of nothing good. Ed didn't have a big family or a lot of friends. So who could possibly be writing him?

"Hey, Wilson," the officer said, as she handed him the paper to sign to get his mail. She smiled as she handed it to him. She knew exactly what it was. She leaned over to him and whispered, "Looks like you're going to have a good Christmas." After he signed by his printed name on the received mail list, she gave him his letter.

It was addressed to Mr. Edward Wilson from the Ohio State Parole Board. Ed's heart began to pound in his chest. Ed looked around to see if anyone was watching. No one was paying him any attention except the C.O. She was eager to see the look on his face when he opened his letter.

Ed opened and read the letter. He scanned through the formal blah, blah, blah. His eyes got big when he read, *Because the nature of your crime was non-violent, we are granting you an opportunity for Sentence Reduction through Judicial Release according to revised code *2929.20.* Ed couldn't believe what he was reading. He felt every emotion possible in less than a minute.

This was great news. But with all good news comes bad news. As he read the terms and conditions, the smile on his face began to fall. Not quite a frown, more neutral. In order to be released early, he had to have a clean record while incarcerated and have a place to stay. He would also be on probation for two years. The probation wasn't an issue, but finding a stable address and having a clean record was going to be a challenge.

Ed came from a small family. It was him, his mom, dad, and sister who lived in Atlanta with her husband and four kids. Ed was raised as one of Jehovah's Witnesses. His father was an elder in the congregation. They were strict parents, but they meant well and wanted the best for their children. Ed knew that going to his sister's place wasn't even an option. She lived out of state and her husband wasn't having it. The only other option was his parents.

Ed knew if he went there, he would have to conform to their way of life. That meant going to all the meetings, participating in the family bible study at home and going door to door preaching the word on the weekends. In Ed's mind, it was like leaving one prison and walking into another one.

The other dilemma was not getting into trouble and keeping his record clean. Ed had a gambling problem in the free world and it followed him to prison. He failed miserably at a check fraud scheme, trying to make some quick money. He didn't make enough to pay off his debt and caught a four-year sentence. Now, on the inside, he fell back into his old habit. He racked up a $250 gambling debt with the jailhouse bookie named Big Low Down. Ed bet on basketball games, football games and tennis matches. He gambled playing cards, shooting dice and playing pool. Whenever there was a chance to make some money with a thrill, Ed was in.

The bookie usually let Ed work his debt off by doing odd jobs for him and his friends. Sometimes, Ed would have to wash and iron clothes or clean their cells. But it was close to Christmas and Low Down wanted cash so he could buy his kids' nice gifts. This put Ed in a nasty trick bag. He had been able to spin Low Down for the last couple weeks, paying him with other small bets he'd won shooting pool, giving him honey buns and ramen noodles. But Low Down was getting impatient, and those honey buns and soups weren't cutting it.

Ed folded the papers up and stuffed them in his shirt pocket. He tried his best to keep a straight face as he walked back to the day room. There were always sharks looking for a victim. Any sign of weakness would be preyed upon. If the other inmates knew he was up for parole, some would make sure he got in trouble so he wouldn't have a good chance of being released. Their thought was, *If I ain't leaving, then nobody's leaving.* Others would try to beg for all of the things he had, like his radio, extra clothes and food from the commissary. Some might try to rob him of everything. Their idea was that he wouldn't be there long enough to report it or retaliate. But, his biggest problem was Low Down. With that $250 debt hanging over his head, there was no way it could be known that he might be getting out in time for Christmas.

"You good?" one of the inmates asked Ed as he walked over to the phone. Ed knew the gut was fishing. So, he hit him with the *I'm good* head nod. There was several people on the phone, so Ed had to wait. While standing there, his mind started running and he began to daydream about life on the outside. This is something he trained himself not to do, but with the possibility of him being released, he couldn't help it.

Bam! The guy in front of him slammed the payphone. Everyone stopped what they were doing and looked in the direction of the disturbance. The inmate stormed off and everyone returned to what they were doing. It was normal to see people get upset and frustrated. This was good for Ed because this guy showed his emotions. Now, the sharks will be focused on him, trying to see why he's upset and if they can capitalize on it.

Ed picked up the phone and wiped the earpiece and mouthpiece with his shirt. He dialed the number. "You have a collect call from an inmate at a Correctional Institution from Ed. If you will accept the charges, press 5, if not, please hang up." *Beeeeeep.*

"Hello, Eddy!" His mom was always glad to hear from him.

"Hey, Ma; how are you?"

"I'm doing all right for an old woman," she laughed. "Is it cold there like it is here in Cleveland?"

"Yeah, Ma; it's freezing cold. How is dad?"

"Oh, I'm sorry to hear that. Your dad is just fine. He's getting dressed now. We'll be headed out to the Kingdom Hall shortly."

"Well, tell him I said hello and I love him." Then he whispered, "I got a letter today from the parole board. I may be getting out early."

There was an awkward silence on the phone. Ed's mom was torn. Even though she hated that he was locked up, she knew where he was. She knew he was eating every day and he called more now that he was locked up then he did when he wasn't. She didn't think that getting out early would help him. Grace knew her son. He was hardheaded and always tried to get over. Serving the whole four years would teach him a more valuable lesson in accountability and the consequence of his actions.

Ed told her the terms of his parole. He needed a place to stay if he got out. There was another moment of silence.

"You know I'm going to have to talk this over with your dad," his mom said, in a sad voice. "And you know what he's going to say."

His father would always quote the same scripture when it came to living under his roof. Ed and his mom said it together. It almost sounded like they were harmonizing.

"Joshua 24:15 states: *...as for me and household, we will serve Jehovah.*"

They both giggled. For a moment, it felt like Ed wasn't in prison. The sound of his mom laughing filled his heart with joy. He told her the date and time of his hearing. He promised to call her and let her know how it went. They exchanged their I love yous. Just as Ed was about to hang up, one of Low Down's boys approached him.

"Yo, let me get a jump on that line, homie?" He was asking Ed to have his mother do a three-way call. Ed swiftly told his mom he loved her and hung up.

"Nah, player, ain't nothing happing over this way," Ed said, as he stepped back, prepared to fight.

"Okay, now, Wilson," the C.O. that gave him the letter yelled to break up the tension. She knew he couldn't afford to get caught up.

"You know you on the books for two and a half," the inmate said to Ed.

"Yeah, I'm on the books with Low Down, not yo' ass. I don't owe you shit."

In the Mix

"I got two pair."

"Well, I got three of kind."

"Damn," the inmate with the losing hand said, as he threw his cards on the floor. He reached in his sock, gave the winner two Twix candy bars and walked away from the table.

The "fever" was getting to Ed. Just the sound of cards shuffling triggered something in him that made him lose control. Ed tried to recite the serenity prayer in his mind to help fight the urge, but it wasn't working. He had gone to Gamblers Anonymous while he was locked up. It helped a little while he was going, but eventually, he fell off the wagon.

The problem in prison is there is always something to bet on. Inmates would bet on fights. They would bet on which C.O. would make it and which one would quit. They would bet on which new inmate would kill themselves and which one would get turned out. Ed had placed bets in all those situations at one time or another.

Ed stood over by the table where they were playing poker. Just to hear them talk was enough for him to lose his self-control. One of the guys invited him to play.

"What's good, Eddy? We got a chair open for you," the man said, patting the seat next to him.

"Yo', you know he's in the bag with Low Down," another inmate at the table said, under his breath.

"I don't care nothing about that shit; that's between him and Low Down. We ain't give out no credit here. It's cash and carry only at this table," said the inmate that invited Ed.

Ed was game. He held up a finger and told the guy to hold on. He walked to his bunk and opened his footlocker. He grabbed four Payday candy bars and a honey bun and then returned to the table. Ed showed he had the goods to play a couple of hands. All the other players at the table nodded in agreement to let him play.

As they played, the regular day-to-day foolishness was going on all around them. Everyone knew what was happening, but were minding their own business. There were people fighting in the showers to settle their differences, while others posted up as lookouts. Ed won the first hand and raked in a couple of Snickers and two packs of coffee.

Some of the Muslim and Jewish inmates started debating the origin of Christmas. They went on and on until the conversation got heated. Others in the dorm began to get irritated. The C.O. walked over to the area they were in to show some authority. She didn't say a word to them; her presence was enough for them to settle down.

One of the inmates on the other side of the day room yelled out, "We go through this bullshit every year. Y'all jailbird muthafuckas arguing over somebody neither one of y'all believe in. What kind of stupid shit is that?"

Another inmate followed up with, "Yeah, y'all don't even celebrate Christmas. Go on somewhere with y'all scared of a ham sandwich-fucking up the holiday spirit asses." The entire dorm erupted in laughter. Needless to say, the Muslims didn't find it funny at all.

It was Ed's turn to deal. As he shuffled the cards, he thought about cheating by second card dealing and bottom card dealing. The players at the table were not rookies. He changed his mind as he saw one player staring at his hand intensely. Ed knew if he tried it and got caught, he could cancel that parole hearing and Christmas. Cheating is like being a liar and a thief in jail; no one would trust you or want to associate with you. It wasn't as bad as being a child molester, but it was still pretty low on the social ladder.

Ed dealt a fair hand and the game played on smoothly. Two of the C.O.'s began to talk about their Christmas plans. One was going to travel out of town to see family. The other one was staying home because he had to work the holiday. A few of the inmates loved to eavesdrop on the C.O.'s . They lived vicariously through them. Other than TV, it was their only connection to the outside world.

Then, there were the inmates that wanted nothing to do with the guards. They couldn't care less what they did for the holidays. For them, it was a constant reminder that they weren't with their loved ones and would be spending Christmas Day with a bunch of criminals.

"Full house, three queens and two nines," Ed said, as he looked around the table to see if anyone had a better hand. One guy rolled his eyes. Ed knew he had him beat. The second player threw his cards onto the table and crossed his arms.

The last player looked at his hand with no emotion. His face looked like it was made of stone. He looked up at Ed like he had bad news for him. Ed wasn't sure what was about to happen. There were a lot of snacks up for grabs and the tension was high in the air. The stone-faced player laid his cards face down and told Ed, "You got it."

Ed was nervous, but he raked in his winnings. This is one of the dangers of gambling in prison. Sore losers can be bad for your health.

"I got to make a phone call right quick." Ed made up an excuse to leave the table. His intuition was telling him to get out of there. No one said a word. They just looked at Ed as he gathered his cookies, candy bars, and snack cakes.

These are the highs and lows that come with an addiction. Even though Ed could have gotten beat up, he still felt the rush from the suspense of it all. He made his way back to his footlocker to deposit his bounty when Low Down stepped to him.

"What's good, Ed? Looks like you made out pretty nice in that poker game? You don't mind if I help myself to a few late night snacks, do you?" Low Down politely reached into Ed's footlocker and relieved him of a couple of candy bars and a pack of cookies.

"I'm going to consider this a good faith payment. But, you still in the whole me $250."

Ed couldn't say a word. He was just thankful that Low Down didn't take all of his winnings. Low knew he had the potential to win more by gambling, so he let him keep a few scraps.

After avoiding two possible physical altercations, Ed needed some comfort. Ed walked back to the phones and waited his turn. When he got to the phone, he wiped the earpiece and the mouthpiece off with his shirt. He dialed his baby momma's number and waited for her to pick up. She didn't accept the call, so he called right back. She declined the call again. Ed slammed the phone down in frustration.

You, Me, We, and Us

Ed called Mika back the next day. This time she answered.

"Yes, Edward," she said, in a snotty tone. Ed wasn't in the mood to argue, so he did his best to circumvent her attitude. He didn't even acknowledge her behavior.

"Hello, Mika, how are you and my baby girl?"

There was silence on the phone. Mika had already spoken to his mother and knew about his parole hearing and him possibly getting out early. She was sick of Ed's lies and his shenanigans. She was waiting for him to ask her to use her address so she could go off on him.

"I'm fine and the baby is fine."

"Can I speak to her?"

"No, she's sleep and I'm not going to wake her up; she had a long day."

Ed was pissed, but he couldn't show any emotion. This would only lead to arguing and her hanging up.

"Okay, well, kiss her for me, please," Ed said, in a calm, loving tone.

"Can you call Damon for me on the three-way?" Ed asked, respectfully.

Mika knew Ed was going to ask for something. Without answering the question, she clicked over and called his best friend, Damon. Damon and Ed were like peanut butter and jelly. They were inseparable as kids and as adults, nothing really changed.

"Hello," Damon answered the phone.

"What's good, boy?" Ed started talking like it was a conversation they had started a couple days ago, but didn't finish. Mika had no interest in what they were talking about so she put the phone down and walked away.

Ed gave Damon the rundown on the possibility of him getting out early and what the terms were. Damon was excited until he heard the conditions of his early release.

"Mannnn, I know you ain't trying to move back home with yo' momma and daddy. You might as well stay there and finish yo' time."

Ed knew there was some truth to what Damon was saying, but Damon didn't know about his situation with Big Low Down. He either had to come up with Low's money or pray he gets out early without Low finding out. To say this was a sticky situation was an understatement.

While they were debating the pros and cons, Ed's daughter picked up the phone.

"Hello, who dis is?"

"Hey, baby, this is Daddy. How's my angel?"

Damon got quiet and let them talk.

"I being goooooood," the three-year-old said.

Ed wanted to cry tears of joy. He hadn't spoken to Mya in several weeks. He talked to Mya for a few minutes. They counted to ten in English and Spanish together. Then, they went over their colors and sang the ABC song.

Mika softened as she smiled, watching Mya interact with her dad on the phone. She wished Ed would get his act together, but he's let her down many times before. She guarded her heart by being mean to Ed. Ed knew he was a chronic fuck up, so he never really pressed the issue.

"Tell Daddy bye-bye," Mika said.

"Byyyyyeeee, daaaadddyy," Mya sang, as she handed the phone back to her mommy. Mika took the phone and told Damon she needed to talk to Ed. Damon and Ed wrapped up their conversation.

"Yo, Dame, don't tell nobody about my parole hearing. I don't want niggas in the streets talking. That shit will get right back up in here through the rumor mill. These niggas are worse than hoes in a beauty salon."

Damon laughed and agreed not to tell anyone about the hearing.

"Thanks, sis, for letting me speak to my boy," Damon said to Mika before he hung up.

Mika wasted no time going in on Ed about him getting out early. But deep inside, she was excited about the possibilities of him getting out in time for Christmas and turning his life around. But fear kept her from showing her true feelings.

"I talked to your mother the other day when I dropped Mya off. She told me all about your parole hearing. You know you can't come stay here. My brother is on parole and he's using this address. Shit, if you make parole, you can't even come over here to visit due to both of y'all sorry ass parole conditions. And please do not sell my baby no lies about you getting out and spending all kind of time with her. She doesn't need to be let down and disappointed like I am."

"You have one minute left on this phone call," the prison's automated recording said.

Ed took it all on the chin. He had to choose his words wisely. Even though he couldn't use Mika's address, he would still need her help if he got out early. She had a car and a good job. Those were two things he needed: transportation and money.

"Mika, you're right, I'm not going to sell Mya any dreams. I apologize for disappointing you in the past. I have a real uphill battle in front of me and I'm not going to burden you with any of it. All I ask is that you allow me to see Mya at least once a week."

Ed knew he couldn't ask Mika for much while he was still locked up. She would only resist and give him a hard time. He had to really soft shoe her until they were face to face. Then he could finesse his way to whatever he needed.

Mika took the bait, hook-line-and-sinker. She dropped her guards immediately.

"Okay, Ed, whatever you need from me, you got it. I just want us to be a family for once."

"Your mom invited me to go to the Kingdom Hall with her; I told her I'll think about it."

Ed knew this was his golden opportunity to say something slick and get Mika under his spell again.

"Maybe we can all go together when I get home and then go out for dinner afterwards."

Mika began to run with the fantasy. She started telling Ed what color dress she and Mya might wear and how Cracker Barrel would be a great choice to eat after the meeting. Ed could hear the excitement in her voice. He knew it would be best to leave her in her fantasy for now.

"Kiss Mya for me; I'll call you tomorrow," Ed said, right as the call hung up.

When Ed got off the phone, he heard some of the guys in the corner of the dorm. They were singing the Temptations' version of *Silent Night*. The echo off the walls made them sound like they were in a concert hall. Everyone got quiet and listened. For a moment in time, no one was locked up. Everyone was home with their loved ones eating and enjoying this day the Lord had made.

Ed was torn inside. Being raised as one of Jehovah's Witnesses, he never celebrated Christmas. But, he noticed how some of the hardest convicts softened their hearts around this time of the year. Even a few of the meanest C.O.'s would be nice during the holiday season.

There was a Christmas movie marathon on the TV in the day room. Home Alone was about to go off and A Christmas Story was about to come on. The inmates were glued to the TV like kids at a daycare.

Ed was only thinking about going home. Either he had to come up with Low Down's money or make parole without him finding out. The stress wouldn't allow Ed to relax and enjoy the season. Plus, Low wasn't one of the shot callers that gave out a pass for the holidays. He was the complete opposite. He needed his money to buy his kids gifts and somebody was going to pay for them one way or another.

Release Date

There was a posting on the board for volunteers. The prison needed help in the visitation room. They needed someone dressed as Santa Claus and the elves to take pictures and entertain the kids that came to see their fathers. Ed saw this as a way to get out of the dorm for a few hours. Low Down's henchman were constantly eyeballing and mean mugging Ed, so he signed up to be an elf.

When they called for all of the trustees to line up to leave, Ed got in line. Low Down saw him get in line. The look that he shot at Ed was terrifying. He knew Ed was trying to buy some time and create some space because of his debt. But he played it cool. He knew Ed would be back in a few hours and that debt would be right there waiting on him.

Condemnation

When Ed returned from visitation, he was exhausted. Those little kids wore his ass out. All he wanted to do was take a shower and go to bed. He went to the showers and two guys were in there jacking each other off. Ed made an about face and headed back to his bunk.

He was sick to his stomach, even though he had seen that kind of thing more times than he cared to remember. *I can't believe I'm in here with these barbarians,* Ed thought to himself. Just twenty minutes ago, those same two men were in visitation kissing and hugging on their kids, wives, and girlfriends.

Sitting there, Ed reminisced when his mother used to make him remember bible verses. It was the dumbest thing ever, or so he thought at the time. Leviticus 20:13: "If a man lies with a male as one lies down with a woman, both of them have done a detestable thing. They should be put to death without fail. Their own blood is upon them."

In a million years, Ed would have never thought he'd live to see this bible verse played out before his very eyes. As much as he hated going to the Kingdom Hall (what other denominations call church), he couldn't help but think that if he had followed their strict guidelines, he would never have seen the inside of a prison. He would have never started gambling. His entire life would have been different. The regrets began to consume him. Ed tried to rationalize his bad decisions to balance out the guilt of not listening to his parents.

"I had more fun than the law allowed, gambling. I've made more money than some people going to work everyday. I met my baby momma in a casino; if it wasn't for gambling, I wouldn't have my daughter."

Ed came up with all kinds of foolishness to convince himself that he really wasn't that bad off and what he had just seen in the showers wasn't that bad.

"Library/recreation," the C.O. yelled.

A lot of inmates started scrambling around getting ready to leave the unit. Ed was one of them. He wanted to look up "how to make parole" on the computer in the library. Making parole was a long shot, but Ed had to put forth the effort.

He threw his shirt back on and got in line to leave the unit. Low Down and a couple of his cronies noticed Ed leaving out again. One of them walked by Ed and mumbled under his breath, "You can run, but you can't hide".

Ed looked straight ahead as if he didn't hear a thing. The C.O. radioed for the door to the unit to be opened. All the inmates walked out, heading in different directions. Ed made sure not to strike up a conversation with anyone. He didn't want anybody to know what he was researching at the library.

Once he got there, he chose a computer on the end. Ed put some books on dog training next to him so it would look like that's what he was interested in. He even typed dog training tips in the search engine to pull up a bunch of sites. After clicking on a few sites, he dropped them on his taskbar.

Then he cleared the search box and entered *what questions will the parole board ask?* Ed was hesitant to hit the enter button. He knew the computers were monitored and they had 'red flag' words programmed into them to prevent inmates from looking up forbidden sites.

After staring at the screen for ten seconds, Ed hit the enter button. The curser spun around and the computer buffered. Then, *boom*, and a long list of sites and forms popped up. Ed felt like he'd just won the pick three lottery for fifty cents box. It was a small victory, but a victory nonetheless.

Ed started reading and taking mental notes. Looking around from the corner of his eyes, he saw someone approaching. With a smooth stroke, he dropped the search box and re-launched the dog training forms.

"What's up, Ed, you 'bout to start training dog when you get out?" the guy said, looking over Ed's shoulders.

"Yeah, I've always been into dogs," Ed said, playing along until the guy left his area. Soon as he walked away, Ed was back to his studies.

Ed read the possible questions that would be asked and the best answers to match them. He closed his eyes and committed them to memory. Whispering them under his breath, they became a part of his subconscious thoughts. Within fifteen minutes, he had them memorized. Ed applied the same technique he used when playing cards. This is one way he was able to win. He memorized which cards had been played; this gave him better odds on the cards he had left in his hand.

Ed read on about how to sit, make eye contact and speak directly to the person that asked him a question. All of these things play a psychological part in influencing the parole board's decision. The most important thing he read was when he entered the room to approach each person, shake their hands and greet them as individuals. He was supposed to do the same thing at the end of the hearing as he made his exit.

It seemed like a lot to remember, but it was simple at the same time. The librarian told everyone they had ten minutes before their time was up. Ed shut down his computer. One of the inmates walked close to him and handed him a sandwich bag full of tobacco.

"Low Down needs you to bring this back to the dorm."

Ed could have shit a brick. This was the last thing he needed. Just his luck that he would get caught a day before going to the parole board smuggling contraband in the dorm. If he didn't come back with it, it would be hell to pay from Low because of his debt.

Because Low was the current threat, Ed opted to sneak the tobacco in. He stuffed the sandwich bag into his pants right next to his dick. He adjusted it so it wouldn't look like he had a hard-on.

His heart was racing as they walked through the corridors. He knew that at any time, an officer could pull him out of line and search him. If they found the tobacco on him, he was going straight to the hole and he could kiss that early release goodbye.

Looking straight ahead as they walked the halls, Ed made no eye contact with any of the officers. He did his best not to look nervous. He stomach was bubbling overtime. The normal walk to back to the unit was less than five minutes, but today it seemed like a country mile away.

Ed's worst fears were waiting for him when they got back to the dorm. The regular C.O. was on her lunch break. One of the meanest C.O.'s to ever walk the earth was giving her a break. Ed knew his ass was grass. This C.O. went above and beyond when doing his job.

"Everyone, turn around, put your hands on the wall and spread your legs." Ed's heart sank. As the officer was patting down each inmate, Ed was praying for divine intervention. Right before the C.O. got to him, Ed let out a silent fart. The shit was toxic.

"Was that you, Wilson?" the officer said, with anger in his voice.

"I'm sorry, C.O., I been holding it since we left the unit; the toilet in the library didn't have no toilet paper," Ed said, with a sincere tone and his head hung down in shame.

"Take yo' stankin' ass in the dorm!" The C.O. pushed Ed in the doorway without searching him.

Ed wasn't sure if that was God showing him mercy or a blessing from the devil in his stomach. Either way, he was grateful. He walked in the dorm, straight to the bathroom. One of Low Down's boys got up and followed behind him. Low never even looked in their direction.

Once in the bathroom, Ed reached in his drawers and pulled out the sandwich bag. He threw it to Low's boy and walked right out. He didn't want to have any conversation with him. The showers were empty, so Ed made his way in there before the next episode of jerk circle started.

As he bathed, he rehearsed his answers in his mind. He was interrupted by one of the guys he was playing poker with a couple of days earlier.

"Yo', come holla at me when you get out the shower, homie."

Ed knew this was nothing good. But when someone calls you out in prison, you must show up. It's a sign of weakness if you don't. Once again, Ed was between a rock and a hard place.

Ed got cleaned up and stepped to the guy that called him out. Ed had a dog look on his face like he was ready for war. He was thinking if he had to fight, he was going all out.

"What's good, Eddy? Why you look like you ready to kill a brick?" the guy asked.

"What's up," is all Ed said in return.

"Damn, gangsta, okay. I'm going to skip the formalities. There's an Ohio State football game on tomorrow afternoon. I know you done tore your drawers with Low Down, but I got an open line of credit for you. You did so well the other day playing poker, I figured you'd be a gentleman and let me try to win some money back."

Ed felt like a drug addict behind the counter of a pharmacy. This was his weakness. Ohio State was a 2-to-1 underdog against Alabama A&M. They were both undefeated and this was the game everyone wanted to see.

Tomorrow was Ed's hearing. If he made parole, it would take two days for the paperwork to go through. That's just enough time to get him killed for not being able to pay two bookies in prison. The best option was to say no. Ed was already in a shit-hole. But, the gambler in him said fuck it.

"Okay, I'll take the bet, but no overs or under. No lines or quarters payouts. Straight bet for $125 for Ohio State to win," Ed said, with a straight face. The bookie laughed like a four hundred pound truck driver from West Virginia. They shook hands and parted ways.

Guilt set in two seconds after the bet was made. Ed felt out of control. He looked and no one was on the phones. They turned off automatically at nine o'clock, so most got off the phone before then.

Ed called his mom first.

"Mom, I've been thinking; I'm ready to turn my life over to God."

"Son, I've prayed for years to hear those words come from your mouth. I knew all that time, love and guidance wasn't in vain."

"Tell Dad I want to start up my bible study again and I'm going to need a couple of his good shirts to wear to the meetings until I get on my feet."

The words that came from Ed's mouth were like smooth jazz to his mother's ears. She was completely hypnotized with hope and expectation. The thought of her son returning to the "truth" before she died was heartwarming, to say the least.

Ed listened to her go on and on about how nice it's going to be having him home. She asked him what he wanted to eat when he first got home and told him to invite his girlfriend and daughter. She rattled off a list of people that she was going to tell at the Kingdom Hall that her baby was coming back.

Ed didn't remember any of the people she mentioned, nor did he care. He had just used the information he got from the library on his mother. He told her what she wanted to hear and let her fantasize about the rest.

Guilt didn't describe the feeling Ed had. The crud on the bottom of a garbage can in a back alley would be better than the taste that was left in Ed's mouth when he got off the phone with his mom. He really wanted to call his girlfriend and try his newfound skill on her. But, he knew his mom was already on the line with her as soon as they hung up.

Ed felt bad about manipulating the system and his parents, but he began to understand that religion and the justice system do it every day for the good of society and their personal interest.

Tito M. Bradley

Born Again

"Chow," the C.O. yelled, as the lights in the dorm came on. Most of the inmates began to move around. Some didn't eat breakfast, so they stayed in the bed. Ed usually slept in, but today was too important. Even though he was exhausted, he forced himself to get up. Ed had been up all night mentally training like a heavyweight contender challenging the champ for the title. His freedom was on the line and he was ready to leave it all in the ring.

The guys were farting left and right as they got ready to go to the chow hall. It was a regular morning routine, so no one was offended or upset. They all understood it was a natural bodily function and it couldn't be avoided. The early morning chuckles from the different sounds calmed Ed's nerves.

Once everyone was lined up, the C.O. radioed for the dorm door to be released. As they walked out on the yard, Ed couldn't help but to think this could be one of the last times he takes this walk. He took in the scenery like it was his first day. He noticed things that he never paid any attention to before. There was barbed wire on the inside of the razor wire on top of the fence. This brought Ed back to the reality that if he didn't give the performance of a lifetime, he could be here for a long time or even die here.

Ed took a deep breath, then exhaled slowly as he entered the chow hall. The smell of pancakes and sausage was in the air. He was glad he decided to eat this morning. Every now and then, the prison would serve something worth eating and this was one of those meals.

"You watching the game today? It comes on at noon," one of the inmates asked Ed as they made their way through the food line.

"I might watch it," Ed answered, trying not to let on how nervous he was about the bet he made last night.

The guy started talking about stats and the odds of who could win and why. Ed tuned him out. He got his tray and found his way to the closest table so he could dig into the hot, fluffy stack of pancakes. While eating, Ed tried his best not to go over the questions and answers for his parole hearing later. He didn't want to over-study and possibly freeze when it was show time.

Ed ate his breakfast like he was at Denny's on a Sunday morning. He took his time and enjoyed every bite. After washing it all down with chocolate milk, he threw his trash away and placed his tray on top of the others.

Walking back to the unit, Low Down walked over to him in a very non-threating manner.

"What's good, Ed?" he asked, casually.

"Shit, just another day in this shit-hole," Ed answered, nonchalantly.

"You know I got eyes and ears all over this jail, right?"

Ed's stomach turned in knots instantly. He just knew the C.O. told Low about his hearing. He assumed Low was going to do something to fuck up his chances. But, Ed was a country mile off.

"I hear you gambling with money you ain't got while you still owe me."

Ed felt relieved, if only for a moment. He could deal with this as long as his chances of getting out were still available.

"You gon' get yo' paper, playa, just hold on," Ed said, with confidence; but, he was really unsure if he could pull off this caper.

Low walked away without saying another word. That was his thing. He never gave any emotion or expression. You didn't know if he was happy, sad or pissed off. The unknown is what kept his foes on their toes. He rarely had to use violence; most never wanted to take it that far to see how dangerous he could get.

Once Ed made it back to the unit, he tried to relax. He couldn't help but look at the clock. Everyone in the dorm was gearing up for the big game. Two inmates got into an argument over who would win and started fighting. The SRT (Special Response Team) came in, beat both of their asses and threw them in the hole. Now, neither one of them would see the game. This brought calm to the dorm. No one else wanted to miss the game, so everyone chilled out in their own spaces.

"Wilson, you got a special visit," the C.O. yelled out.

Ed looked in her direction and she winked at him. She didn't want to let anyone in the unit know he was up for parole, so she lied aloud to cover for Ed.

He gave her an appreciative head nod and got ready to go. Most people assumed he was seeing his lawyer or pastor, so they paid him no attention. Low didn't even bother with him to bring any more contraband in.

Ed went to the bathroom, relieved himself and then stood in front of the mirror. Looking at his reflection, he tucked in his shirt and buckled his belt. After splashing water on his face, he popped a peppermint in his mouth and made his way to the door.

"Good luck," the C.O. said, as she radioed for the door to be released for Ed to exist.

"Thank you," Ed replied, as he stepped out, on faith and the dorm, simultaneously.

Ed was floating on air as he made his way across the prison yard to the administration building. He had complete tunnel vision. Once again, he began to go over the questions and best possible answers in his head.

He walked into the building and notified the secretary that he was there for a parole hearing. She got on the phone and informed the board members that he was there. There was an eerie silence in the hallway where Ed sat and waited to be called in.

Ed kept looking at the clock on the wall. It was 11:45. Both games would be starting at noon. One with Ohio State vs Alabama A&M and one with the State of Ohio vs Ed Wilson. They were both a long shot and Ed had everything riding on them. He felt the same rush of excitement and fear that he got when he was gambling. It was his drug of choice and he was on cloud nine.

A man stepped into the hallway. "Mr. Wilson?" he asked.

"Yes, sir," Ed answered, like he was in boot camp for the Marines.

"Please come in and have a seat; the board will see you now."

Ed's heart was pounding a mile a minute. As he entered the room, only one person smiled as they greeted him. It was an older white man. This threw Ed off. There was a black woman on the board, but she was reading his file and never looked up as she said, "Good afternoon, Mr. Wilson."

Ed looked at the clock on the wall. It was 12:15 pm. Time was flying and it was time to play ball. Ed spoke to each person, looking directly at them with confidence. His poker face was flawless, but inside, he was nervous like a hooker in church.

The questions began to fly at Ed a hundred miles an hour. Like Barry Bonds in his prime, Ed was knocking them out of the park. The parole hearing was like a well-choreographed Tango dance routine. Then, the million dollar question was asked.

"How do you feel about the crime you committed and the effect, if any, that it had on the community?" This was asked by the same lady that didn't look up when he entered the room. Most of the time, this is the very question that tripped people up and causes the board to deny them parole. But, Ed was prepared and was ready. Without missing a beat, the answer flowed from his lips like a love poem written to his childhood sweetheart.

"First of all, I regret we even have to have this parole hearing. I was raised in a solid family structure with values and high moral standards. As we sit here, I'm embarrassed and ashamed of how I've disappointed my parents and shamed our family name. The crime of fraud that I committed was out of pure selfishness and greed. My desire at the time was to get easy money to support my bad habit of gambling. Through the classes and counseling that I have received here, while incarcerated, I've learned to admit I have a problem, know what my triggers are and adopt new ways to avoid repeating the unacceptable behavior. The crime that I committed caused a great deal of stress to my victim and unnecessary workload on the banking system. Not to mention that I myself have now become a finical burden to the State of Ohio. With that said, I request of the board that I be afforded the opportunity to apply the things learned here and return to society where I know I can be a productive member."

The board sat in amazement. They were not ready for the answer they received. Even the woman that asked the question looked up at Ed, then at other members of the board before she continued writing in her notes.

The chairperson asked the board did they have any further questions. They all said no. None of them showed any expression of how they might vote. Ed felt that he said everything right, but he was unsure of what the outcome would be.

"Thank you for your time, Mr. Wilson. Please have a seat in the hallway while we deliberate."

Ed thanked each person individually before he left the room. His stomach was in knots. Ed had heard this process could take up to thirty days to get an answer. Their telling him to step outside while they deliberate made him feel like their minds were already made up. Ed sat there and gave up hope.

"Excuse me, C.O., can you tell me what time it is?" Ed asked one of the officers walking by.

"It's 1:48 pm," the officer replied, never breaking stride.

It has to be halftime by now, Ed thought to himself. He really wanted to ask the officer what the score of the game was, but before he could ask, the officer was gone. The thrill was all but gone. The state of limbo had Ed in a sour mood. Not knowing what the score of the game was and not having the parole board decision was mental agony.

The door opened and one of the board members told Ed to step in. This was that moment. It was like having seventeen in blackjack and asking for a hit. The odds of getting a three is one and seventeen. Ed braced himself for the hit.

"Mr. Wilson," the black woman on the board finally spoke. "At this time…" Ed just knew he had blown it. "…we will ask you to return to your unit while we review your disciplinary records. The computer was down and we were not able to access them. We will have an answer for you soon as the system is up and running."

Ed was relieved and disappointed at the same time. He wanted to know. But, he still had a chance. He didn't have any major rule infraction on his record, so he wasn't worried about that. But the fact that he bet the long odds on the football game had him still feeling desperate.

Ed thanked each person on the board again for their consideration and made his way back to the dorm. By this time, it was late in the fourth quarter.

"How did it go?" the C.O. on the unit asked as Ed walked in.

"Good, I think," Ed responded like someone had just stolen his bike.

The C.O. try to give him some words of encouragement, but it wasn't sinking in.

"Yo, Eddy, you missing a hell of a game, my nigga," one of the guys yelled from the day room. The day room was packed. All the inmates had their snacks of dry, sweet cereal they had saved, chips and cookies from the canteen. Their eyes were glued to the TV. Ed stepped into the dayroom to see the score. The first person he locked eyes with was Big Low Down. He gave Ed a player's head nod and continued to watch the game.

The score was 28 to 28 with three minutes left on the clock. Ed couldn't believe what he was seeing. The highlights they were showing from earlier in the game were pure classics. The game had been a real dogfight. But now Alabama A&M had the ball and they were running down the clock. They were gaining first downs on almost every possession. It was like taking candy from a baby. Ohio State could not stop their running game. They had all kinds of trick plays.

Alabama made their way to the Ohio State's 40 line. It was 1st and 10 with under two minutes to go in the game. They snapped the ball. The quarterback took two steps back and pitched it to the running back to his left. The running back smashed through the defensive line and was tackled on the 15-yard line. It was 2nd and five. The QB yelled, "Hike," and attempted to do a sneak play and run the ball himself to get the first down. Ohio State stopped him dead in his tracks. The crowd went bananas. Alabama A&M had been running over them like a freight train all afternoon. It was 3rd in 5 with 55 seconds on the clock. Alabama wanted to get a little bit closer and more in the center of the field to kick a field goal and win the game. Ed's mind began to race just as fast as his heart.

God, please let Ohio State hold them so they can go into overtime, is what Ed was praying for.

The offense line was stacked. They only had one receiver on the QB left side. The defense pulled up to play tight and blitz. The Ohio State coach signaled for the safety to drop back - just in case.

The QB said, "Hike," and everything was in slow motion for Ed. The QB rolled out to his right like he was going to hand it off to his running back again. But this time, he kept the ball. That running back ran past the QB and

125

became a blocker as the QB circle behind him. The entire line shifted to the left. By this time, the one wide receiver was more than halfway to the end zone. The Ohio State defense was closing in on the QB. He knew he didn't have a chance to make the five yards to the 1st down, so he took his second option. While in motion and with 49 seconds on the clock, he hurled the ball toward the receiver, who was now in the end zone. The ball floated in the air for what seemed like an eternity. The receiver saw the ball coming to him perfectly. With outstretched arms, he prepared to end the game with the winning catch.

Without warning, that safety in the backfield cut across, leaped in front of the receiver and intercepted the ball. Ed couldn't believe what had just happened. The safety came down with the ball running like a runaway slave. He bobbed and weaved his way through and around Alabama players like he was made of silly putty. One he made his way past all of them, he turned on the jets.

Everyone, including Ed, was screaming. "Run, run, run, run, run, run!" Ohio State scored a touchdown with 4 seconds left on the clock. They kicked the field goal just as the time ran out. The entire prison was celebrating. Even the C.O.'s were high-fiving each other. It was only December 21st, but it might as well have been Christmas Day.

A letter was brought to the unit by another C.O.. It was the parole board's decision. Ed was looking for the bookie that owed him $250. He was already spending the money in his mind. First, he was going to pay off Low Down and then buy his daughter something nice. The bookie called Ed's name. He was standing by the showers. Ed walked over to him smiling like he won a million dollars.

The bookie gave Ed some dap and told him, "Good game," like he actually played in it.

"My boy got you," the bookie said, as he pointed into the bathroom.

This wasn't out of the ordinary. The bookies rarely touch the money. He was more of a Mafia don. He didn't do it; he simply got it done. Ed stepped into the bathroom where he saw an inmate counting a large amount of money. It wasn't uncommon to see an inmate with a couple dollars they had snuck in, but this was on another level.

"$250, right?" the guy said, while counting it out.

"Yeah, that's right," Ed said, as he exhaled a sigh of relief.

The guy handed Ed the money with his left hand. As Ed reached for the money, he felt a sharp pain enter his back, then another sharp pain on the other side of his back. He wanted to yell out from pain, but he couldn't. Both of his lungs had been punctured with a shank. His lungs filled up with blood every time he took a breath.

Ed fell to the floor, while trying to swing at the man that was counting the money in front of him. The pain was excruciating. Ed laid on the floor thinking about how he almost made it home for Christmas. His mother's face crossed his mind as his vision became blurry. Thoughts of his daughter broke his heart in two as he laid on the shower floor, dying. His final thoughts were of how excited Mika was about them all going to the meeting and then dinner as a family.

"Happy Holidays, nigga," one of the hit men said, in a menacing voice.

The other bookie and Big Low were in cahoots the whole time. The person that Ed pulled the fraud scam on that got him locked up was a big time hustler. The hustler put a hit on Ed. It didn't matter who won the football game, Ed was never going to see Christmas morning.

"Wilson, Wilson," the C.O. yelled as she walked around looking to give him his letter. Upon finding him dead, she called for backup and the prison was placed on lockdown.

All of Ed's belonging were packed up and sent home with his parents when they came to ID the body on December 25th. The C.O. gave his mom the parole decision letter. Initially, his mom wanted to throw it away, but curiosity got the better of her. When they got home, she sat at the kitchen table and opened it.

Mr. Wilson, it is with great pleasure that we, as the Ohio Parole Board, have agreed to grant you an early release…

Ed mom's face streamed with tears of sorrow and joy. It pained her that her only son was killed, but for her to know that he had turned his life around and was going to return to God gave her some peace of mind.

THE END

The Gift We Didn't Want

Chapter 1: Family Ties

Our family has always been referred to as the black version of the Brady Bunch. My father Tyrus, much like Brady, met, fell in love with and married my stepmother, Ne'Asha, whom I affectionately refer to as my mother since my birth mother has never been a factor in my life. My stepmother and father, much like Brady and Carol, also came into the relationship with children. I, Tymir Rawlings, am my father's only child, while Siyan Simmons was my new mother's only child.

One thing Siyan and I had in common was a missing parent. Just as my biological mother had never been a constant force in my life, neither had Siyan's father been in her's, leaving us to become solely dependent on the only parent we did have. The bonds shared between us and our parents seemed unbreakable.

From the moment, our parents united as a couple, the loyalties built within those bonds shifted. Siyan was five years old when we were first introduced, while I was seven. The two-year age difference between us may not have been considered much to others but, to Siyan and I, that age difference might as well have been in dog years.

Granted, when I first met Siyan, I didn't like her, as she often came across as a brat. All she ever did was cry and it irked my soul. Her tears seemed to be a magic potion for our parents. Every time she cried, they came running.

According to them, she could never do any wrong, which caused me to resent having her around. I began hinting at my resentment, yet our parents didn't take notice. When hinting didn't work, I began threatening Siyan with bodily harm. I know that some will consider my actions bullying, but I never truly planned on hurting her. I only wanted to scare her. My techniques still didn't work. What amazed me was the fact that Siyan never told on me for threatening her. I couldn't understand why her she wouldn't tell on me, knowing that our parents would've easily taken her side. With that, my antics still didn't cease.

Being that we were both an only child, we were used to playing alone. Siyan often enjoyed playing with her dolls, playing dress up with old clothes, heels, and makeup, while I enjoyed playing in dirt, climbing walls, and breaking things. One of Siyan's favorite things to do was throwing imaginary tea parties, which I found both boring and stupid. My father always encouraged me to join in and play with her in order to make her feel as comfortable as possible, but I didn't like it.

Her tea parties made me feel all girly inside, so I avoided them whenever possible. On the few occasions that was not possible, I created ways of making the parties a little more suitable for me. I did things such as knocking over her dishes, pushing her dolls out of their seats, and even going so far as to rest my feet comfortably on her table out of spite. I knew it would aggravate her, but having to participate in those damn tea parties aggravated the hell out of me. It was a fair exchange.

My actions became a regular routine every time I was forced to participate in one of Siyan's tea parties, yet she still refused to tell on me. It seemed like the more I tried to get rid of Siyan, the more she and our parents seemed to grow closer.

Over time, their bond seemed to strengthen, leaving me the odd man out. I couldn't stand that my father loved her as much as he did, but there was nothing I could do about it except pout and complain, which our parents deemed as nothing more than glorified temper tantrums. My fits, as they typically called them, often went ignored until the moment our parents announced they were getting married. It was then that everything came to a head.

All our parents ever talked about from that moment on was their upcoming wedding. I hated it. They'd often talk with me about my upcoming duties as the ring bearer, yet I had absolutely no interest in hearing any of it. My father would constantly tell me how important my role was to the entire day going off without a glitch and I'd simply roll my eyes. I wanted no parts of their big day and one day, I finally found the courage to tell my father.

"Dad, why are you getting married?"

"Because we love each other, son. Is there something wrong with Ne'Asha and I wanting to get married, son?"

"No. Well...I don't know."

"What do you mean you 'don't know,' son? It's okay to say what's on your mind. I'll respect your feelings, man to man."

"But, I'm not a man yet, Daddy."

"You will be one day, son, and here's one of your first lessons in manhood.

Men express themselves when they disagree with something. They don't hold in their feelings while throwing temper tantrums in hopes of someone else reading their mind or deciphering their thoughts. Now with that being said, what is the real problem, son?"

"Well…Ne'Asha's nice, Dad, but I don't really like Siyan."

"Well, why not? Talk to me, son. Has something happened that I'm not aware of?"

"She's a girl, Dad! She always wants to do girly stuff. I don't want to play with dolls, makeup or dresses, and I hate her tea parties!

You guys are always making me play with her and I don't like it. She never does anything I want to do. Whenever she cries, you guys come running but, when I cry, you tell me to suck it up and quit crying. She always gets to have her way and that's not fair, Daddy."

"Son, I know things have changed a lot around here recently, but I don't think Siyan means you any harm. I asked you to do all those things with her so that she would feel welcomed into our family. With Ne'Asha and I now planning to get married, you're going to become Siyan's big brother. Being her big brother comes with certain responsibilities such as a being a comforter, a protector, and an encourager, which I know you're more than capable of doing. I wouldn't trust you with a job if I didn't think you could do it.

I'm sure that Siyan may also be feeling a little nervous about us all becoming one big, happy family, but it's my duty to reassure the both of you

136

that we'll be just fine. We'll get through; that's what families do. You don't have to worry about anything through this transition, son, and you have my word on that. You can take everything I just told you to the bank, son, and that's a fact. So, are we all good now?"

"I guess so."

"Your answer leads me to another lesson in manhood, son. Never guess at something. When you make a decision about something, you should always be certain that's what you want to do. Before making a final decision about anything, always weigh out both the pros and cons of the situation, while also ensuring you never base your decision off your emotions at the time. So, with that in mind, are we good, son?"

"Yes, Dad. We're good. You and Ne'Asha can get married and I also accept Siyan as my new little sister."

Chapter 2: Gliding into Manhood

Ever since my father sat me down for our man to man back when I was just seven years old, I began looking at myself differently. His words that day allowed me to see that I was truly a man in the making, which only fueled my desire to be more like him.

The bond between Siyan and I also seemed to strengthen over the years, but that was only after I began embracing my new role as her big brother. Of course, we still argued, battled, and even fought occasionally, but it was all done out of love. While we may have fought each other at times, no one else could do it and that was a fact. When it came to fighting others, we were a united force. Nobody could lay a finger on either of us without consequence from the other. Some things Siyan did still worked my nerves, however. Her tea parties were one of those things, though, I'd learned to participate in. I'd grown rather fond of the smile that graced her face when I did.

A bonus to my new role as her big brother was that she now wanted to be included in some of the things I enjoyed. At first, it seemed like a cool idea, but as we grew older, I became much less thrilled with the idea of having her around for certain activities.

She particularly had a thing for wanting to hang out with me and my friends whenever they chose to hang out at my house. We never allowed her to do so, though. My friends and I were known to be a little mischievous from time to time, so they didn't want to run the risk of her telling on us. That left me with the task of keeping her away whenever possible. While I knew that my sister would never rat us out, I still went along with my friends for the sake of saving face.

Of course, Siyan never liked it, but she had no choice but to deal with it. When my friends weren't around, however, Siyan and I shared some enjoyable moments. One of our favorite pastimes was gathering around the TV every Saturday for several bowls of Honey Smacks cereal and all the Saturday morning cartoons ABC had to offer. We'd laugh and laugh until one of us wound up with milk flying from one of our mouths or noses. Those were some of the best times ever. Things were going well for us as a family until start of my freshman year in high school. It was then that all my focus and attention shifted.

One Saturday afternoon, while hanging out with my friends at the local arcade, we spotted a group of girls standing off to the corner watching our every move. When we moved, so did they, always making sure to never be too far from us. While I was certain that my friends noticed them, they seemed unbothered by their presence. Neither of them acknowledged the girls, instead, choosing to enjoy the various video game competitions. Ignoring the girls would prove to be a much harder task for me, however. Each time one of the girls flipped her hair, smirked, or laughed, I took notice. Not to mention, every time one of the girls looked in our direction, I met them with eye contact.

Being watchful had always been my specialty, so I always made sure to pay attention to my surroundings. My friends seemed to be used to girls swooning over them. I, however, was not. That type of attention was new to me. I'd recently began to take notice of how pretty girls could be and two of the girls from the crowd really stood out. I didn't know their names at that moment, but it didn't stop me from making a mental note to find out who they were as soon as the opportunity presented itself. While I admired both the girls for their beauty, it was something about the tall, chocolate one that caught my eye.

From the moment I laid eyes on her, I couldn't seem to shake the thought of her. I'd never envisioned myself liking chubby girls before, but I couldn't help being drawn to her, as a moth to a flame. She consumed my thoughts from that day forward. Each time my friends and I hung out in public, I secretly hoped we'd somehow run into her. I knew I'd have the courage to make a move if we did. As luck would have it, that opportunity would come much sooner than I anticipated.

Video games were something my friends and I enjoyed, with the *Grand Theft Auto* franchise being a favorite. On this particular day, my friends and I had headed out to Rivergate Mall in search of *Grand Theft Auto III* as it had been released the weekend before. We'd already been to 100 Oaks, Hickory Hollow, and Opry Mills Mall in search of it, but to no avail. We hoped for better luck on this trip. However, after three full laps around the mall, we still hadn't gotten what we came there for and I was irritated.

Instead of going after the game, my friends were running through the mall like wild dogs let out the cage for the first time. Roaming wildly in circles was pointless. Seeing no purpose in their antics, I was ready to go. Just as I prepared to tell my friends, I stopped dead in my tracks.

There, right in front of me, stood the two girls from the arcade. Both looked good enough to eat, yet again, it was the pleasantly plump, tall, chocolate beauty that held my gaze. Her presence alone captivated my attention. Standing there in awe, I probably looked like a goofball, but I didn't care. Nothing was going to stop me from seizing the moment!

Trying my best to look cool, calm, and collected, I casually strolled over to the girls.

"Hey, ladies," was all I managed to get out before being met with attitude from the girl I later deemed as the light-skinned diva.

Apparently, she was used to getting all the attention, so she naturally assumed that I was trying to get with her. It wasn't hard to see why most of the attention came her way as she was easy on the eyes: light skin, slim build, and auburn shaded eyes. Not to mention she had booty for days. She was definitely beautiful, but her attitude proved to be a real turnoff. Most boys would've done anything just to have the pretty girl that everyone wanted on their arm, but I was different. My father had not only taught me, but he had shown me that true beauty comes from within. A person's inner spirit had to match their outer appearance for them to be truly beautiful in my eyes.

Shifting my attention, I turned my gaze back to the true gem that stood in front of me. Standing there, I took in every vivacious curve of the girl before me. She was truly a sight to behold. Her ebony hued skin oozed power while her deep-set, almond shaped, mahogany brown eyes radiated strength. Her body language revealed her shyness, yet I saw so much potential in her. Her appeal was so great that I wanted to kiss her right there even though I didn't even know her name.

Realizing that I could get easily get lost in her eyes, I knew it was time to make my move.

"Hey."

Quickly casting her eyes toward the ground, she replied, "Hi."

Not wanting to lose my nerve I continued. "My name is Tymir. I know that we don't know each other, but I was hoping that you'll give me the chance to get to know you. If it's okay with you, we can start off with me learning your name."

From the way she blushed, I could tell that she wasn't used to getting this type of attention. She came across as the friend that skinny girls often asked to tag along with them so that they felt better about themselves. The type of friend that skinny girls felt they didn't have to compete with. Judging from her demeanor, that concept was accurate, as it left her feeling unworthy of my attention.

"M-m-my name is U'Neshia."

"U'Neshia; that's different. I've never heard that name before. I know this is spur of the moment, but I was just about to head over to the food court where my friends are and I was wondering if you and your friend would like to join us for something to eat?"

I must've struck a nerve with my last comment.

"I have a name and if you must know, it's Krysta!"

"Well, nice to meet you, Krysta."

"Yeah, whatever, but I'm down with whatever U'Neshia wants to do. Plus, my feet hurt from all the walking we've done and I am a little hungry; so, lead the way."

Her arrogance annoyed the hell out of me, but I couldn't complain since I was going to be able to spend time with U'Neshia. I could only hope and pray that Krysta didn't sabotage my time with U'Neshia by making everything about her. Allowing them to take the lead, we headed off in the direction of the food court.

After catching up to my friends, I made the proper introductions before turning my attention back to U'Neshia. Neither of us were hungry, so we opted for cookies from The Cookie Store. I led the conversation between us to give her time to warm up to me. It didn't take long before the exchange of information began flowing freely between the two of us. The more we talked, the more she opened up. Each time she laughed, a piece of my heart melted. This girl truly had my mind gone and I couldn't believe it.

This was my first real experience with a girl and I already felt sprung. I didn't care, though. U'Neshia was a rare beauty and I couldn't let her slip away. Before heading our separate ways with our friends, we made sure to exchange phone numbers. I found myself entranced with the lasting impression she left with me.

We never got that video game that we came to the mall for that day, but I wasn't disappointed. That day, I gained so much more than *Grand Theft Auto III* could ever offer me. I couldn't wait to get home to tell my mother and father all about it!

Chapter 3: Stepping into Responsibility

U'Neshia and I were officially an item by the time school started in August and everyone in our school knew it. We found fun in just about everything we did together: walks in the park, dates to the mall, movies, and arcade, even our nightly phone calls. There was never a dull moment with us.

Being with U'Neshia felt good. I enjoyed bragging about her and showing her off, especially at school. I was never ashamed to be seen with her and I think that served as a confidence booster for her. Each day, we walked to and from all her classes together with me refusing to leave from the doorway until she gave me both a hug and a spit swapping kiss. Sure, it may have caused me to be late to class a time or two, but I didn't care. My lady was worth it in my eyes. Things between us were definitely hot and heavy.

Even my parents liked her, especially Ne'Asha. She'd often invite U'Neshia over to the house for dinner so that she could spend more time with us. She also allowed her to tag along with her for personal spa and shopping dates so that they could get better acquainted, woman to woman. My family even began regarding her as a part of the family, which filled my heart with joy.

Things were going so well with us that, after just six months of dating, we decided to take our relationship to the next level. Sex was something neither of us took lightly as we were both virgins. We'd touched on the subject before during conversations where we both agreed that sex should be reserved for the person you're in love with. We both felt we'd reached that point in our relationship, so it made perfect sense to cross that line.

U'Neshia was nervous originally, but after some much needed reassurance from me, she agreed to allow me to take the lead. Over the next few weeks, we discussed when and where our first time would happen before finally settling on the first weekend in September since my parents would be out of town that weekend. I did my best to create a romantic atmosphere for her. I went as far as to light candles and spread rose petals all over the house. I wanted our first sexual encounter to be a memorable one. What U'Neshia and I shared could only be love, which was why I took extra precautions with her.

Before entering her forbidden tunnel of love, I ensured I had the condom on properly while also reassuring her that everything was going to be all right. I'd done my research so I knew my entrance into her womb would initially be painful but the more she relaxed, the easier things would go. As she lay beneath me with traces of fear etched in her face, I shuddered with anticipation. This was actually about to happen. For as much as I reassured U'Neshia that everything was going to be all right, I was just as nervous. I wanted everything about this moment to be perfect.

With the condom still intact, I entered my woman for the first time. My face couldn't express the pure delight I felt once I was inside her tavern of paradise. It took everything in me not to indulge in her goodness without regard. The feelings her womanhood gave me caused a desire to stroke her recklessly deep within me, even though I knew it would cause her a great deal of pain. I refrained from doing so out of love and care for her.

Once she grew accustomed to the way my manhood felt inside of her, she allowed me the opportunity to dive deeper inside her walls. I couldn't have been any more thrilled by her choice. The deeper she allowed me to stroke, the more passionate I became. My passion and eagerness caused my strokes to be more than I intended, leading to several deep, penetrating strokes. Her apprehension seemed to fade the more our encounter continued with only slight traces of discomfort lingering within her eyes.

There were no words to describe the sensation my body felt as it released its seed. Magical. As I came down from the floating high of our special moment, I began slowly easing my way out of her as the tip of my penis remained quite sensitive. I held my penis in the palm of my hand and was shocked at the sight! Sometime during our magical moment, the condom managed to break, leaving several parts of my penis uncovered.

Fear, dread, and sadness immediately replaced the feelings of passion I'd felt mere moments before. Regret seemed to cover U'Neshia's face as well as I noticed tears threatening to fall from the corners of her eyes. I could only imagine the thoughts running through her mind as they were probably the same ones running through mine. Even though I, too, was scared shitless, I tried my best to once again reassure her that everything was going to be all right. However, from that moment forward, things weren't going to be that easy.

U'Neshia

It had been six weeks since my first sexual encounter with Tymir and things had been rather smooth for us until two weeks ago. It was then that I'd randomly started becoming fatigued. At first, I thought I may have not been getting enough sleep at night, but the symptoms remained even after getting a full night's rest or taking a nap during the day. I knew something was off, yet I was afraid to find the answer.

Scared of what could be wrong with me, I preoccupied myself with planning for my sixteenth birthday party, which was right around the corner. In the past, I'd never done anything special for my birthday but, for some reason, I wanted for this birthday to be different.

Since my mother never did anything special for me, either, as she often treated me as if I didn't exist, I'd hoped to spend my birthday with Tymir and his family. Tymir, along with his family, were the only ones to show me exactly how it felt to truly be loved for who I was and to this day, I'm more than grateful for their presence in my life. I can't imagine where I'd be without them and I never wanted to.

Even with my mind distracted by all the party planning, I couldn't seem to shake the nagging feeling of something being off with me. My body didn't feel right and I knew that I couldn't put off finding out what was going on any longer. I had an inkling of what may be going on, yet I chose to remain in denial. Nevertheless, I knew what had to be done. There was no other choice other than to purchase a home pregnancy test so that I could find out my fate.

The Gift We Didn't Want

Worry, fear, and apprehension consumed me as I headed to Lynn's Drugstore on the corner of Shelby and South 6th streets to purchase one. Making it there and back without issue, I quickly proceeded to the bathroom and locked myself inside as I prepared to find out what lay in wait for me and my future.

Not wanting to waste another moment, I hurriedly sat down on the toilet, took in a deep breath and slowly released a short stream of pee before ripping open the pregnancy test. Gripping the plastic end of the stick, I placed the test just under my vagina, making sure the absorbent tip lay directly in the flow of my urine. Once it was properly in place, I restarted my flow of urine ultimately saturating it before placing the cap back over the absorbent tip and placing it on the sink to await my destiny. Was I going to be someone's mother? If so, what was I going to do? Would Tymir still want to be with me? Was he going to stay or would he leave me? So many questions ran through my mind as I sat there waiting on the results to come back. With all that was going through my mind, one would have thought it took a lifetime for the results to come back instead of the short five minutes it actually took.

Trembling, while filled with anguish, I picked up the test to see three blue lines staring back at me. Despair overtook me as I realized two of those lines were in the shape of a plus sign while the other one stood solid on its own. Pregnant. I was pregnant and there was no doubt about it. There was absolutely nothing I could do to change it. Definitely not the birthday gift I'd hoped for, but the one I'd been given nonetheless.

Unsure of what my next move should be or exactly what the future held for me, I needed to vent to someone to get this burden off my heart. My mother may not have been the best choice for receiving advice on parenting, but she was the only option I had at that moment. While she'd never played her role as my mother very well in the past, she could at least be a listening ear and that trumped everything in that moment.

Walking into my mother's room, I found her sitting on the side of her bed. The heavy drooping and reddish tint of her eyes revealed that she'd just finished up one of her infamous smoking sessions. Being that she was under the influence, I figured I could run my current dilemma by her without much feedback or consequence. I was sadly mistaken. As I sat there, pouring out my heart, she flared her nostrils while staring back at me with contempt.

Things took a turn for the worse the moment she heard the word pregnant. By the time I'd finished revealing my dilemma, I found myself being kicked out of her house for good. Her words hit me like a ton of bricks. To say that I was shocked would be an understatement. In the back of my mind, I'd expected her to be a little upset or even a bit angry, but I never would've thought she would kick me out of the house. Originally thinking she'd spoken out of anger, I hesitated on making a move. Finally coming to the realization that she was serious, I began packing as much of my belongings as possible into a backpack. With one last look, I took in the house I'd occupied for the last fifteen years of my life. Not exactly sure of my next move, I headed to the only place I felt I could go: Tymir's house.

I had no idea what I'd say to him, nor did I know how he'd respond to our newfound dilemma. But, he was the only one I felt I could turn to. I could only hope that his family would be understanding of my situation and take me in. Upon making it to Tymir's house, I found him at home alone and I was grateful for that. It afforded me the opportunity to fill him in on all that had happened, including the news of us now having a bundle of joy on the way.

The Gift We Didn't Want

Wasting no time, I broke down, proceeding to tell him everything that had happened from the moment I began feeling unusually tired to the moment my mother kicked me out of the house before bursting into a fit of tears. The sight of me in tears proved to be too much for Tymir. He attempted to do everything in his power to console me, including wrapping me up in a bear hug while squeezing me tightly. I sobbed into his shirt.

After roughly five minutes or so, my sobs started to calm, giving him the opportunity to fully dissect everything I'd told him. I stood on pins and needles as I awaited his response, but nothing could've prepared me for his reaction. Hints of joy, excitement, and delight covered his face as he took in the fact that he was now going to be a father. Ecstatic and thrilled were the only words to describe the expression sprawled across his face. Although we'd found ourselves in quite the predicament at such a young age, he didn't seem to mind. His reaction to our situation was the very reason I decided to leave him with the task of informing his parents of what we'd gotten ourselves into. I knew they weren't going to be happy about it, but they had to find out one way or another. Plus, I felt that it would go over better if the news came from Tymir instead of me.

Later that night, Tymir, his parents, and myself sat down around the living room. Tymir and I held hands while sitting on the loveseat as he began filling his parents in on what was going on. My chest filled with both anticipation and air as I held my breath, patiently awaiting their response. From the frantic looks splattered across each of their faces, it was easy to tell that they were caught completely off guard by our news. Not to mention, it was also clear to see that they weren't too thrilled with us.

Devastation seemed to resonate throughout the living room as Tymir and I both lowered our heads. We weren't necessarily ashamed of our actions, yet the sight of disappointment displayed on his parents' faces still saddened us. No one spoke for a moment, allowing silence to linger before Ne'Asha finally spoke.

"I'm not really sure how to respond to this news you guys dropped on us. Neither I, nor Tyrus, expected to hear anything remotely close to what you two just dropped on us. To say that we aren't disappointed would be to tell a lie, simply because we had high hopes for the both of you after high school. Now, we're not saying that you won't go on to accomplish great things despite having a baby, but what we are saying is that having a baby will complicate things. Life, from this moment on, for the both of you will never be the same." Sighing out of frustration, she continued, "Now although we're disappointed with the outcome of your actions, there's no way for us to go back in time and change things, so we're just going to learn how to get past it and deal with what's to come as a family. Now that we've gotten that out of the way, let's get something else understood. Tyrus and I may be disappointed with the two of you, but we're not heartless. There is absolutely no way that we'll allow you to be out there homeless, U'Neshia, especially since you're now carrying our grandchild."

It was in that moment, I finally let out a sigh of relief.

"We'll just convert the spare bedroom into your room so that you'll have somewhere comfortable to sleep. Also, since the two of you are opting to keep this baby, the both of you are going to need to get jobs to help financially prepare for his or her arrival and thereafter. Are we clear?"

Before I even had the chance to respond, Tymir spoke up. "I'll work. I don't want U'Neshia working while she's pregnant. I'd much rather her focus solely on getting through the school year and delivering a healthy baby."

While I don't think his parents fully liked the idea, they agreed to it, which I was more than grateful for. Over the next few weeks, Tymir put in countless job applications before finally landing one at Sbarro's Pizza inside the food court at Opry Mills Mall. From the start of his very first day on the job, he worked his butt off, often asking for overtime whenever possible to ensure both I and his unborn child didn't want for a thing.

Whenever school wasn't in session, he even volunteered to fill in for other employees that didn't want to work their scheduled shift. Although working and going to school proved to be a hard task, Tymir still managed to maintain A's, B's, and C's in all his classes. He was truly doing a wonderful job at managing his responsibilities.

Two months had passed since finding out I was pregnant and things seemed to be rolling rather smoothly for us. Christmas was now right around the corner and everyone looked forward to spending the day together, filled with loads of laughter and fun. Tymir and I were especially excited as the doctors had informed us the we were merely a few weeks away from possibly finding out the sex of our unborn child. The doctors didn't want us to get too worked up just in case the baby decided to be stubborn. We didn't pay them any mind. The only thing we'd heard out of everything they'd said to us was finding out what gender our baby was. We knew in our mind that our baby was going to let us see what it was.

While the thought of becoming parents initially scared the hell out of us, we'd both warmed up to the idea along the way. I knew that we were going to be all right. I felt secure that Tymir would make a great father as he'd grown up with a great role model and leader in his father Tyrus. He was definitely a great example for one to pattern themselves after, but that wasn't where our solid foundation stopped. Ne'Asha, too, was a wonderful role model and inspiration. I knew that I could always turn to her if ever I needed any advice or help along the way. Our baby was truly going to be loved and well-rounded.

Tymir and I wanted nothing more than to stare into our child's eyes, while letting him or her know that we'd always be there no matter the circumstances. Who knew that fate would have other plans for us?

Chapter 4: The Unexpected

Here it was, Christmas Eve, and I was still out last-minute shopping. Since I'd gotten paid the day before, I'd chosen to go out for a few last-minute gifts as a token of my love and appreciation for my family. Since I received an employee discount on anything I purchased at Opry Mills Mall, I decided to head there to do my shopping. One thing I knew for sure was that being an employee at the mall sure had its perks.

Finally, after several rounds of shopping, I was satisfied with the gifts I'd picked out for my family and couldn't wait to see the looks on their faces when they opened them on Christmas morning. Unfortunately, those things would never be.

I'd just finished purchasing the last gift on my list when my stomach began reminding me of its need for food. Thinking back on it, I couldn't remember eating anything since breakfast that morning, so I knew it was beyond time for me to grab a bite to eat. I wasted no time heading in search of food. As I headed in the direction of the food court, I couldn't decide what to eat Just as I rounded the corner near where I worked, I overheard two guys arguing. I didn't think much of it initially as it was quite common for an argument to break out in the mall. Figuring it was probably over some girl that was most likely sleeping with the both of them, I continued on my journey for food.

I couldn't help but to laugh at the thought of her playing both guys as I made my way through the food court. The arguing got louder as I made my way across the food court, yet I still chose to pay it no mind. Guys were known to get loud when trying to show out in front of a girl or their friends. Not wanting to make eye contact with anyone, I kept moving through the food court. Just as I reached the middle of the food court, gunshots rang out, inciting pandemonium throughout the mall.

Footsteps, screaming, crying, and panic were all that could be heard inside the food court for quite some time. When the smoke cleared, I lay sprawled out in a pool of blood on the floor of the food court. Things had happened so fast that I never saw it coming, nor was I given the chance to react. The first bullet pierced me in the neck, yet it didn't stop there. After firing several shots at his intended target, the gunman attempted to escape out of the double doors located directly behind where I'd been standing. His intended target wasn't willing to let him escape without consequence, leading to more gunshots being fired wildly in the direction of the fleeing shooter, ultimately leading to four more bullets ripping through my body. I never stood a chance.

There I was, another young black man in the making that just so happened to be on the right path, dead before my time because of senseless gun violence. I wasn't a thug out there in the streets selling dope on some type of get rich quick scheme, nor was I a child out there looking for some type of mischief to get into that wound up finding trouble. I wasn't even one of the parties involved in the original altercation, yet I still wound up losing my life. I was truly an innocent bystander in this whole ordeal, but what made matters worse was that I couldn't even be considered a person in the wrong place at the wrong time because I was exactly where I was supposed to be doing exactly what I was supposed to be doing. Nothing about what I'd been doing up until that moment was wrong. I was simply a young African American king striving toward making a better life for my unborn child and its mother. A young man set on making his parents proud. Becoming a future success story was my only goal. I only desired to be the guy that loved his girlfriend, along with being the young adult yearning to see the smiles put on his family's faces from his random gestures of kindness. The child with a beautiful soul was the only thing I could be described as. The one whose life was stripped away from him far too soon.

Christmas was supposed to be a joyous occasion, full of good times and laughs. But, from this moment on, Christmas for my family would never be the same.

Chapter 5: The Mourning After

A time of joy, that's exactly what Christmas was supposed to be, but for my family, that was never to be again. Due to the unfortunate events of the day before, my family could no longer revel in the happiness associated with unwrapping gifts on Christmas morning.

Unfortunately for them, they were given the one gift they truly didn't want, which was a Christmas without me. Several bullets were what led to my demise, robbing my family of my presence. Smiles could no longer grace their faces as heartache and pain filled their hearts. No one even bothered to gather around the Christmas tree to exchange gifts as everything surrounding this day now served as a painful reminder of what they'd lost the day before.

Each family member took my death hard, yet U'Neshia showed it the most. She refused to come outside her room unless she was going to the bathroom and although she carried our unborn child inside her womb, food was the last of her concerns as she refused to eat anything. Instead, she chose to remain trapped inside the confines of her room, bawling her eyes out. Her tear-stained pillows revealed that she'd been crying since the moment my parents informed her of my tragic fate. My death had truly rocked her world, leaving my mother and father to wonder if she'd ever rebound from it.

Our unborn child seemed to suffer from my death as well. The tightness of U'Neshia's belly showcased the fact that our unborn child was also in distress, which troubled my parents. It was far too early for her to deliver and they feared her having a miscarriage as she was only three and a half months along. She still had a very long way to go and they had to find a way to help her grieve properly. They couldn't bear the thought of her losing the only piece of me they had left. The tragedy of my death had already cost them far too much and even though our family's grief was in its earliest stages, my parents were going to have to find a way to get a handle on it before they lost someone else.

While no one's level of grief could be compared to another's, Siyan appeared to take it just a bit softer than U'Neshia. Maybe she didn't show it outwardly to the extent U'Neshia did, yet it didn't mean she wasn't just as broken and devastated. Her grief seemed to be more internal as she had been quite distant since getting news of my death. Attempts to console her by our parents had been shunned, leaving them to wonder if she'd ever speak after that fateful day. It had only been twenty-four hours since my death, yet it had already changed my little sister into a shell of her former self. The pain was proving to much too hard for her to bear.

Ne'Asha, the one to always be in control of things, tried her best to come across as strong, but her attempts weren't fooling anyone. Although she wasn't my biological mother, she was the closest thing I had to it and there's nothing like a mother's pain. This woman nurtured and cared for me as I grew up, while showing me unconditional love, so I knew she was hurting. Losing me hurt just as much as it would have if she'd lost the child she birthed.

Her grief was a little different from everyone else's. She seemed to break down in spells versus all at once. Those spells often occurred when she was off to herself. She always tried to come across as strong when in the family's presence, yet even the strong crack under pressure at some point. She'd tried to contain her crying spells to the confines of her bedroom, but it was proving to be a very hard task. Her pain was beginning to become more evident in other spaces around the house as she'd often find herself staring off into space just before the floodgates opened, allowing streams of tears to flood her face. Her pain was becoming much harder to contain, yet she'd always been the strength of the family. What happens when being strong was no longer an option? Her heart was breaking and no matter what things looked like on the outside, it would only be a matter of time before she broke.

My death had really taken a toll on my father, Tyrus. From the moment reality set in, he became numb. Other than answering the necessary questions, he rarely spoke. His mind seemed to be working in overdrive as he struggled with the reason this happened, as no answer seemed sufficient. There was no acceptable reason. No one had the right to take my life. I didn't deserve the fate I'd been delivered and somebody needed to pay. He'd never been the type to condone violence, but I'd be lying if I said he hadn't thought about making someone else's family suffer the way mine was. In the back of his mind, he knew that wasn't an option, but it didn't stop him from wanting justice. It didn't feel right that my family now had to go on without me while the killer or killers still walked this earth with breath in their bodies. Maybe some time later in life, he could possibly forgive my killer or killers, but that time was a long way away.

For now, he could only operate out of the stage of grief he currently resided in, which was a combination of several stages, including shock, anger, and depression. Acceptance would come, but only after I was put in the ground. He hadn't shed a tear since learning of my death, which served as further evidence that he was still in shock and struggling to process my death. Perhaps, after my funeral, he would finally be able to gain some type of emotional release, allowing him to finally cry and grieve. He needed to feel the hurt as it will ultimately be the only way for him to come to peace with what happened to me. If he doesn't let it out in some form or fashion, he'll wind up lashing out at others who had nothing to do with the cause of my death.

I knew that most men grew up under the adage that men weren't supposed to cry, but that couldn't be further from the truth. A man that can allow himself to be vulnerable is the truest form of a man. My father had always taught me that true men found ways of expressing themselves, even if it was painful to do so. Sometimes, crying was the only way to do that very thing.

Each member of my family dealt with my death in different ways. The one thing they shared was the wish that I'd come walking back through that door on this dreaded Christmas morning, but that could never be. No matter how much they begged and pleaded, they would never be granted that gift. Their worlds were shattered and no amount of love or support could ever put them back together. A lot of sleepless nights were to come, along with several moments of feeling empty and hollow inside from this day forward.

There was nothing my family could do to get prepared for what lay ahead and I hated it for them. I may have no longer been present in the flesh, but my spirit still lingered and I hated seeing them as they endured this pain. I could only hope they'd sense my presence or feel my spirit and know that I was still with them. I needed them to know that I'd forever be watching them from above. I'd now become their guardian angel and I missed being with them just as much as they missed having me around. While that Christmas in particular would be spent mourning the loss of me, I could only hope and pray every Christmas after would be spent celebrating my memories while also giving my child something to smile about. I know they'll forever be haunted by the tragic nightmare of my death during the holidays, but I desire for my death not to overshadow the fact that the gift of family remains with them in my child and its mother. The mourning after is very real, but hopefully, the morning after will once again inspire joy within my family.

Epilogue: Existing Versus Living

It had been three years since my tragic death. For my family, the wounds and void felt from my loss is still very fresh. They'd found some solace in the fact that my killers had been both caught and charged with reckless homicide, with each shooter receiving the maximum sentence allowed, which was twelve years a piece. It was peanuts compared to what my family felt they should have received, but in all actuality, there wouldn't have been enough time in the world that could've been given. No amount of jail time could have given me my life back and because of that, my family would truly never receive any justice.

Holidays since my death had also proven to be rather difficult, yet my family managed to get through them for the sake of my son who came roughly six months after my death. Tymir ReShawn Johnson had been born on June 20, 2004 which also happened to be Father's Day that year. It proved to be the ultimate gift for my father, Tyrus. While Father's Day was naturally a hard day for him to deal with, it turned out to be a very blessed one. Celebrating being a father had taken on a new meaning as he was now a grandfather. His life, from that moment on, had new purpose and for that, I was grateful. My son looked so much like me that it was scary. It was almost as if my spirit and soul passed into him as he even smiled like me. Everything about him reminded my family of me, which brought about joy. Being in his presence was the first time they truly smiled in a while. I couldn't keep from smiling as I watched from above because I desired so greatly for them to be happy again.

U'Neshia wanted to give our son my last name, but that wasn't plausible in Tennessee. However, he didn't need my last name to be a part of the family. He was my seed and they knew it. He was their last piece of me left and nothing in the world could keep them from fully enjoying a great life with him. In the three short years he'd been alive, he'd managed to come in and steal their hearts. He was their second chance at getting things right and they were more than willing to take it.

So much had changed for my family since my death, yet they were managing to cope. Before baby Tymir was born, they were merely existing without a purpose, unwilling to look toward the future. He gave them a new outlook on life. Before his presence came into their lives, they had no will to live on without me. The only thing they knew, up until baby Tymir's birth, was that they'd been robbed of one of the most vital parts of their lives. After his birth, however, they were forced to live on because he didn't deserve a life of depression. He deserved a family full of love, if for nothing more than the fact that that's what I would've wanted for him. Our son deserved a strong mother and I knew U'Neshia fit the bill. She may still suffer through moments and emotional breakdowns when thinking of me, yet I knew she'd pull it together for our son. If ever she seemed not to be able to get a grip on things, my parents and sister would be right there to support her. She'd never have to go through this thing alone because she was now a permanent part of the family.

As I witnessed our son running through the house that holiday season from above, I could only smile. He was happy and thriving, which was my only wish for him. He didn't seem to have a care in the world and I wished he could stay that way forever. Deep down, I hated that he would have to grow up and one day be told the truth of what happened to me on that fateful day. I could only hope it didn't change him or make him resent the world as I only wanted a normal life for him. I also could only pray that rage didn't consume him. I knew that the news wouldn't be easy for him to take, but it would be dead wrong of them not to tell him. Regardless of the pain it might bring, he had a right to know.

That Christmas Eve back in 2003 my family suffered tremendously, but nobody suffered more than my son. Because of that fateful day, he, too, had been given a gift that no child should ever receive. Although he hadn't even been born yet, he received the painful gift of having to grow up without me. Three years had passed, yet the pain still cut so deep. Because of that tragic day, I was never able to witness his birth, nor did I get to the chance to see him hold his bottle for the first time in the flesh. That day also caused me to miss out on seeing him roll over for the first time as well as witnessing his first time sitting up on his own. I never got the chance to see him crawl or the opportunity to stare in awe as he took his first steps, nor did I get to hear him speak his first words. All those things occurred within the first eighteen months of his life, so one can only imagine how much more I was forced to miss out now that he was three preparing to turn four. He would soon be getting ready for his first day of PreK and I wouldn't be there to see him off to school. I could only imagine the pride I would feel that day but, because of gun violence, I was taken from him.

It truly breaks my heart to know all the emotions he'll be forced to go through because of someone else's senselessness. Emotional hard times and tears can be associated to my family's Christmas, yet they're still reminded of the fact that it's a day to be grateful. No, they can't be grateful at the loss of me, but they can be grateful for the time they did have me, along with the memories of the good times we shared. They can also be grateful for the piece of me that's still here on earth because some families don't even have that. While I am missing out on loads of things physically, I'm still right there with them in the spirit. Only my body left them because I'm still there in their hearts. The other advantage to my situation is that I am no longer qualified to experience suffering through perilous times while on earth. My soul is finally free. No one else can cause me any harm.

There's a moral in this story, however, and it's quite simple. As humans, we never know when it's our time to go; so, we should cherish every moment like it's our last. We should be grateful for every breath we take and thankful for all the opportunities that come our way. Christmas is not about the gifts that lay under the tree, but the gifts that many of us often take for granted. The gift of sight, for example, or the use of our limbs and most importantly, the gift of family. Not everyone can reach out and hug their loved ones and many of us take the fact that we can for granted. Families of gun violence victims across the world would give their lives just to see their loved ones one more time. So, if one has family still living, they should count their blessings.

For my family, this story is quite tragic. But for yours, it doesn't have to be. Take heed to my story and cherish those around you, for they can be here today and gone tomorrow. Bullets have no eyes and those closest to you can be lost in the blink of an eye. Please put down the guns and learn to enjoy living life before you wind up causing another family to receive an unfortunate gift that I'm sure they don't want.

THE END

Christmas Memories

December 24, 1985

"*It's Super Plumber Boy and I need your help saving the world from the diabolical Turtle Aliens*." That one line managed to slither its way into the kitchen for the umpteenth time that fucking day, driving me fucking crazy with its stereotypical Italian accent drenching the character's every fucking word. I swore that if I heard that damned commercial one more time I was going to shoot the damned TV with my 22 caliber pistol.

"Man, fuck Christmas," I mumbled, hoping my son didn't hear me from the next room where he quietly sat in his wheelchair watching *Rudolph, the Red Nosed Reindeer*. It broke my heart every time I looked at my son sitting alone in that damned wood paneled living room in that fucking wheelchair, just staring at that piece of shit black and white TV. The picture kept blinking as if someone were making it flinch out of fear of being hit, which I did do from time to time to get the picture to come in clearer. But, my son didn't care about that shit. To him, everybody's TV acted up. Just like he thought everybody would go to bed once in a while without eating anything but salty crackers and cream cheese. Hell, the poor little bastard even thought that God made him crippled to give him the power of love to others. His mom fed him that bullshit to try to make him feel extraordinary, to shield him from the negative effects that his disability brought. God bless his mom for that, but she was only babying the kid and making him blind to the cruelty of the real world.

169

If you ask me, his mom is preparing him to be a bitch-ass nigga. You think the world is going to cater to his ass just 'cause he's a cripple? Hell no! This fucking world will eat him alive if I don't teach him how to be a man. Whenever I don't kiss or hug my shorty, it's because I'm trying to toughen his ass up, but his mom keeps nagging that not showing our son any affection will make him become distant and withdrawn. Fuck that. I'm trying to raise a man, not a damned sissy.

I've come to terms with the fact that I'm the one to blame for my son being disabled. I've been carrying this guilt for eight long years, trapped within its hellish walls as it ate away at my soul, bit by bit. Back in December 1978, I ran with a crew of four stick-up kids. We called ourselves the Wrecking Crew. The moniker was corny, but you couldn't tell our asses anything. We thought we were hot shit back then, robbing anything on two feet. That shit was gravy until we decided to hold up this Italian joint near Union Street. I swear, none of the cats in my crew had any idea that the restaurant we were going to knock off that night was owned by Sal Romano, the head of Delaware's crime family at the time. If my Puerto Rican ass would have known that information, I would have backed out of the job with a quickness; unfortunately, that wasn't the case.

The memory of that day began to warm itself in the film projector in my mind. Suddenly, the empty chairs that surrounded the kitchen table were filled with images and sounds of my boys playing a rambunctious game of Dominos as *Earth, Wind, and Fire's* hit song, *September,* played loudly, encompassing the entire house with a cheery vibe that clashed with the sinister plan brewing in our minds.

"*Capicu,* motherfuckers!" Santito yelled, slamming his last domino piece on the table, making it wobble with the force of its boom.

"Aww, hell nah, nigga! We ain't playing that Puerto Rican shit up here," said Otis, in a facetious tone as he smiled from ear to ear. "What the hell's a capicu anyway? It sound like some voodoo shit if you ask me," he continued, looking toward Big Mike for backup.

"Nigga, don't look at me; you're on your own on this one. You do know that I'm married to a Puerto Rican broad, so I know all about this particular type of domino game," said Big Mike, between fits of laughter that made his entire body jiggle like a bowl of Jell-O.

"Man, fuck you, Mike," said Otis, getting deeper into his feelings. Noticing Otis' facial features turn into a scowl, a voice that was buried deep in my mind said, *Julio, you better explain that capicu shit to him before he snaps.* As if I needed more incentive to explain what capicu meant, my mind took me back to a house party where Otis shot a dude in the head over a TV episode of *Good Times.* According to Otis, he shot the dude because the guy was talking some crazy shit about the young female actress who played the role of the sister, saying that she fucked every dude on the set of the show. That's how petty Otis was. If he didn't like what you were spewing, pow! The dude would send you to your maker. Hence, why I started to explain what capicu meant in a game of dominos.

"Relax, man! That just means that the winning domino that was thrown down has the same number of pips as the first domino that was used to start the game."

Otis sucked his teeth and cut his eyes at me. "Like I said, nigga, we ain't playing that Puerto Rican shit up here," Otis repeated, directing his attention back to Santito. I could already see Otis' hands moving rapidly toward the back of his waistband where the butt of his pistol was sticking out. As luck would have it, however, one of our wives in their drunken mania bumped into the record player, smashing it onto the floor into a million pieces.

"Yo, what the fuck, Sandra!" Otis barked at his woman from the kitchen table, giving her a look that said, *Bitch, I know it was you that knocked down that record player.* With that, Otis' mind was completely off the capicu incident and I was grateful, blowing out a sigh of relief.

Desperate to change the topic, I cleared my throat and made my way closer to the table, hoping my three partners weren't too drunk off my wife's homemade coquito. Shit, Lord knows all I wanted was for my boys to be clearheaded for the big score we were going to pull that night.

"Yo, this shit is tastier than a motherfucker! What do y'all call this drink?" Otis asked, downing the last of the cold, white, alcoholic beverage from his clear plastic cup.

"We call that coquito; it's Puerto Rican eggnog mixed with a shit-ton of Bacardi. Shit, if you call yourself Puerto Rican and don't serve that drink around Christmas, than your ass ain't considered Puerto Rican." Santito said this as a matter of fact, daring Otis to snap at him. Sensing the animosity build up again between Otis and Santito, I quickly changed the topic to our big score that night

"Enough of this petty bullshit," I cut through the animosity that seemed to be thickening like homemade slime in a bowl. "We need to focus our attention on our big score tonight," I continued, hunching over the table to speak directly to my crew.

"Fuck, it's about damn time we get down to talking business," said Big Mike from the end of the table, rubbing his eyes as if he had awakened from a deep slumber. He cleared his throat and began to speak in a baritone voice, befitting of a man of his stature. "According to my dude on the inside, he will let us in through the 'Employees Only' entrance in the back of the kitchen, but we gotta wait till 8:45 pm when the entire kitchen staff goes out to the dining room to sing Happy Birthday to some old asshole who's celebrating his eighty-fifth."

"Damn, why do we have to wait so late to stick up the joint," Santito whined. In response to his question, Big Mike gave Santito a cold stare that passed a chill through all of our spines a look that let us all know that if we weren't serious about the job at hand, he'd be happy to kill us all and do it his damned self.

"Nigga, use a little bit of common sense. It's Christmas Eve, which means the restaurant will be packed during the day. Shit, I don't know about y'all, but the less cats I gotta kill, the better. That's why we're moving in at night. According to my man on the inside, there will only be fifteen people attending that old geezer's birthday party, which means that the party is private and the place will be closed for anyone who didn't RSVP. I don't know about y'all, but seeing as the restaurant will be packed with customers during the day, I can't help but think of the amount of cash they have held up in that place. Also, keep in mind that all of the banks are closed for the holiday and the owner of the joint will keep all of that money in a safe in his office until Wednesday. My man says that he knows the combination to the safe. All we need to do is make it seem like he wasn't in on the robbery and pay him his cut," Big Mike said in a matter of fact tone.

It all sounded like a simple job to pull, but something didn't sit right with me. I got the feeling that we were in over our heads.

"Hold up, you want to hit that little Italian joint that's on Union?" I questioned Big Mike, failing to hide my incredulous tone that was dripping with fear.

"Yeah, nigga, that's the spot. Why; you got an issue with hitting that particular joint?" Big Mike asked, causing his well-kept mini-afro to shake a little under the sudden movement of his head as he cut his eyes at me. "Julio, if you've got any issues with this hit, your ass better stay put, Jack, cuz I ain't gonna have this shit fucked up over some cold feet bullshit. So, you're free to back out now if you want." As he was saying this, bits of silver glitter had fallen into his afro, making Big Mike resemble the fourth ghost that Charles Dickens forgot to mention in *A Christmas Carol* the Ghost of Hood Christmas. I had to literally bite my tongue until it bled to keep from laughing my ass off right then. *Damn, I've gotta tell Yadira to stop hanging those sparkly mistletoes around the house,* I thought to myself, desperately trying not to laugh.

"Did you hear me, nigga?" Barked Big Mike, dragging me back to reality.

"Yeah, man, I heard you. You ain't gotta get all rowdy. I was just asking cuz that joint's near Little Italy, and everybody knows that every business in and around Little Italy is owned and operated by Sal Romano," I said, trying to rush away the fear from my voice.

"Do I look like I give a fuck?" Big Mike said, arrogantly. "Besides, haven't you heard that Puerto Rican crew from New York practically wiped out Romano's entire organization, including Romano himself? Shit, the

174

streets say that those crazy Puerto Rican niggas ran up in Romano's pad and sliced him, his wife, and kid up really good. My man down at the Wilmington precinct says those Puerto Rican cats literally made minced meat out of Romano and his wife and kids, so much so that the cop had trouble identifying the bodies!"

I could feel the excitement and astonishment radiate from Big Mike as he went on with his story.

"According to the streets, those crazy motherfuckers known as the *Cucos*, the Boogiemen. The cat that runs the crew goes by the name Ismael Zepedas, a young cat who use to work under Nicolas Baxter, New York's biggest heroin distributor; even bigger than the Mafia itself. Crazy, right? How one black man had the power to overshadow an entire organization."

Glued to his story, I couldn't help but wonder if Big Mike was working with the Zepedas crew. Shit, the way he was talking about them made it seem like he was fucking the dude! Big Mike kept spinning yarn with so much enthusiasm one couldn't help but marvel at the tale. Shit, back in seventies, it was unheard of that a lowly Puerto Rican crew would take out an entire Mafia family. Hell, in those days, Puerto Ricans had to work with the black crews, but to hear that there was a Puerto Rican crew on the rise now, that was sure as shit something to behold!

"Holy shit, a group of Boricuas took out the Delaware Mob. Damn, that takes some *cojones*." I added, noticing that everyone at the kitchen table was as engrossed in the story as I was. We damn near resembled a group of campers around a fire listening to someone tell a scary story.

Christmas Memories

"And you know what else," said Big Mike, putting emphasis to his words. "The entire crew did the job with machetes!" A giggle of shocked amazement escaped Big Mike's mouth as he ended his story.

Silence enveloped us as we all digested what we'd just heard. The only sound in the room at that moment was the melancholy chorus of *Silent Night* flowing through the kitchen doorway.

"Papa, that's how we Ricans get down, baby!" Santito exclaimed proudly, causing me to smile.

"What the fuck, man? That damn song sounds so depressing," said Otis, extremely irritated. "Yo, turn that shit off!" He barked into the living room. The sound and tone of his voice seemed to create a demon that encompassed every inch of the house, killing off the Christmas spirit that was once alive. "Fucking broads, man, always partying while serious business is about to go down," huffed Otis, causing my blood to boil. But, I didn't have time to care about Otis' temper tantrums. I was more focused with the business at hand. However, if the dude labeled my wife a broad again, it was on.

"Say hi to your uncles, Ray," chimed the sweet voice of Yadira by the kitchen doorway, holding my baby boy upright by his chubby little arms, aiding him to walk. The pitter patter of Ray's tiny feet smacked against the linoleum floor with each step. Every man at the table was silent as they watched Ray and Yadira slowly make their way toward me. I swear, there wasn't a mean mug in the room. Shit, even Otis' crazy ass cracked a smile and anyone that knew him knew that smiling wasn't the dude's forte. As Ray and his mother walked closer toward me faint rays of sunlight began to peek through the kitchen windows, illuminating the entire room.

"Come on, *papito*," I said to my son, in voice that oozed baby talk, urging him to walk toward me. My heart instantly melted as my son's round, cherub-like face cracked a smile, sending a warm wave of love cascading over the entire group at the kitchen table. At that particular moment, we weren't crooks, gangsters or thieves, but ordinary men who were filled with an unbridled love that was beyond explanation. It was then that Yadira let go of my son's tiny hands and let him walk toward me all by himself. The pitter patter of his feet seemed to punctuate the love that was emanating from our hearts, like a baseline to a hot beat. Making his way toward me, little Ray fell abruptly to the floor face first, making a grotesque plopping sound as he hit the linoleum. Before anyone could go to my son's aid, the windows to the kitchen began to shatter as rapid gunfire whizzed through the room, taking out Otis and Santito instantly. Big Mike and I were lucky to get out alive with only bullet wounds to our arms.

Hiding under the table until the rain of bullets subsided, I caught a glimpse of my son lying face down and motionless, with a pool of blood surrounding his head. At that moment, my whole fucking world came crashing down around me. Fuck my safety; I needed to get to my son! With my legs feeling like gelatin, I ran toward my son. Honest to God, I can't figure out how my entire body didn't get riddled by bullets. To this day, I somehow believe that God himself was protecting me with his saintly robes wrapped around me. Arriving at Ray's lifeless body, I noticed that he had a bullet wound on the right side of his head slightly above the temple.

"No, no, no!" I screamed, letting my rage and desperation escape my being, creating a morbid symphony that would play its melancholic melody throughout my life for years to come. At that point, I was completely oblivious to the fact that the bullets had stopped whizzing in the room. The main focus was my son. Without giving it a second thought, I scooped Ray into my arms and ran out the house like a bat out of hell, forgetting about the well-being of the others that were in my house at the time, including my wife.

As I ran down 5th Street, making my way toward St Francis Hospital, I noticed Ray was breathing shallowly, which was a good sign. Shit, best believe that I was thanking God aloud the moment I entered the emergency room and my son was still clinging on to his life. A blast of warm air encompassed my entire body as we entered the hospital. It was as though God had wrapped my son and I into a warm blanket that was fresh out of an industrial dryer. I know that the warmth I was feeling at the time was just the hospital's heating system on full blast, but under the circumstances, the warmth that encompassed me was reassuring. It made me feel as if everything was going to be all right.

Seeing me with a bloody baby in my arms, a ton of nurses and doctors came to my aid as quickly as possible. It was as though they were expecting me to come in with a half dead child in my arms. In all honesty, I was impressed with how fast the medical staff handled the situation. Watching my baby boy being put on a stretcher and rolled away into emergency surgery is perhaps one of the hardest things that I have had to witness in my life.

"Sir, we need to have a look at your arm," said a nurse with concern masking her face.

"What?" I said in dazed voice, breaking out of the fog of my reverie.

"Sir, your right forearm has a bullet wound in it," said the nurse, pouring more concern into her voice.

178

"Oh, so it does," I said in a nonchalant voice, not realizing that I was in a state of shock. Seeing the crude, pulpy, bloody hole burrowed into my forearm brought me back to the harsh reality of my situation, and with it, the excruciating pain of my wound. Looking back, I think that the adrenaline coursing through my body prevented me from feeling any type of pain whatsoever (fuck, it was eighteen degrees that day and I didn't feel a wisp of cold air on my body as I was running all the way to hospital). Now that my bullet wound was brought to my attention and the initial shock had subsided, my entire right arm was pulsating in pain. Suddenly, the Christmas decorations that were displayed in the emergency room seemed out of place. Right in front of where I sat was a picture of a rosy-cheeked Santa smiling from ear to ear with ruby red lips that to me, seemed to be covered in blood, as if Santa had just finished eating the raw carcass of one of his reindeer and forgotten to use a napkin to wipe off his lips after he was finished eating. This was an emergency room two blocks away from the ghetto; what the fuck was a fat white man's picture doing posted up to a wall smiling?

Beside the smiling picture of Santa, there was an artificial Christmas tree decorated to the nines. Hell, the fucking thing even had real candy canes hanging on its branches with ropes of popcorn wrapped every which way. Living in the ghetto all my life, I never saw a more beautiful tree. Oddly enough, while my mind was still transfixed on the Christmas tree, the doctors had extracted the bullet from my arm and had me laying in a room with the TV show *What's Happenin!* Playing on mute on a thirteen inch wood paneled television that was bolted to the highest point to the wall that was facing me.

Looking over to my right, I saw Yadira sitting beside my bed with mascara running down her face, making her look as though she was some kind of banshee.

"Hey, babe," I said, in a whisper as her beautiful hazel eyes grew big with the happiness from seeing me awake. Without a word, however, the happiness that shone in her eyes suddenly faded. It was as though her soul was sucked out of her body leaving just a shell.

"What's wrong, Yadira? Tell me!" I yelled frantically, remembering that our son took a bullet to the head. With all the courage that I could muster, I asked if Ray was dead, but a tidal wave of relief washed over me when she said that he was still alive. Despite the good news, though, Yadira's mask of sadness stayed firmly placed on her face. Fear suddenly had a vice grip on my chest as I asked about the well-being of my crew.

"Santito and Otis are dead, but Mike is still alive. He was shot in the arm," she said, in between sobs. "There is one other thing. The doctors have told me that the gunshot wound that Ray has suffered will leave him wheelchair bound for the rest of his life." The wind was knocked out of me, as if someone had come up and punched me in the gut. At that moment, I could feel an overwhelming urge to jump out of that bed and run to my son's side, but that's when I realized that one of my legs was in a cast. The doctors explained later that during my race to the hospital, I was hit by a car and kept moving with the baby in my arms. Shit, let me tell you, the body's adrenaline is a crazy thing because I don't remember feeling my leg break, let alone what caused it. I guess you could say that I was 'in the zone' at the time.

The sound of footsteps penetrated my reverie, causing me to focus on the doorway to my room. Joy flooded through me as Big Mike's huge frame walked through the doorway with a mean mug expression on his face. Taking notice of the expression on his face, Yadira got up and exited the room as if on cue.

"Julio, how you holdin' up, man?" Big Mike's baritone voice came booming toward me with the warmth of a person that has just left a wedding rather than one who was almost shot to death. As he came closer to the foot of my hospital bed, I noticed that his left arm was in a white sling, but he wore a huge grin on his face despite his injury.

"There ain't a damn thing to be smiling for, man. Wipe that shit-eating grin off your face," I said, angrily. Seeing that grin on his face made me wish he had died in the fucking shootout.

"Hold up, nigga, don't kill the messenger. Shit, I come bearing good news," he said in a jovial tone. Like a high school kid preparing to sing his solo at a glee club Christmas recital, Big Mike cleared his throat and announced that the fuckers who shot up my pad were killed by the Zepedas crew in retaliation. According to Big Mike, the motherfuckers who shot up my pad were a hit squad sent by the Romano Family. Apparently, the inside man we had working in the Italian restaurant wasn't so loyal. He had dimed us to Sal, giving him the heads up about the heist. The same cat who snitched on us, however, gave up the whereabouts of the motherfuckers who shot up my pad once they tied his ass to a chair and carved up his face to the point that it was literally hanging off a piece of flesh from what was left of his ear.

My attention span weaved in and out of the conversation like static on a car radio. I couldn't help but think about the well-being of my baby boy. I also couldn't help thinking that if I hadn't agreed to meeting up with my boys at my pad that day, things would have been different. My son wouldn't

181

have been laid up in the hospital with a fucking bullet wound in his head. I only caught the end of Big Mike's rambling when he said that Santito and Otis' wife were safe.

"Not a scratch on them. They're just a little shook is all. My wife made it out okay, but Lord knows that shit is gonna fuck with her mentally," said Big Mike, plopping himself down in the chair that Yadira sat in minutes ago. "Man, you know that we are in debt to Mr. Zepedas, right?" Big Mike's question began to sound distant as the memory of Christmas Eve 1978 started to relinquish me into the year 1985. The damn *Super Plumber Boy* commercial began to play again, helping to dissolve the image of that memory a lot faster. Shaking the cobwebs that particular memory left behind, I made my way to a pea green corduroy armchair that was situated beside my son's wheelchair. Hearing me plop down in the chair beside him, he averted his eyes from the TV and looked straight at me.

"*Papi*, is Santa gonna bring me a Fun Station for Christmas this year?" I could feel my heart tearing itself to pieces as my son's question drilled itself into my brain.

Lord knows, at that moment, all I wanted was to say, "Yeah, little man, Santa got you." In reality, however, all I could say to him right then was, "You know damn well that I can't afford to buy you a video game." Ray's little face crumbled into a rubble of sadness, tugging at my heartstrings. Trying to hide my emotions from Ray, I disguised myself in anger by saying, "Ray, you need to learn that in this world, you rarely get what you want, so fucking deal with it." I sat there and watched two teardrops slide down each cheek. That shit was so painful to watch. It felt like I was witnessing Ray's heart break itself apart, piece by piece. Needless to say, I felt like a real dick

182

telling my son that, but that's what he needed to hear. Shit, I wasn't gonna raise a fucking sissy.

"I miss Mom," said Ray, trying hard to hold back his tears.

"Why? So your mom can baby you like she always did? Newsflash, you little shit! Your fucking mother walked out on us. She left me and abandoned you for some dyke named Rosie." At that point, I was out of the armchair and hunched over my son's wheelchair screaming in his face. With my fist clenched and ready to knock his block off, I quickly told myself to calm the fuck down. As if trying to hold me back from hurting my son, this shrill ringing of the phone caught my attention. I silently thanked God for that minor interruption. Shit, if it weren't for that ringing phone, I would have probably killed my son right then and there. Putting my fist down, I left my son quietly sobbing in the living room and answered the beige phone by the kitchen doorway.

"Yeah?" I barked in the phone.

"Well, hello to you, too, nigga," Big Mike said, jokingly, on the other end trying to stifle a giggle that escaped through the cracks of his serious tone.

"Don't start with me, Mike. You know damn well that today ain't my day, man," I said, hoping that he got a clue and would think twice before busting my balls.

"Man, you need to get over that shit; it was seven years ago. Your son's alive and healthy, Julio, what more could you have asked for?" Big Mike said this in a nonchalant tone, as if what happened to my son in '78 wasn't that big of a deal.

"What more could I have asked for," I yelled into the receiver. "For starters, I could ask for Ray to have a normal life! Do you realize that he won't be able to fuck a girl when he gets older because his dick doesn't work?" There was silence on the other end of the phone, letting me feel the thickness of guilt blanketing the entire conversation.

"Man, that was a shitty thing for me to say," said Big Mike, breaking the silence.

"Just forget about it, man. What the fuck did you call me for anyway," I said, changing the subject.

"Today's our lucky day, nigga!" Big Mike exclaimed, cheerfully. "I got a call from one of Zepedas' goons. Apparently, Ismael has a job he wants us to do tonight. His goon has already given me the details…"

"How much is the he paying to get the job done?" I said, interrupting Big Mike while trying not to sound overzealous.

"Damn, slow your roll, nigga! I'll swing by your pad in fifteen minutes," he said, hanging up the phone abruptly.

"Yeah, this better not be a fucking wild goose-chase," I said to myself, as I hung up the phone.

Fifteen minutes on the dot, Big Mike came busting through the front door with a bunch of bags under his arms and a filthy Santa hat that was a bit too small sitting jauntily on his head. The little white pompom at the end of the hat's tail was gray with dirt and age, making me think of a Santa Claus I used to see when I was a kid, sitting on the porch of an abandoned house drinking whiskey straight out the bottle. Shit, I could still see the man's raggedy, moth-eaten Santa suit if I closed my eyes.

"I come bearing gifts!" Roared Big Mike in his baritone voice, bringing me back from my memory. He made his way toward Ray with a shopping bag full of books, laying it across his lap sideways. A ton of books spilled onto the floor from the bag's opening.

"Whoa, Iceberg Slim and Donald Goines novels?" Ray exclaimed in excitement. His little face was beaming with joy as he looked up at Big Mike.

"I remembered how you like reading, so I picked up a couple of 'hood classics for you," beamed Big Mike, patting Ray on the head with his huge right hand.

"Wow, you even got me *Never Die Alone*," squealed Ray in excitement. "My dad told me that this was his favorite Donald Goines title," said Ray with increased happiness oozing out of his voice.

"Hey, what do you say," I said sternly to Ray, prompting him to remember his manners. Looking at me with a mixture of respect and fear, he opened his frail arms to embrace Big Mike. As Big Mike hunched over my son to hug him, I couldn't help but think of a giant bear mauling a victim.

"Thanks, Uncle Mike," said Ray, his voice sounding slightly muffled within Big Mike's hug.

"Don't worry about it little man; anything for you. You're my homeboy; you know that. Hey, but I need you to do me a solid, though."

"Anything, Uncle Mike, name it," said Ray, with complete and utter determination.

"If you ever decide to write a book, make sure you dedicate that shit to me," said Big Mike, playfully jabbing Ray in his belly, gently hitting all of his ticklish spots.

Shit, I ain't going to front. I could feel an aura of envy encompass me as I saw Big Mike interacting with my son like that and I felt angry that he knew that my son liked to read. I had no clue that Ray was a fan of reading. Hell, that was fucking me up. Why didn't Ray share these things with me? I was his father, damn it, not Big Mike! Visions of him reading to Ray and seeing Big Mike act overenthusiastically whenever he would read one of the stories Ray wrote in his composition books had me fucked up. There were times that I felt that he bonded more with my son than I did. I had no idea that Ray was into reading urban fiction. For God's sake, he was only seven years old!

"Yo, congrats, man. Ray just told me that he got the highest reading and writing scores out of the entire school," said Big Mike as he removed his Santa Claus hat, revealing a freshly groomed high-top fade that replaced his well-kept mini fro of the seventies.

"Yeah, thanks," I said, nonchalantly as I got a can of beer from the fridge. "Dude, you want a beer," I asked, nodding toward the fridge.

"Nah, I quit drinking a couple of years back," said Big Mike as he sat down in one of the chairs at the kitchen table. "Man, I had to quit drinking," he continued. "Between Natasha's addiction to crack-cocaine and my addiction to Jack Daniels, we were tearing each other apart, literally," said Big Mike. "Shit, things got so bad with us that I ended up sending her to the emergency room back in June because I gave her the ass whopping of a lifetime. Fuck, I was only preventing her from overdosing. Besides being hooked on crack, she's also using heroin as well, which has her looking like a motherfucking zombie and shit. I'll tell you, dude, it has been a grueling struggle dealing with this bitch. Thank God we weren't able to have kids because they would be the ones suffering the most throughout this shit." With all of that being said, Big Mike began to slouch in his chair, as if what he had just shared with me had drained him of all his energy.

"Man, that's rough," I said, trying to muster up what little sympathy I had left in my heart. On the real, though, I ain't give two shits about what he was going through with his wife. I was still pissed about the fact that when my son was laid up in the hospital struggling for his life in a damn incubator, Big Mike was all hyped about being down with Ismael Zepedas' crew. At the time, he couldn't have cared less if Ray had died. The sad thing or in this case, the funny thing, is that Zepedas went ahead and made Big Mike some sort of a lackey, cleaning up whatever mess needed to be dealt with. It was evident, though, that he was unhappy with the with his place in the Zepedas Family. Shit, every time he would stop by my pad he'd be bitching and moaning about how he was fucked over for a promotion within the family, but I couldn't have given two shits about his position in the Zepedas Family. That's what he gets! Shit, aside from being partly my fault, Big Mike holds the brunt of the blame for Ray being disabled because he was the one that recruited me as one of the goons to rob the Italian place on Union. Like I said before, if I would have known that we were going to rob Sal Romano beforehand, I would have never agreed to do the job.

"Yo, earth to Julio," Big Mike barked, dragging me out of my thoughts. "Nigga, you haven't heard one word that I just said."

"What?" I said, in a tone drenched in confusion.

"Exactly!" Big Mike said, annoyed and sucking his teeth. Seeing that he now had my full attention, he began to speak.

"As I was saying, I need your help on this particular job. Zepedas wants to shoot up this dude's spot. According to the boss, this Dominican cat came down from New York and is trying to muscle in on the boss' crack spots and he's not having that shit, obviously. Just so you know, we're supposedly running up on a Christmas party with some of his boys. If we go in there, guns blazing by midnight, nigga's boys will be so drunk, the element of surprise won't leave them any time to fire back. Plus, it's said that the dumb fuck doesn't allow guns at his parties. Man, it's gonna be like shooting fish in a motherfucking barrel," said Big Mike in between chuckles.

"Hold up. How do you know all of this information and who the fuck is this cat?" I said, with a shit-load of skepticism surrounding my thoughts. *Man, this entire hit could be a setup to get rid of Big Mike,* I thought.

"First off, nigga, that's a stupid question. Everybody around Hilltop and North side know that Zepedas use to fuck with a Dominican cartel before he rolled with Nicholas Baxter and his crew up in Harlem," said Big Mike in a matter of fact tone. He seemed to forget, however, that I had been out of the game since 1978. Hell, I was so far out the loop when it came to the streets, that I didn't even know where to get my hand on some good ass coke or illegal weapons. I guess you could say that I went soft and became a square once Ray was confined to a wheelchair.

Noticing the lost expression on my face, Big Mike says, "Damn, I forgot that you've been out the game for awhile." He clears his throat and continues, "The dude that we're gonna hit tonight goes by the name Caesar, but he is known to the Latino cats in the game as Caesar el Rey."

"Caesar the King?" I repeated in English, trying to figure out why that moniker sounded so damn familiar. Then it hit me as if the entire ceiling had just caved in on us. "Holy shit, wasn't that the cat who shot up an entire project building full of motherfuckers on Christmas Day back in '75," I asked, letting the grizzly details of that event flood into my mind. If memory served right, Caesar and his crew went in Oak Street Projects, guns blazing, all while Andy William's *It's The Most Wonderful Time Of The Year* played through a huge speaker in the bed of a pickup truck one of his goons were driving around the parking lot. When the carnage was over, forty-five people were dead and many others wounded. Among those that were killed, was an eleven year-old boy named Trois who suffered from spina bifida. According to some of the cats that were lucky enough to make it out of the building, they caught a glimpse of Caesar throwing Trois off the roof as the echo of his voice rang out, "Fly, little nigga, fly!" It was later said that the reason Caesar and his crew shot up the place was because he found out that his side chick was fucking a dude that lived in that building. I couldn't believe that a man would do all that damage over a damn side chick. What was even more fucked up about the matter was that the side chick's dude wasn't in the building at the time of the shooting. He was at his mom's house in Philly that day. Shit, I wonder if they ever killed that dude. Nobody ever saw him again.

With the image of Trois flailing his skinny arms all the way down to the pavement playing itself throughout my mind, I blurted out, "That Caesar faggot's going down tonight."

"That's the spirit, nigga," said Big Mike said, putting his dirty Santa hat back on his head.

As the night grew longer, déjà vu set in. Talking shit with Big Mike really felt like I was reliving that horrific Christmas Eve in 1978. Shit, I'm not going to lie, I half expected bullets to come crashing through my windows and take us both out. I kind of welcomed that notion.

"Yo, you remember how off the wall Otis used to be? He ain't give a shit about nothing, man," Big Mike said, nostalgia glazing over his eyes. He continued bringing up more memories of Otis. "Hell, you couldn't even say anything wrong about Thelma from Good Times; he loved that chick," Big Mike said, with a chuckle.

"That he did. Don't you remember he shot a dude at a party for talking shit about her?

"Oh yeah, that's right," he said in a fit of laughter. "Goddamn, I miss that nigga." Big Mike puffed up his cheeks and let out a long sigh. It was as though he was expelling the sorrow he had for Otis through his mouth.

Throughout that walk on memory lane, I couldn't help but think about Santito. The mere mention of the dude's name would send Big Mike into fits of rage. You see, not too long ago, during an argument with his wife, she revealed that Santito was dicking her down a couple of weeks before he died and Big Mike was still salty over that.

"We gotta go," said Big Mike, looking up at the clock. I followed his gaze and saw that it was midnight on the dot. What happened next is a complete blur. I don't remember the ride to the hit. What I do remember, however, is pulling up to a bunch of row homes on Fifth Street and kicking down a white door that was in need of a coat of paint. Once the front door was kicked loose off its hinges, we went in there, A-R 15s blazing. We shot anything that was in our path, including children. When there was no more

190

movement in front of our guns, we surveyed our surroundings and saw at least thirty or more people laid out in the huge living room with bullet wounds in their heads and chests, smoke still rising from them.

"Got 'em!" said Big Mike, pointing out Caesar's body from the rest of the corpses. Caesar's torso was slightly slumped over to the right while his lower half was naked with a chick's face pointed directly to his groin.

"Shit, at least he went out happy," I mumbled.

"Oh, shit, it's a Station!" Exclaimed Big Mike, holding a half opened gift in his hands with the silver Fun station logo exposed.

Suddenly a cloud of selfishness held me in my place, causing me to turn my gun on Big Mike. "That shit belongs to Ray," I said, shooting Big Mike in the side of his head. As police sirens wailed in the gloom of night toward the scene, I made my way to the car and drove away, game console in hand, singing, "You are my sunshine," as I imagined my son's face beaming with a smile.

THE END

A

Cold

December

Chapter 1

I thought the two-hour flight from Los Angeles would ease some of the tension I felt about returning to Seattle. When I stepped out of the airport, though, the feel of the cold weather brought back all the childhood memories I'd tried to bury. When I aged out of the system at eighteen years old, I bought a one-way ticket to California and never turned around. Seattle had nothing for me. It was filled with good memories that were lost in the bad ones. It had ripped everything from me. Pulling into Comet Lodge Cemetery, I exhaled. How ironic; this was the last place I'd visited before I left nearly a decade ago and it was the first place I visited when I returned. I stared at my parents' tomb stones. There, lay a part of my heart in the ground.

"I know it's been awhile. A very long while." I chuckled, trying to prevent the tears from falling. "I just never found a reason to come here. I know it sounds crazy, but it hurts too bad. It's extremely hard to deal with you two not being here. But, I came back with a purpose. I will get whoever did this. I will get peace and revenge for the Shaw family, even if it kills me."

I walked off. Early on, I learned to detach my emotions from situations. But, when it came to my parents, I couldn't. So, it was best I removed myself from the situation. I sped out of the cemetery making my way to the north side of Seattle, South Beacon Hill. Everything about the place I used to call home was different.

1268 McAllister Ave.

It was the place I used to call home. It shaped my childhood and changed it forever. It was the last place I saw my parents alive twenty years ago. It looked the same as it did twenty years ago. The house reminded me of the young, carefree girl who stood hours by the picture window of the bright yellow house waiting on her father to come home. Now, I was a woman with a heart full of hatred and revenge for the man with the heinous laugh and scar down the side of his face. He had ripped life from me. I was back to take his. Pulling myself out of my emotions, I sped off, heading to my intended location - Seattle Police Department.

***

"Hello. I'm looking for Detective Young. You can tell him it is Detective Shaw from LAPD," I requested from the desk sergeant.

"Welcome to Seattle, Detective. I will let Detective Young know you are here." She smiled.

"Thank you," I replied, hitting the decline button on the incoming call from my captain back home. Captain Mason was a tough ass. He wasn't too thrilled about me leaving in the middle of an ongoing investigation, trying to bust one the biggest serial rapists Los Angeles had ever seen. Although I loved my job and busting the sick bastard that got off on raping old women was a priority for me, finding out who killed my parents was something dear to my heart. I made a choice and took the next flight out; and I wasn't leaving until I got peace for my family.

"Detective Shaw. Thank you for coming down on such a short notice." A young, geeky, black man in a tailored suit approached. "I am Detective Young."

"Nice to meet you. I was shocked by your call. I have called dozens of times over the years about my parents' case. Everyone told me it was closed and there hadn't ever been any leads. Why the sudden change?"

"Let's head to one of the back offices. I was assigned to go over cases that involved a Detective John Swartz. Upon going over a few cases, your father's name came up a few times as a follow arresting officer."

"Detective Swartz was my father's partner for years. They attended the academy together and everything. His daughter Sarah and I spent plenty weekends over each other's houses."

"That's what I found out. My father also attended academy with them both. He speaks highly of them both. I started to review your parents' case. The night your parents were killed, you told officers your mother received a call from your father. Do you know what he told your mother?"

"I am not sure what my father told Mama, but it changed her whole mood. She told my brother and I to pack a bag because we had to leave. A few moments later, a knock was at the front door. When Mama didn't answer, whomever was on the other side tried to force themselves in. Mama told me to go hide in the security tap that my daddy created. When I came out, Mama was dead and Junior was laying with a bullet in his chest. Right above his heart."

"It was believed that your parents' death had something to do with a case. Swartz and your father had dealings in the streets with a thug by the name of Scar."

"Because he has a scar down the side of his face," I blurted.

Young's brow furrowed. "How did you know that?" He questioned, searching my eyes.

"Read my statement again from the night of my parents' murder."

"All the other original paperwork was lost or, I think was stolen, from the file. All we have is the paper that stated that your mother received a call. I found you on accident. After watching the press conference regarding that serial rapist you guys in LA are dealing with, I put two and two together by age and name. I figured you had to be that same Shanae Shaw."

"Why would someone steal my statement?" I asked, puzzled.

"That, we have no clue. My suspicion is that someone is trying to cover up your parents' murders, along with a few others. For years, Detective Swartz's name has come up linking him with a few drug dealers. Nothing anyone looked into. We locked up a local heavy hitta a few weeks back. He informed investigators that he'd had Swartz in his back pocket for years. Swartz kept him and his boys informed when raids and hits were being conducted. Until they got greedy and they tried to cut him off.

"A dirty cop?"

"The dirtiest. We have reports of money laundering, extortion, witness tampering and murder."

"What does Swartz being a dirty cop have to do with my parents' deaths? Because I know damn well you aren't suggesting that my father was also dirty cop."

"The total opposite. Your father was a very dedicated police officer. From my understanding, your father put in a transfer two weeks prior to his death. My theory is your father got wind of what Swartz was up to and confronted him. There was a note attached that stated another officer saw your father and Swartz having a heated discussion the day your parents were killed. The only thing is we don't have is a name. The name was ripped off."

"Wait. If I am following you correctly, are you saying Swartz had my parents killed?" My insides felt like someone had lit a match inside of me.

"My informant told us that Swartz ordered hits for a few people. When Swartz needed someone murdered, he would help him with it. Many of the people Swartz had killed were drug dealers who wouldn't pay him, people who threatened to turn him in, and police officers that got in his way." Young continued, "He couldn't pinpoint him ordering the hit on your parents. But, he pointed me in the direction of a thug named Scar that used to do hits for Swartz back in the day. I haven't been able to get anything on this Scar. No criminal record of anyone linked to the name Scar. You mention the name Scar in the streets and everyone gets a case of amnesia."

I heard Young talking, but I had checked out. My father treated Swartz and his family with the utmost respect. Hell, he had always treated them like they were our family. *What did my father know that got him killed?*

"I don't know what it is about this dude that has the streets so quiet. He could stand right next to me and I wouldn't know it because I don't know what this dude looks like besides a scar down the side of his face. Hell, my informant couldn't even remember what side."

"The left side of his face," I blurted.

"Wait; you have actually seen this man before?" Young rose in his seat.

"I watched him kill my daddy. I will never forget his face."

"So, let's back things up. Tell me what happened the night your parents were killed."

I sat back and closed my eyes. "It's usually cold here in Seattle around Christmas. On this particular day, it was oddly colder than it had ever been in my ten years of life. It was Christmas Eve. The Temptations' Christmas album played in the background. Every year, Mama played the same album. Mama, Junior, and myself stood in the kitchen baking cookies, waiting for Daddy join us. Sean laid in his infant crib sleeping. The time was nearing eleven o'clock and Daddy would be coming home any minute. The house phone rang. Mama sang hello into the phone. Instantly, her mood changed. Her once joyful tone went flat as tears formed in the corners of her eyes."

'What do you mean?' Mama questioned sternly, never letting her tears fall. Her smile was now replaced with a frown. *'Sylvester, you better hurry here now,'* my mother demanded of my father, slamming the outdated Crossley pink phone down. It was the only thing Mama had left as a gift from her mother after their house burned down from her childhood.

'Junior, Nae. Go to your room and pack a small bag. I need you to do it fast. Daddy is on his way. We have to leave,' she informed us with tears in her eyes.

'But, it's Christmas,' I whined. Being the only girl, I was a spoiled brat.

'Shanae Melissa Shaw. I don't want to hear none of that. Do what I say and do it fast. Without all that damn lip,' Mama raised her voice as she stared at me for a moment before she turned away and moved around the kitchen.

'Okay,' I replied under my breath, with my shoulders hung down. Christmas was my favorite time of the year and, in my young eyes, Mama was ruining our family tradition. We always sang Christmas songs, made cookies and once midnight hit, Daddy would let us open one gift. Like the brat that I was, I stomped up the stairs, trying to hold back the tears. Flopping on the pink day bed, I grabbed the Barbie duffle bag from the closet, stuffing two days' worth of clothes inside. Grabbing my favorite Barbie dolls, I made my way back downstairs. Mama was still moving around like a mad woman all over the kitchen. Beads of sweat dripped down her Hershey-colored skin. I wanted to ask her what was wrong. There was something different about the way she was rushing around.

There was a knock at the door.

Mama peeked out the living room picture window. From the window, you could see who was on our porch. *'Fuck,'* she cursed. She turned toward us, her long, slender index finger covered her full lips, signaling for us to remain quiet. She used her other hand and pointed upstairs.

A knock came again. This knock was louder than the first one. Mama's eyes grew wide. I remember seeing her chest rise and fall rapidly.

'Who is it?' Junior questioned. At sixteen years old and close to six feet tall, Junior was militant. He had no choice but to be with the father we had. He was built to carry on the Shaw legacy.

A Cold December

The sound at the door grew louder. But, it no longer sounded like a knock. The person on the other end was using something to try and break into the house. *'Go hide!'* Mama yelled. The panic in my mother's voice scared me. *'Nae, you hide and don't come out until I tell you to. Remember, like daddy taught you.'* Mama's eyes were wide with concern as she spoke to me. Wrapping my arms around her, I hugged her tight. Somewhere in the back of my young mind, I knew something bad was about to happen. My little feet moved swiftly up the stairs to my parents' bedroom with Sean tucked in my tiny arms. I punched in the code and climbed into the space just as I heard the familiar sound of Daddy's shot gun being cocked and then Mama's voice, *'You must be asking for a death wish coming in here.'* I closed the door, isolating me from all the sound.

I don't know how long it was, but it had been a good while since I crawled into the space and there was no sign of Mama or Junior. Sean had waken and fallen back asleep. Climbing out, I laid Sean, who was still asleep, in his playpen in my parents' bedroom. I moved down the stairs slowly. I didn't hear anything. I made it downstairs and the first thing I saw was Mama. She was laid out on the kitchen floor. Her big, round brown eyes were wide open with a single bullet hole to her forehead. For some reason, Mama looked at peace. I couldn't even cry. I closed her eyes.

'Nae, Nae,' I heard a whisper. It was Junior. He had been shot. My heart beat rapidly as I ran to the house phone to call the police. My fingers shook uncontrollably as I tried to dial 911 on the outdated phone. I heard his voice. I turned my head, looking for the direction it was coming from. I heard it again. It was Daddy. I sat the phone down on the counter and made my way closer to where the voice was coming from.

'Daddy!' I yelled, happy to see him through the picture window that was wide open now. With everything going on, I knew my daddy would protect me. I don't remember if I finished giving the operator our address. The door was hanging from its broken hinges. I locked eyes with Daddy. A smile crept on his face. I couldn't smile because I saw the man eyeing him, coming from across the street. Rat-a-tat, tat-a-tat! was all I heard. *'Daddy!'* I cried. As I watched my father, Sylvester Shaw, Sr, a decorated police officer for the Seattle Police Department, fall to the ground. A single shot to the back of his head. The man holding the gun glared at me. His dark eyes held no emotion. A large, ugly scar decorated the left side of his face making him look more dangerous. He laughed. It was a heinous laugh. It was filled with so much evil that I can still hear it today, just as clear as then. A cold December in 1998 ripped life from me and my siblings. Most celebrate it as Christmas."

"You are one tough cookie. Many children would be bat shit crazy witnessing what you did at just ten years old."

"Who said I was sane?" I chuckled.

"I mean, we are all a little touched in some way. Where are you brothers?"

"After our parents' deaths, they separated us. We didn't have any family. Sean was adopted right away being he was so young. I tried to find him once I got of age, but they wouldn't give me any information on his whereabouts because the adoption was closed. When Junior turned eighteen years old, he enlisted in the Navy, just like my father wanted. Before I moved to California, I tried to look for him, but he was overseas. I've kinda pushed it to the back of my mind and consumed myself with nothing but work. Thinking about it…it's too hard for me. So, I don't."

"You know that will not change anything."

"I know; but, we have our own way of dealing with situations. So, where is Swartz now? I would love to have a chat with him." I switched the subject.

"That may be too risky for the case." Detective Young stared into my eyes as if he could read my mind.

"It won't. My father and Swartz go way back. I haven't been here in ten years. It will be like catching up with an old family friend. Trust me. I got this, Detective." I smiled, breaking the stare-down with the geeky looking detective. I stood up, preparing to leave. "Does he still have lunch at the deli on Old River Road?"

Young seemed stunned by the question. "You remember a lot."

"Like I said, Swartz and my father go way back. Our families often swapped dinner dates at each other's homes. Plus, that was Daddy's and his favorite lunch spot. Is he still with his wife, Karen?"

"She left him a few years ago. He was caught with a stripper who disappeared without a trace a few weeks after Karen filed for divorce."

"What about the kids? I know everyone is all grown now. Does anyone still live here?"

"Sarah is the new district attorney. Kevin is the fire chief down at Station 19. Little miss Megan is the troubled twin who has been in and out of trouble that Daddy has to cover up since she was 16 years old. Morgan is doing fine. She moved away to attend law school right after her parents divorced.

"Damn. Well, push your informant for some more information on Scar. I will go run inference with Swartz. Let's link up for dinner and see what we can piece up."

"Detective, I may look young and I am sorta geeky looking, but I can read a person very well. I am good at my job. Don't do anything that can cost you everything you worked so hard for. It's not worth it. I know you want to seek justice for your parents. We will. We just have to do it the right way."

"That's why I am here. See ya later." I half smiled, walking off. I didn't give a damn what Young was talking about. I came to Seattle to find out what happened to my parents and I intended to do just that. If Swartz had anything to do with it, I would handle him the way I saw fit.

Chapter 2

Shanae

I pulled onto Old River Road and parked directly across the street from the deli. Through the window, I spotted Swartz sitting at a table in the back, occupied with another. Removing my suit jacket and throwing it over the backseat, I placed my shield and the holster that contained my service weapon into the glove box. I made my way inside the deli. Walking past Swartz and his guest, I took a seat behind them. Swartz was in a heavy conversation with a young white kid with filthy shoes and holes in his pants, whose hair looked like it hadn't been washed in days. He didn't notice me sitting behind them. Pulling out my phone, I snapped a picture of the two and sent it over to Young.

"One of them low-lives ratted me out. After everything I did for you fuckers. Without me, all you bastards would be locked up. Now I have these muthafuckas all down my throat and shit, searching through my accounts and cases I worked," Swartz raspy voice spat.

"Swartz, what the fuck does that shit have to do with me? I pay you good money to make sure the school turns a blind eye to me pushing these pills. Now, I have Dean Wilson sending the campus police to my dorm room to search and I am losing clients, which means I am missing out on money. Get it together or this weekly pay will end," the kid in the filthy shoes spat back.

"I still run this shit. Don't your little rich, white, spoiled ass forget that. I can see to it that you make the Channel 5 news. I can see it now, *Judge Richard Billow's Son Busted for Supplying Opioids to Students at*

Washington University." Swartz laughed. "Now I still want my fuckin' money and I want it on time. In the meantime, I will speak to Dean Wilson."

"If I go down, you go down. Remember that shit, Detective," Filthy Shoes spoke, sliding an envelope across the table to Swartz. Nice doing busy with your crooked ass. I want the Dean off my ass or I will have my dad on yours." Filthy Shoes laughed as he stood to leave.

"We'll see about that," Swartz chuckled, as he watched the kid leave.

"Are you ready to order?" The host approached.

"Yes, can I get a pastrami sandwich on toasted rye bread with a slice of tomato and avocado?"

"Anything to drink?"

"Just water."

"Okay. My name is Sam; your order will be out as soon as it is done. If you need anything, just let me know." Sam smiled as he moved over to Swartz's booth. "Detective Swartz. How is everything?"

"Good like always, Sam."

"Detective Swartz like John Swartz?" I questioned.

"Who asking?" He turned toward my booth. He had aged. His salt and pepper hair was balding and he now had a pot belly. Looking at Swartz made me think what Daddy would have looked like today.

"It's me, Shanae."

"Shanae Shaw? Sylvester's daughter?" He squinted his eyes.

"Yup, Angela and Sylvester's baby girl."

"I be damn. You all grown up. I thought you moved away."

"I did. I am here visiting. How is the family?"

"Everyone is fine. Off living their lives. Karen divorced me and remarried some man."

"Sorry to hear that. I've called a few dozen times to see if they had ever found someone in my parents' murders. Did you guys just give up?"

"We didn't give up. We pushed in those streets for a name. But, your father was…" He paused, scratching the balding spot at the top of his head. "Shanae, your father was a dirty cop. There is no telling who killed him. He was my partner and I loved him like a brother. I know that it is hard to hear, but it is the truth. I would love to bring in the bastard that took his life. But, no one ever talked."

I couldn't believe this dirty bastard was sitting here trying to tarnish my father's good name. Against my better judgements, I had to ask this bastard what he knew to gauge his reaction. "What do you know about a man named Scar?" I questioned, my emotions taking over.

"Who?" Swartz shifted in his seat. He avoided direct eye contact.

"The night my parents were killed, I saw the man." I watched Swartz's eyes widen like that was the first time he had heard that. I asked around and they told me there is only one man here in South Hill that has a scar like that, which is why they call him Scar. Have you heard of the name? I'm going to visit the station today and see if they ever had an encounter with a man named Scar or anyone that has a scar on his face."

"Shanae. South Beacon Hill isn't like it used to be. It is very dangerous. I will look into it. I have never heard of a Scar. But, do me a favor, sweetie. Don't go in these streets asking for information. You will find yourself in something you can't get yourself out of. Asking too many questions around here can get you killed, even if you are the police. Look what happened to your father and many others."

"Thanks for the advice. I have hired a private investigator to look further into it. I will get the bastard who killed my parents."

Swartz chuckled. "Stubborn, just like your father."

"I call it passionate, like Daddy." I smiled.

"Well, you enjoy the rest of your day. Here is my card." Swartz slid his card on the table in front of me. "Call me if you need anything, or you can find me down at the station. How long are you here?"

"Until I get answers on my parents' murders," I spoke, looking him dead in his eyes.

"Well, it looks like you are back home. Welcome," he smirked. "Let me know if you get any leads."

"Sure will," I lied. I wasn't going to tell him shit, but what he thought he already knew. I watched Swartz walked out the deli, instantly pulling his phone out of his pocket. He dialed a number and brought the phone to his ear. I couldn't read his lips well, but by the creases in his forehead and hand gestures, I could tell he wasn't pleased with my presence. His fuckin' bad.

"Here is your pastrami on rye with a slice of tomato and avocado. Is there anything else I can get you?" The host approached, breaking me from my ponder.

"No, this is all. Thank you," I replied.

Young said Swartz was out on suspension, but Swartz talked and slid me his card like he was active. My father would always say that 'great men always speak with confidence.' Swartz spoke as if he knew he would be reinstated. "What are you up to, Swartz?" I sat and ate my sandwich, replaying Swartz and my short conversation.

"Shanae," I heard a voice call out. I looked up to see Reggie Tate. Reggie was a childhood friend and my high school crush.

"Reggie Tate. How are you?"

"I'm good. How about yourself? You look like you haven't aged a bit."

"Thank you. I am good. I wish my body felt like I haven't aged." I smiled. Reggie had aged well and was still fine. Standing roughly around six feet tall, his skin the same color of Skippy creamy peanut butter. Soft curls adorned the top of his head. His beard and mustache were cut low and well maintained. His brown eyes still left me mesmerized like back in high school.

"Well, you are still beautiful." He smiled, showing off his perfectly aligned smile.

"Well, thank you. You are not too bad yourself. Still out here looking like Rico Suave. You still have women throwing their panties at you?" I laughed as I looked around. In high school, women went crazy over Mr. Reggie Tate.

"Not hardly. I am still waiting on Miss Right to be Mrs. Tate. How about you? Moved out to sunny California. Husband and kids?"

"I am married to the job. Detective with LAPD in the homicide department."

"Followed in your daddy's footsteps."

"Yeah," I replied, pulling my eyes from Reggie. Every time someone mentioned my father, I got a little emotional punch to my gut.

"I'm sorry I brought it up. I know it was a hard time for you and your brothers."

"It was."

"Since you are home, it would be nice for you all to meet up. I can only image how you all feel every December."

"You know where they are?" I questioned. I hadn't seen Sean since he was a baby and Junior in almost a decade.

"Yeah, Sean was adopted and they changed his name. He is the spitting image of you and your mother. He is currently incarcerated at SeaTac. Junior lives not too far from here. He has a wife and kids. He suffers from PTSD after coming back from the service. I check on them both every once in a while. My mother couldn't get over what happened to your mother and father. I still can't believe they never found out who did it. He was a police officer, for Jesus Christ's sake."

"I think they don't want to find out," I blurted out before I knew it, Swartz and my conversation heavy on my mind.

"Why do you say that?" Reggie questioned, with a raised brow, taking a seat in the booth across from me.

"What are you up to these days?"

"I am currently running for councilman of the 43rd district."

"Our old neighborhood?"

"Yes, South Beacon Hill is nothing like it was when we were growing up. I want it to get back to what it used to be. I have to start with the community that raised and shaped me."

"That is very true. Well, councilmen, how is your family relationship with John Swartz?"

"My parents will not speak his name. Why do you ask about him? Didn't I just see him speed away from here?"

"It was. I heard the department has suspended him."

"Who did you hear that from? We have tried to get Swartz off the police force for years. I know he is a dirty cop. But, they never can get anyone to flip on him."

"Wait, what? I was told he wasn't currently working."

"That's news to me. I saw him just yesterday down at the precinct. Who are you working with?"

"I received a call from a Detective Young a few days ago telling me he was re-opening my parents' case and had some new evidence. I flew out here and met with him today. He told me all about Swartz being a dirty cop and how they had an insider telling them all this stuff Swartz did and how he was being investigated."

"That may be very true, but, he is still an active detective for Seattle Police Department."

"None of this is making sense. Unless someone wants Young to think Swartz is suspended."

"I am not sure. But, Shanae, be careful. Swartz is nothing to be fooled with. I have heard the stories and none of them are pretty.

"I just had a conversation with him. Well, briefly. He told me my father was a dirty cop."

"Now we both know that isn't true. The whole community loved your father and all the good he did around here. That man is full of shit. Take everything Swartz says with a grain of salt. Many that have been here for years are not fond of him. How long are you here for?"

"Until I find out who killed my parents."

"Please let me know if I can be any assistance to you. Please don't go asking too many questions. You can get yourself hurt, Shanae. Everything isn't what it seems around here."

"Same shit Swartz said," I chuckled.

Reggie's brow furrowed. "He told you not to go asking questions because you can get hurt?"

"Yeah." It was something about the way Reggie looked at me when I mentioned Swartz's comment. "Why?" I questioned, still unfazed by Swartz's comment.

"Shanae, he was threatening you. Does Swartz know you are a cop? Who is this officer that called you? Swartz has a lot of people in his corner out of fear of him."

"Detective Darron Young and I didn't tell him. I purposely left my service weapon and shield in the car."

Reggie pulled out his cellphone. "Hey, sis, can you do me a favor and get me all the information you can find on a Detective Darron Young? I mean, everything you can find."

"Reggie. I am confused. Why are you getting information on Young?"

"He is a detective, yet he tells you Swartz was suspended and I know for a fact that isn't true. Call it a hunch. But, I don't feel too good about this, Shanae. You know it was a rumor that Swartz..." He paused. His eyes shifted from the gaze he held with me previously. "That he had something to do with your parents' murder. A few years ago, I heard my parents talking about it." His eyes met mine and there was something behind his glare that I couldn't put my finger on.

"Young didn't blatantly tell me that; but, he suggested that Swartz had something to do with it."

"I don't have to tell you to be careful. You already know that with you being a police officer. I am sorry. Correction: a detective." Reggie smiled again, making me want to cream in my pants. "You know I have had crush on you since we were young."

"Really? I didn't know that. You have always been the chick magnet."

"Yet, you never noticed me."

"I did, but I didn't think you would want a Plain Jane like myself when you had the whole cheer squad in high school dropping their panties for you on the daily."

"No man truly wants the woman everyone has had exclusively as his."

"Why didn't you ever say something?" I questioned.

"Although I seemed like this cocky jock, I feared rejection and I wasn't sure how you would respond. So, you go for the girls you know will not reject you instead of those you think possibly will. It's a dumb logic, but I was young. When I finally gained enough courage, you told me you were moving to California."

"I remember the day we crossed paths and I told you that I was leaving. You just wished me well in California. You know you miss one hundred percent of the shots you never take." I smiled coyly.

"You are right about that. So, what do you have planned for the night?"

"I am supposed to be meeting back up with Detective Young after he speaks with his informant. You said you knew where my brothers were. If you are not too busy with running around being the next councilman, do you mind taking me?"

"I have a meeting I can push back. Let me make a call." Reggie stood and headed outside with his phone in hand. I watched as he paced around with his phone glued to his ear. I pulled out my phone from my pocket to use the idle time to check a few of the dozens of messages Captain Mason had sent throughout the day. He was ripping me a new asshole for leaving.

"Something wrong?" Reggie questioned. I hadn't even heard him walk up.

"No, it is just my captain at home. Were you able to reschedule your meeting?"

"I was. Is everything okay?

"It's just my captain; he is really pissed at me. I left during one of the biggest cases of my career. I had a choice to make and I made it." I dropped a twenty on the table and stood.

"I get it. Getting justice for your parents' murders."

"That's what I told myself before boarding the plane. But now, this is much more. There is something bigger going on around here."

"I can tell you that," Reggie chuckled. It was something about Reggie's statement that made me stare at him for a moment.

"Did you want me to drive or did you want to?"

"I wouldn't ask you to drive me around town. Plus, you are a visitor in my city for the moment. You traded South Beacon Hill in for sunny Los Angeles, remember?"

"Whatever." I rolled my eyes as I followed Reggie to his car.

Chapter 3

Reggie

I couldn't help but steal looks at her as she moved her fingers swiftly on her phone unbeknownst to my lust. She was still as gorgeous as the day I first laid eyes on her. It was the summer of 1997 when my family and I moved to McAllister Ave. I was the new nerd on the block. I had big, Coke bottle glasses and my mother always made me dress like I was going to church. Instantly, they joked and called me the light-skinned Steve Urkel. Shanae welcomed me to the community with a smile. I had been crushing on her since. When we got to high school, I convinced my mother to let me get contacts so I could ditch my glasses. I came into my own and women fell at my feet. I was also the star running back at South Hill High School. Shanae stayed to herself after her parents' deaths. It wasn't until I ran into her after graduation where she was looking as beautiful as ever, did I realize she was the woman I wanted, but it was too late. She told me she was leaving Seattle for California. Like a coward, I tucked my tail and wished her the best, never telling her I was secretly in love with her and her chocolate brown skin that was always so radiant. Here she was in my presence, ten years later, looking just as gorgeous as the ten-year-old girl with the flying pigtails I had met all those years ago.

"Here we are," I announced, as we pulled up to the house Shanae's older brother Sylvester Jr lived in with his family. I watched her pull her eyes from her phone. Instantly, I could see the perplexed look in her eyes. "He will be happy to see you. Trust me." I offered her a smile.

"It's just been so long." Shanae exhaled deeply. "I feel bad for waiting so long."

"Which makes this moment even more special. Let's go."

"How do you know he will be happy to see me? I up and left him alone to deal with this shit every year by himself," she questioned, avoiding eye contact with me. "I'm sure every year he goes back there and replays what he could have done differently."

"Because we have had this conversation a few times, he wanted to come look for you, but he never gained the courage. He felt like him being the oldest, he failed you and Sean. Your father raised him to be a man and a man takes care of his family. He enlisted in the army like your father wanted, but he didn't look out for you and Sean. He has guilt there. So, like I said, he will be happy to see you. Both of you can let go of the guilt and be there for Sean because right now he needs both of you. He is in some deep stuff with some local gangbangers and the police."

"Okay. I know I am asking a lot, but can we see if we are able to see Sean?"

"Yeah, we can go up there. I have a friend there that should be able to get us in. He doesn't go by Sean anymore. When he was adopted, they changed his name to Jacob. Jacob Carter."

"Does he know who his real parents are?"

"Yes, he knows where he comes from and everything about the great man your father was and all he did for his family and community."

"Okay," Shanae exhaled deeply, finally getting out of the car. I could tell by her hunched shoulders that she was still nervous about the reunion with her brother after all of these years.

"It's going to be okay." I smiled, grabbing a tight hold on her hand as we walked up. Shanae looked down at our hands in each other's and smiled softly. It was pure and the most beautiful smile I had seen in a very long time.

Chapter 4

Shanae

It felt like my heart was going to burst through my chest. I hadn't been this nervous in a long time. Although Reggie tried his best to ensure me that Junior would be happy to see me, I couldn't help but still be nervous and scared of what his actions would be when we laid eyes on each other. It had been close to a decade since we had last seen each other. As I stood next to Reggie waiting for someone to answer the door, my palms began to sweat. Reggie still had a tight grip on my hand.

"Who is it?" A tiny voice yelled from behind the door.

"It's Reggie. I am looking for Sylvester."

"One moment. Daddy, it's for you," the tiny voice called out again. I could hear the locks being unlocked on the door My heart began to race. When the door opened, I felt like I was looking at a ghost. Junior was the spitting image of our father. I could feel the tears forming in my eyes.

"Shanae?"

I couldn't speak, so I simply shook my head up and down.

"Oh, my God. I have been praying for this moment." Junior wrapped his arms around me and when I heard him cry, I could no longer hold back the tears. You never know how much you are missing something until you finally get it again. I hadn't felt this safe in anyone's arms outside of my father's.

"Come inside." He moved to the side to allow Reggie and me inside. I laid eyes on the pretties little girl with the chunkiest cheeks I had ever seen.

"That there is Bella. My daughter. Bella, this is your Auntie Shanae I told you about."

"The one that lives in California?"

"That would be me," I smiled. She looked like a lighter version of Junior.

"Malibu is in California. That is where Barbie lives."

"That is true. Malibu is in California. Maybe one day you can visit. When I was your age, Barbie was my favorite."

"Daddy, we have to go visit Auntie Shanae in California so we can go see Barbie together."

"We will, princess. Can you go get Mommy for me?"

"Yes," Bella replied, as she pranced off in her pink, plastic Barbie heels.

"She is adorable."

"Thank you. Do you have any kids?"

"No. I am married to the job."

"What do you do for a living?"

"I am a detective with LAPD. How about you? Last I heard, you enlisted in the military."

"That's what he wanted for me. I see you followed in the old man's steps and joined the police force." Although Junior smiled, I could see it was a forced smile. He wasn't happy.

"What is it you wanted to do in life? I know that's what Daddy wanted for you. But, what is something you want to do?"

"I don't know. No one ever asked me that. Why did you become a detective?"

"Watching the greatest police officer I ever knew be killed right before my eyes. It was my mission to put men like the one who ripped our family apart away."

"That day changed my life. Serving in the military was like keeping his dream for me alive. I am sorry, Shanae. I failed you. As your older brother, I should have been there for you a little more. I got lost in my own sorrow."

"Don't be sorry, Junior, it was a difficult time for the both of us. You watched Mama be killed and was damn near killed yourself. We cannot change the hands of time and what happened in the past. All we can do is live in the moment and build the future."

"I am down. Have you seen Sean?"

"We are headed there next. I ran into her at the deli and you were closer," Reggie interrupted.

"Can I join you two?"

"Of course. When was the last time you seen him?"

"Right before he got locked up. He been running with the wrong crew. He found me after he found out he was adopted. I filled him in on what the Shaw family represented before our parents were killed."

"I am interested in seeing him. I haven't seen him since he was a baby."

"It will be like looking in a mirror. He looks just like you and Mama. So, what brings you into town and how long will you be here?"

"I came because I received a call they were re-opening our parents' case. They had some new information. But, I found out today everything isn't what it seems. So, I will be here until I find out who ripped our family apart and made me hate what is supposed to be the happiest time of the year. I haven't celebrated since then."

"Damn. It used to be your favorite time of the year."

"Used to. Now, it is a yearly reminder that my parents are not here. And before today, it was a reminder I had no contact with the only two living members of my family."

"Every year, I go there and think of new ways I could have done something for Mama. After today, you won't have to worry about that. Because I am not letting you out my life for another second, even if I have to come out to California to lay eyes on you. You have that Shaw blood in you, so I know you are going to find out who killed our parents. When you do, nail their asses."

"That's my plan. What do you know about dad's old partner…"

"Swartz?"

"Yeah, him."

"Not much. He checked in on me a few times over the years. Nothing more than that. His name doesn't attach to anything really good around here. Many in this community hate to see him coming. Rumor is, he is somewhat a dirty cop. Why did you ask that?"

"Has a Detective Young come around here asking you any questions about that night?"

"No, I haven't spoke to anyone in years regarding the case. I call every once in a while and I am always told the case was cold because they hadn't gotten any new leads."

"Same shit they always tell me. Which is why I was surprised when I got a call that they wanted to reopen the case only for me to get here and the case file has missing documents. I am very curious as why Young never reached out to you about that night, you live here, and he is aware of that."

"I have my sister working on finding out who this Detective Darron Young is. I don't know what it is, but something about this seems off. Things are not adding up," Reggie blurted. "He told her that Swartz was suspended from the force. But, I was there yesterday over something that occurred in the neighborhood and Swartz was there on duty, interviewing a suspect."

"Maybe he was suspended afterwards."

"Young said it had been weeks. He told me once I got here, that while combing through Swartz's cases, they came across Daddy's name as his partner from back in the day. When Young found out he was dead, he looked into his case and then found us. With me being a detective, he called me."

"Okay..."

"Well, he also informed me that he thinks Swartz had something to do with our parents being killed."

"What?"

"Yeah, his theory is that Swartz ordered the hit because Daddy found out he was a dirty cop. According to the records, Daddy put in for a new partner. I ran into Swartz not too long ago where he suggested Daddy was killed because he was a dirty cop and that's why there hasn't been any arrests or breaks in the case."

"That's bullshit. There is no way Daddy was a dirty cop. The whole city loved him. People who knew him still speak nothing but good about him."

"Same thing I said. Everything since I got here today has been off. It is like they don't want to find out who killed them. Like it doesn't mean shit to them that, at a young age, someone killed our parents in our faces."

"Those people don't care about us. Shanae, I know you are a cop, but with everything you told me, please be safe. The police around here aren't really worth a damn."

"Same thing I told her. Swartz already tried to pass off a threat as a friendly safety tip."

"He told me not to go around asking too many questions. I can get hurt."

"Does he know you are a cop yourself?"

"That I do not know. I didn't tell him that, but he is a cop. I am not hard to find within a simple search in any police database."

"Sorry it took so long. I was on a call." A brown-skinned woman with a wide smile emerged down the stairs.

"Not to worry. This is my wife, Kelly. Honey, this is my sister, Shanae."

"Nice to finally meet you. Sylvester always talks about the moment he could lay eyes back on his sister."

"It's been a long time and overdue. I am happy to see him."

"Maybe now we can get him to get out this Christmas funk he is always in. Hopefully, if you are not too busy, you can stop by tomorrow."

"I don't celebrate Christmas." I offered a soft smile, hoping she would drop the topic.

"Shit, you, too. Just like your brother. Christmas is about family. Many people wish to be in your shoes with their families for the holidays," Kelly expressed.

"Christmas has different meanings for everyone. You may feel the way you do, but I feel a different way. Now, can we just drop the topic?"

"I understand that; I am just trying to understand what happened in your childhood that you two don't like to celebrate Christmas. I thought it was weird when Sylvester told me that. I thought it would change once we had kids. But no, it's gotten worse and now you are here saying the same thing. Sylvester always just shuts down when the subject is brought up. I know nothing of his childhood, but that his parents died and he grew up in foster care. Did your father kill your mother or perhaps, the other way around?" Kelly questioned.

"Kelly. I told you when I was ready, we would take about it. Leave it alone," Sylvester spoke up. I was glad he did because I was two seconds away from putting my new found sister-in-law in her damn place speaking ill of my parents.

"That's what you always say, Sylvester."

"Kelly, I know you may not mean any disrespect, but, you should watch the questions you ask. My father was a wonderful husband and would've never hurt my mother; and my mother was a devoted wife that loved her husband." I tried to remain calm because the smiling beauty that came down the stairs wasn't the one in front of me. She was looking for a modern family; Sylvester and I had lost faith in that.

"I'm sorry; I didn't mean it like that. I just want some understanding. I never know what to tell the kids when they ask why Sylvester becomes someone different around Christmastime."

I stared at Sylvester, who seemed to be lost in a trance. He had mentally checked out of the conversation. It was a look only I would understand because I too, shared the same trait of mentally escaping while the body was still in the present.

"Kelly, give it some time and when he is ready, he will tell you why we don't celebrate Christmas any longer."

"So, at some point, you guys did?"

"Yeah," I replied. "That was a long time ago. I had decided I was done with the conversation with Kelly. I hadn't been in her presence but five minutes and she had pissed off every fiber in my damn body with her white-washed black ass. She was a damn airhead. "Reggie, are you ready to go? I don't want to miss seeing Sean before I have to get back to work."

"Whenever you are ready."

"I'm ready. Vee," I called out. It was my childhood name for Sylvester. He just sat there still staring at something in the distance.

"Shaw!" I called out a little louder and firm in tone.

"Yes!" Sylvester replied, standing to his feet. I, too, rose to my feet so that I could be eye level with him. He was a trained solider.

"What the fuck?" I heard Kelly whisper. I cut my eyes at her. There was so much about the man she called husband that she did not know.

"Are you still going with us to see Sean?" I questioned, turning my attention back to Sylvester.

"No, not today. Call me tomorrow so we can hang out. I'm going to lay down," he spoke before walking off and up the stairs.

"Now he will be in there for days," Kelly released, sounding defeated. I felt bad for her.

"I will try my best to stop by tomorrow. Just let him have his time. This is a very difficult time for him."

"Why?"

"It just is. When he is ready to talk, he will. Give him some time. Pressure is something that he doesn't need," I spoke before heading for the door.

"Your parents really fucked you guys up."

228

"What did you say?" I turned around to make sure I heard her correctly. Reggie grabbed my arm.

"What in the hell happened in that household that fucked you guys up? I never heard of someone just not celebrating Christmas that wasn't a damn Jehovah Witness. I am tired of trying to explain to my kids why he just completely ignores them around this time," Kelly spat. "I can't take it. I know he seen a lot of shit while he was in the army. But, when Christmas comes, he is just different. He is withdrawn."

"Maybe you should have found out more about the man you laid down and had babies with. I will give you this warning, Mrs. Kelly. Don't ever ask my brother that question and especially not with that tone. You will fuck around and find yourself dead," I spat, watching Kelly's eyes widen in fear. I was seconds from putting my own foot in her ass. "Be gentle with him."

"Why won't he tell me?" Kelly cried. I actually felt bad for her. It was difficult trying to love someone who was sheltering their heart. Sylvester was trying his hardest to remain normal, but his pain was forcing the people he loved away from him. I knew the situation all too well; the only difference with me was I didn't give a fuck.

"Because…it hurts too bad."

"What hurts? How can I help him if he doesn't want to talk about his childhood?"

"Give it time. He just needs time to start talking about it."

"Okay," Kelly wiped her wet eyes as she walked behind us to the front door.

Halfway to the car, I turned around and saw Kelly still standing at the door. "We don't celebrate Christmas because it is a constant reminder that it was the day our family was ripped apart. It was Christmas when our parents were killed…in front of us." I could hear Kelly bawling behind me as I got into the passenger side of Reggie's car.

Chapter 5

Shanae

Reggie stared at me. "Don't you think that is something Sylvester should have told his wife?" Reggie questioned as we drove off.

"She needed to know. He is not going to tell her. He can't. He hasn't dealt with it. He just found ways to mask the pain. Can you imagine a day starting out with so much joy and family only for it to end on life support? When you finally are stable, they inform you that your mother and father are dead. And the only family you have left are separated from you."

"No, I can't imagine that pain."

"People think time makes it easier. But, it doesn't. Some days are better than others. It's those moments that you want to celebrate something and it hits you like a ton of bricks that you don't have anyone to celebrate it with. Had my parents died of some illness that attacked them rather than some fuckin' coward taking their lives, we probably could deal with their deaths a little better. It's been twenty years and nothing. No arrests made. My father was a damn cop and damn good one and no arrests? That shit alone makes me question the Seattle Police Department."

"So, you think that someone within the department knows what happened to your father?"

"I don't 'think.' I know they do. What I am confused on is who actually did it and why the others helped cover up what really happened."

"What if the department truly doesn't know?"

"They know something. Remember, I am a cop. There is not just one cop behind this. They have help. It may not be the whole department, but, it's a few. I am sure of that."

"You can be right or you can be wrong. What is your game plan to find out the truth?"

"That I don't know. I know it is going to take me some time. I must sit back and watch. But, one thing I do know is that I will not be leaving Seattle until I have justice for my family. My brother is suffering and if he doesn't fix it, his wife is going to leave him. Or worse, she is going to apply too much pressure and he snaps and kills her. The military fucks with people's heads. They condition you for war. Your brain never turns it off."

"I never looked at it that way."

"That's why many veterans suffer PTSD. They see so much shit. Sylvester was diagnosed with it before he even enlisted. I just want my parents' deaths to finally feel like it was justly resolved. At this point, I need it to be. Sylvester needs it so he can move forward. He has been living with this guilt for twenty years."

"What if you get hurt in the process?"

"That's just a risk I am willing to take. Every day, I leave my apartment with the hopes of returning, but with the mindset that I potentially can die. It comes with the oath I took to the job." I could feel Reggie's eyes prying into me as we pulled into the prison gates. For some reason, I found his brown, dreamy eyes prying into me kinda sexy.

"Seeing Sean is going to be different than seeing Sylvester. Sean doesn't have any memory of the family because he was so young."

"I am aware of that. What is he in here for anyways? This is a federal prison?"

"Being with the wrong crew, getting into some stuff, tryna find himself out here in this world. I know you see it a lot with young boys tryna find a place to belong with no real guidance. When the woman who raised him died, he felt alone and went off in the street."

"Damn. I feel bad because I should have come back for him years ago. I was just so caught up in my own shit."

"You can't beat yourself up for something you can't control. Like you just said, you cannot change the past, but you can make sure the future is better. Focus on the future."

"You are right."

"Can you call the warden and let him know Reggie Tate needs to speak with him?" Reggie requested of the officer sitting at the front desk.

"Sure can. One moment."

"What do you plan on saying to him?"

"I don't know. I'm really not a good communicator when it comes to my emotions. On the job, yes. But in my personal life, not really."

"You seem like a natural to me." Reggie smiled. I was here for a sole purpose and could not be distracted with being smitten by Reggie and all his sexiness. But every time he smiled at me, my hormones went wild.

"Mr. Tate, what can I do for you?"

"Warden Jefferson. This is Detective Shaw out of Los Angeles. We need to speak to Jacob Carter."

"It will only be for a few moments because we are about to go on lockdown."

"That will be fine," I spoke up. "I just want to be able to look him in his face and let him know I am here for him for whatever. I can always come back at a later time."

"Are you family?"

"It's a long story," Reggie interrupted.

"Okay; give me a few moments to get him brought down. I will have one of my officers get you set up in a conference room."

"Thank you, Warden."

"Anything for the new councilman," the Warden smiled. I am not sure if Reggie caught it, but the warden's comment came off extremely sarcastic and the smile was forced.

"Right this way," a young, Latina, female officer spoke, leading us to the back to a conference room.

"What is the deal with the warden?"

"What do you mean by that?"

"His comment was sarcastic as hell and that fake ass smile when he said 'anything for the new councilman.' You two have history?"

"Something like that. His sister is my ex-girlfriend." Reggie avoided eye contact with me.

"What happened between you two?"

"We can talk about that later. Here comes Sean," Reggie spoke. From where he sat, he could see the people who were approaching the room. When he entered the room, it was like seeing a ghost for the second time that day. Sean was the spitting image of my mother and myself. We could've been triplets.

"You have ten minutes," a tall, white officer spoke sternly, handcuffing him to the table.

"Thank you."

"What's up, Jacob? Remember when we had that conversation about your birth parents and siblings?"

"I do. This my sister?" He asked, staring me in my eyes.

"How did you know?"

"Looking at you is like looking at myself in a female version. The shit is wild," he chuckled.

"Same shit I thought when you walked in the door. We actually look just our mother."

"Do you have any photos?"

"I do. This was the last picture we took as a family. It was right after you were born." I pulled out the only family photo I had, sliding it across the table. I always kept it in my wallet.

"Damn. We looked like a happy family. Like the Huxtables." Sean smiled and it melted my heart. This day was way too fuckin' emotional for me.

"I don't know about the Huxtables. But, we were a tight-knitted family. Our father was a dedicated cop to the Seattle Police Department and our mother was a devoted wife. She worked in the nursing field until she gave birth to you. She wanted to be able to attend our school activities, so Daddy let her become a stay-at-home mom. In my eyes, everything was perfect until the day they were murdered and our young lives were ripped apart."

"What happened? Who would want to kill them?"

"That, I still do not know. That is why I am here in town. It is my mission to find out what happened to them. So, let's talk about you. Why are you in here?"

"I found out I was adopted at twelve years old when the women I knew as my mother was diagnosed with cancer. On her death bed, she told me. Her husband had left right after she was diagnosed. Turns out, he had another family on the other side of town. She couldn't have kids, which is why she adopted me, but he could and decided to have his own elsewhere. After her death, they contacted him since he was listed as my father. He told them I was adopted and not his kid. That it was something his wife wanted, not him and he already had three kids of his own to take care of. He signed over his rights and I was put back in the system. So, I started to ask my case workers questions about my birth family and why they didn't want me. I was given a name. Once I found that, I started asking questions. I was getting nowhere. Growing tired and wanting to belong, I started hanging with some kids in the group home with me, getting into a lot of stuff I wasn't supposed to,

236

which led me here. When they busted us, I had nothing on me. Dude I used to work with said it was a crooked cop who got pissed he wasn't paying him what he wanted weekly and decided to make an example out of us for everyone else to see he wasn't to be fucked with. While here, Reggie started to visit me and told me he knew my real family and that I was born Sean Shaw and not Jacob Carter."

"Do you happen to know this cop's name?" I really wanted to know if Swartz was behind this or if there were more dirty cops within the Seattle Police force.

"Swartz. He was known for shaking down the local streets dudes for money; hell, from what I heard in here, he even took a few dudes' product when shit not going his way. Swartz is as shady as they come."

"Does Swartz know you by Jacob or Sean?"

"Everyone knows me as Jacob. The only people that know I was born Sean and not Jacob are Reggie and my girl. Well, outside of you and Sylvester. The adoption was closed,, so they don't have that information unless they have a plug in the DPSS office. Why you ask that?"

"You are aware our father was a police officer?"

"I am aware of that."

"Swartz used to be our father's partner. I also have reason to believe he had something to do with our parents' murders."

"Whoa. Why do you have reason to believe that?"

"I was contacted by a detective from Seattle PD - that they were re-opening our parents' case."

"You are a detective, right? Out in California?"

"Well, they told me they were investigating our parents' murders and that they received some new information. So, I came out here and basically everything you just told me I was informed of. But, I had a little run-in with Swartz and he seems to think our parents' murders were never solved because our father was a dirty cop. Which is pure bullshit and I know that as a fact. But, I will be in town until I find out the truth. It's been twenty long years and I will not let it go on any longer without being solved." I felt like a broken record, constantly repeating myself.

"If you weren't a cop, I would say you on some gangsta shit. Many people underestimate these Seattle streets. But, you been in Killa Cali for a minute, so I'm sure you know how this shit goes. Swartz has a whole team behind him. They protect him. So, be careful." Hearing Sean warn me of Swartz fueled me to bust his ass and see to it that he is stripped of his title as a police officer. He didn't deserve to have the same title as me.

"Don't worry about me. I can handle myself. How much longer you have in here?"

"I was given six years; I have been down for a year. The thing is, I wasn't caught with anything and was railroaded at court. Swartz had an officer say they took all of this stuff off me, but it's not true."

"He isn't lying. I forgot the officer's name. I have it written down at my office."

"They never gave me his name. They still haven't issued me paperwork. I do remember what he looked like. Tall, dark, short fade. A geeky looking dude. He wore a nice tailored suit, though."

"I will consider it. Our time is almost up. I know you live by this street code, but I want you to think about it. I need what you just told me to nail Swartz."

"I know what this means to you and I would love to help fuck him over if he indeed fucked our young lives up with having our parents killed. But, I'm no rat. I told you that as my sister, not a detective. I could never walk around here."

"You don't have to; I can get you set up with a fresh start in California. You can live being who our parents birthed and named Sean Shaw; and Jacob Carter can be left right here in Seattle. All I am asking is that you think about it."

"Time's up!" The officer spoke, coming back into the room. "It was nice seeing you. This is my card. Call me if you need anything and again, just give it some thought."

"I will give it some thought and holla at you."

"Thank you," I replied, as I watched the officer escort Sean out.

"How soon can you get your hands on the officer's name that arrested Sean?"

"We can go to my office and grab it or I can have my sister look up Sean's case."

"Can you do that, please?"

"Yeah, why?" Reggie questioned, looking at me.

"Because I think it's Young." The Latina officer opened the door for us to walk out. "Sean described him to the tee. Black, low fade, geeky looking and tailored suits. That's Young."

"Damn." Reggie ran his hands through the bed of curls on his head.

"If Young is in cahoots with Swartz, what is the purpose of him bringing me here?"

"To tell you the truth, Shanae, I'm confused on all of this. Did I know Swartz was up to shady stuff here? Yes. But, this is deeper than I could ever imagine from someone who is supposed to serve and protect the community."

"Not much surprises me these days. Leaves me stunned, but not surprised." We made it to Reggie's car and as soon as we were inside, his cell phone began to ring.

"Yeah, how long has he been on the force? Can you find information on where he grew up? I want everything down to his parents' names? I also need you to check the arresting officer for a Jacob Carter and what evidence that they had against him," Reggie spewed into his phone. "She is pulling up Sean's case now. As far as Young, he just transferred here a few months ago."

"From where?"

"I have her looking into that."

The more information I was finding out, the more it was starting to make sense. Young was new in the department and was probably bullied by Swartz to do the shit he wanted him to do. Or, he had the power to send him packing back to where he came from. I had seen it many times before. I was still missing a piece on how I was connected to this all.

"Thank you. That's good and bad news. Get me everything you can find on him. Call me when you are done." Reggie started the car.

"What did she say?"

"Detective Young was the arresting officer. Swartz was the lead detective on the case. He reported that during the bust, they seized two pounds of powder cocaine, ten thousand dollars in cash and a fully loaded 357."

"Did anyone verify this evidence?"

Reggie looked over at me and then back to the road. "Swartz and another officer that I am sure was under his supervision."

"I haven't been here a full twenty-four hours and all I have heard since I been here is about fuckin' Swartz. Can you drop me to my rental car? I need to get to the hotel and take a shower."

"Okay, but I am coming with you. This is sounding more and more like a set-up."

"I can handle myself, but whatever." Swartz was a pain in my ass and I hadn't heard from Young since we departed. Sliding the phone from the glove box, I dialed Young again but the phone went straight to the voicemail once again. "I find it odd that now I can't even get Young on the phone."

"Follow your gut. He is going to call when he is trying to make his next move."

"Yeah, I just wish I knew what that was."

"You are ahead of them. They don't know you have linked them. When Young does call, keep it cool and act like you don't know anything. Keep it like you just landed and still trying to figure everything out."

I listened to what Reggie was saying, but I wasn't in the mood to hide shit anymore. I wanted justice and I was ready to bust shit wide the fuck open.

Chapter 6

Reggie

The sway of her hips hypnotized me watching her move around her hotel room in the plush hotel provided robe. I had been so busy with work in the last few months the desire for a women's flesh hadn't crossed my mind until I laid eyes on her. I wanted her, I have always wanted her. It was taken everything in me not to grab her in my arms and lay her on the bed and kiss her from her full lips, down her neck to her plumped breast down to her wide baby making hips until I landed at her most prized possession. I wanted to fest on her mound until she released all the built-up tension she was going through. I wanted to please her with my tongue until her juices coated my tongue.

"Maybe you should take a little nap. You are so tensed."

"I can't think about sleep. All I can think about is what is their next move, what they are up to and why they are up to it. Sleep will have to wait." Rubbing her hands down her face. She leaned back in the chair.

Planting myself behind her. I massaged her shoulders. "I understand you want to get them and you will. You are to determined not to. But, you have to put yourself first. All this stress and tension is not good for you."

"Where you learn to give a massage like this." Shanae chuckled. Closing her eyes and letting her neck fall. "This shit feel's good."

"Just a little something I was blessed with." I couldn't help but move my hand further down her neck, when she didn't stop me, I kept going until I cupped her full breast in my hands as I bought my lips to her neck. "I've always wanted to do this?" teasing her earlobe with the tip of my tongue I made my way further down her stomach until my fingers reached her well manicure mound.

"Aah," She signed. With my lips, still to her neck I used my right hand to fondle her breast, my right hand moved in circular motion around her clit. She was so fuckin' wet. Just the thought of becoming one with her had my manhood rock solid. I wanted her, no I needed her." I moved slow, then fast, then slow again. Shanae squirted in the chair below me.

"Cum for me," I whispered in her ear slipping my index and middle finger inside of her the flood gates gave out her juices coating on my fingers. Making my way in front of her. I brought her face to mine. Our lips locked as I carried her to the bed. Burying my face between her long chocolate legs. I feasted until her legs locked around my neck rocking her hips she fucked my face until her juices released.

"Take off your clothes." She demanded.

Following her demands I slowly unbuttoned my shirt, then took off my under shirt admiring the chocolate beauty sprawled out basking in the pleasure I just given her. She was so fuckin' beautiful and naturally built like a brick house. Removing my slacks, then my briefs finally giving her all of me in the flesh. She smiled using her index finger she called me over. Following her commands, I made my way closer to her.

Sitting up on her knees. She greeted me with a kiss. "Now I'm about to show you what I made of." She smiled pushing me down on my back. Our lips met as she slowly leads me inside of her wetness. Inch by inch she welcomed me, and I tried my hardest not act like a twelve-year-old boy and cum just from sticking the tip in. from the mirror behind us I watched her dark flesh bounce on my manhood. It was a beautiful sight. Our bodies collided like we had taught each other sexual prior to this. There was no doubt in my mind, Shanae was born for me, and me for her. I wasn't letting her slip out my hands this time. She was mine, I was hers and I wanted this feeling forever.

Chapter 7

Shanae

I felt bad about leaving Reggie in the room sleeping. But, when Young text me, I had to hurry and leave. I couldn't wait and miss the chance of missing out on what Young knew. Since Young knew the car I was driving, I left my keys in my hotel room with Reggie and took his car. I sat down the street from the address Young requested me to meet him at. I arrived earlier than requested. I needed to see what was coming and going before I walked inside. There wasn't any movement in the house.

"Hey," I answered, knowing the Seattle number calling was Reggie.

"Where are you?" His voice wasn't as lovely as it was before.

"I'm sorry. I had to leave to meet Young. I couldn't wait. You were sleeping peacefully and I didn't want wake you."

"Are you meeting him at 16543 Willow brook Way?"

"How do you know that?"

"My sister called while we were sleep. Detective Young was a transfer requested by Swartz. He grew up here, but when his parents divorced, his mother moved him and his siblings to Nebraska. He joined the force five years ago. Six months ago, there was a transfer requested by Swartz and approved by the captain. His father, Clifford Young, lives there. He never left South Beacon Hill. I am having my sister find everything she can find on Clifford Young."

"None of this makes sense to me. He seemed like he was fixated on getting Swartz out the department."

"He wanted you to think that. Shanae, do not go in there alone. I am calling a friend of mine on the force to come down there. This is a set-up."

"We don't know who is a part of this with Swartz and Young down at the station. So, I'd rather just handle this on my own. I can't risk thinking someone is on my side, but they are not and working with them. All my life I was taught to survive. This will be no different."

"Shanae, I let you slip through my fingers once; I will not let it happen again or let anyone do anything to you. I may not be a police officer, but nothing of this is making sense and the way things are going, it looks like they are out to get you. Shanae, I have loved you since I was ten years old. Call it faith that I walked into the deli today because I haven't eaten there in months. Please do not go in that house until I get there."

Reggie had butterflies filling my stomach. I hadn't felt anything for the male specimen in a long time. Most men couldn't take dating a cop or just couldn't hold my attention for a second date. But, there was something about Reggie that made my heart speed up. I had been crushing on him since I was a frail little thing, flat chested, with flying pigtails. It was bittersweet to have him all this time later accepting me with all my flaws, but I couldn't let that stand in my way of what I came to do.

"I am in your car. If you are not here in fifteen minutes when I am supposed to meet him, I am going inside. There is a gun in the middle console that is loaded. Don't come in without it."

"A gun?"

"You already said we don't know what they are up to. Go in expecting the best, but prepared for the worst."

"I'm on my way."

"All right," I replied, ending the call with Reggie. A light in the house came on, but I still couldn't see any movement. A car pulled into the driveway and someone stepped out. As the figure moved into the light, I saw it was Young. Stepping out of the car, I closed the door lightly so as to not make a sound that would cause anyone to look out of the window. I made my way down the street. Scrolling through my call log, I dialed Young.

"Hey, it's dark out here. Uber dropped me off. I'm not sure where I am. Why did you want me to meet you here? Who lives in this neighborhood?"

"My informant. Let me come outside and get you."

"Okay," I agreed, ending the call with Young. I quickly text Reggie, letting him know that I was going in. Everything about it seemed off, but I wasn't turning around. I had come too far. I was going to see this to the finish line. From where I stood, I could see Young step out of the house.

"Hey," I called out to gain his attention from a few houses away.

"Where is the rental?"

"It caught a flat. So, I just hopped into an Uber. I will have it fixed tomorrow. So, has the informant given you any new information?"

"Something like that. How did the meeting going with Swartz?"

"I didn't catch him. The waiter said he had just left."

"Oh," Young replied, his eyes shifting like he knew I was lying.

"Yeah, wished I had. But, seems like I will be here for some time. So, I will be able to catch up to him."

"That may not be true. You should wait until you speak with the informant. There may be a crack in the case sending you back to sunny California. Or, maybe you can become a permanent fixture back here."

"I will be on the first thing smoking back to California once this is done."

"So, you say," Young laughed it off.

"I do say." I smirked, looking at the brittle smile plastered on Young's face.

"Ladies first." Young held the door open for me and as soon as I walked in the house, I instantly had an eerie feeling. The pale paint on the walls was chipping and the house reeked of a funny smell that resembled a hospital or a rehabilitation center.

"I need to get something from my bag. He is waiting on you. He is in the last room on the right-hand side," he instructed as he went the opposite way. I left the door half cracked and sent a text message to Reggie. I stepped in the room and instantly our eyes met. It took everything in me not to race across the room and slap the smirk off his face.

"We meet again." The smile was still on his face like he was happy I walked into his trap.

"Very clever of you. I mean you two." I could feel the barrel of the gun pressed against my back."

"Walk in the room and walk slow," Young instructed.

Slowly, I walked into the room where I could survey it in full. There was a figure laying in a hospital bed in the room, which was probably why it reeked of medical supplies.

"Had you just minded your damn business and stayed in Los Angeles… You're like your father."

"Is that why you killed him? See, you two thought you had it all figured out. But, I knew I was walking into a trap. See, I did a little more snooping. I know you requested a transfer for Young six months ago. I am just trying to figure out how you, Young, had your name listed as one of the arresting officers in a case from a year ago. Because I know when your parents broke up, your mother moved you all to Nebraska. But, your father, Clifford Young, still lives here. This house is registered to him."

"You did some homework."

"I was supposed to. I am a fuckin' cop and a damn good one. Unlike you two. You jumped around on the force while you were out there in Nebraska. Homicide, narcotics and special victims. You moved to a new department before they were able to suspect you for some of the shit you did. When they were close, you transferred here. You are a dirty cop. As dirty as the fat, bald fuck in the corner. I just have one question because that's what I can't figure out. What do I play in this all?"

"Clifford Young is my father. I wanted to be closer to him since he doesn't have much time left. But, I couldn't do it alone. So he told me he could get it done. But, of course it was conditional on doing something for him. You wanna guess what that was?"

"Getting me here."

250

"You are correct."

"But, why?'

"To find the little bitch I should have killed twenty years ago." The figure in the bed spoke slowly, turning around. His dark eyes met mine and they were still the most evil eyes I had ever seen in my life. "Had I known you would grow up to follow in daddy's steps and be a pain in my ass, I would have killed you like I did everyone else." He had that heinous smile plastered on his face. He was still evil and ugly.

"Clifford Young is Scar. Scar is your father." I laughed. "Hence your face when I said I saw my father's killer. But, you already knew that. You should have killed me then because now, you have no choice but to kill me. Because, if you don't, I will kill you and hang these two with years in state prison where every damn inmate will know you are both cops."

"You have it all figured out," Swartz chuckled, sitting back with his arms folded across his chest.

"What I still don't understand is why did you kill my parents?"

"Because, just like you, your father wouldn't keep his mouth shut and mind his fuckin' business. When you go looking for something, you find it; it just might not be what you are expecting. It cost him his life."

"My mother?"

"Sweet Angela," Swartz licked his lips. "I can still see her pretty, chocolate face. You know I should been your dad. I met your mother first."

"So you had my mother killed because she married my father and not you?"

"No, because she loved your father too much. She wouldn't just let him die and that be it. She would have searched, called and drove me crazy. I hated to see her go, but she had to. She was a casualty of her love for her man."

"Junior?"

"He lived. His weak ass shouldn't have tried to get in my way," Scar spoke up.

"Junior lived and did everything your father wanted for him."

"Why was I spared?"

"Because it was a fuckin' mistake," Scar laughed.

"And next, you are going to ask me about Sean, huh? Oh, I mean, Jacob Carter?"

"His arrest was no accident. You knew his identity."

"This is my fuckin' city. I know everything."

"Put the gun down or I will blow your fuckin' head all over these walls," a voice behind Young spoke.

Reggie stepped out of the shadows, making his presence known.

"Councilman Tate."

"Swartz, I would say it was a pleasure, but that would be a lie. Seattle PD is outside. I know all about what you two have been up to. It ends here, Swartz."

"I will not say it again. Put the gun down." I knew the voice, but I couldn't place it.

"I'm not going to jail," Young's voice squeaked as he turned the gun on himself. POW! His body fell forward, almost causing me to lose my footing. Swartz reached for his gun, but Junior already had his gun to Swartz's head.

"Don't even fuckin' try it."

I could see Scar reaching for something. Having no choice, I dived onto Scar.

"Bitch," he called out. Using the butt of the gun he managed to pull from under the sheets, he struck my face.

"Fuck," I yelled, dazed by the impact of the gun. I knew if he gained full control, I was dead. Junior was dead; Reggie was dead. Mustering it up, I struck Scar, knocking the gun from his hand. I didn't stop. I kept striking him and then, everything went black.

Epilogue

I regained consciousness a few hours later with Reggie and Junior right at my side.

"Hey there, gorgeous. We been here waiting on you."

"What happened?"

"Swartz's gun went off and shot you. It is only a flesh wound. The hard impact knocked you unconscious. They said all your vitals are stable. You should be good to go by morning."

"What happened to them? Are they dead?"

"Junior shot Swartz right after he shot you. He will be okay. The police have him here somewhere," Reggie spoke. "Scar was arrested. He is suffering from Stage 4 pancreatic cancer. He doesn't have much time left to live. And you are aware that Young killed himself."

"Twenty years later and we finally have justice. Merry Christmas, Shanae." Junior smiled and it was a genuine smile. He finally got his smile back.

"Merry Christmas, Vee. I love you."

"I love you, too. Thank you for telling Kelly. I could never find the words to tell her."

"I am my brother's keeper. I always got you. Don't ever forget that."

"You don't ever forget that I am my sister's keeper," Junior replied.

"Merry Christmas, Reggie."

"Merry Christmas, beautiful," he leaned down and kissed my lips. It was the best Christmas gift I had in years.

On a cold December Christmas night, I found justice for my family love in my heart.

THE END

Daddy Christmas

Daddy Christmas

Once upon a time, long ago and as fairytale sounding as this opening, I was told a story about a jolly, fat, black man who rewarded good children at the end of each year. It was long and boring, as most of the fairytales I'd heard were; so, I honestly didn't retain enough of it to share. I was focused on trying to stay awake with exaggerating yawns that pissed off the storyteller. I did, however, hear enough of the story to know that something was missing; there wasn't a bad guy. Who in the hell tells a story about a hero without mentioning a villain?

Hopefully, this doesn't put a timestamp on my age, but there weren't any social media outlets or search engines available at the time to check out his selfies. Somehow, pictures of him still began to surface everywhere and I wasn't impressed. A vast amount of them were lousy, cartoon depictions that I was sure the artists had wrong. If the story I was told was true, then those rosy cheeks in the drawings were, in fact, purple bruises from him smiling all the damn time. The white, fluffy beard that looked as if it were made from cloud scraps should have had a beige, eggshell tint from the lack of maintenance. He ran a warehouse that operated twenty-four hours a day, seven days a week, with no days off. The dude didn't have time to hit the barber for a trim. Maintaining that whiteness would have been impossible; it would have been covered in dirt and grit. Like Jesus, his picture had gone 'viral' before 'viral' existed and like Jesus, the description given didn't match the pictures but that didn't stop the popularity of him, either. I even met a white man at a department store ringing a bell to collect donations dressed like the cartoon image. He was a perfect match of the picture, however, he must have heard a different rendition of the story; he was begging! I was told that this man didn't need shit from anyone outside of his

elves. He wasn't rich in currency; he was rich in laborers, which made him no better than slave masters. He, too, profited off the backs and sweat of others.

They called him Santa Claus in the streets, but I knew that was an alias. His name was Kris Kringle; he was a pimp from out north and those pimps never went by their government names. Good ole Saint Nick to some, Father Christmas to others. I'm sure he preferred being called Daddy Christmas and if he was as comfortable with his weight as he was portrayed to be, I can guarantee he'd answer to Big Daddy Christmas, too. There was no fooling me when it came to his full-time profession. A tailored, red, fur-trimmed suit, a hat that matched, and German army steel-toed boots. Because of his choice of attire alone, I visualized an overweight pimp in a city plagued with violence, and that's exactly what Memphis, Tennessee was.

Strangely, I found comfort in his lack of tact. Screaming, "Ho, ho, ho!" as he crept into houses and got what he wanted first, a plate of cookies with a tall glass of room temperature milk. Cookies and milk were a slick way of saying tits and twat, which is exactly what this man packaged and sold for a living.

My imagination was limited to enhancing images I was already familiar with, but I was sure Elder Flynn's secret identity was Santa Claus. I watched him knock off three full Thanksgiving plates, leaving crumbs in his beard and he pinched each woman's ass who served him. As I continued to listen to the storyteller's words, I pictured the oldest man in our North Memphis, neighborhood traveling to every place called home, by way of magical deer to deliver gifts all over the world in just one night. Nope, the story wasn't adding up. I tried and failed to believe that if it wasn't Elder Flynn, there was a compassionate pimp that carried a list of the nice children's names whom he blessed with whatever their little hearts desired. The naughty ones, whose names weren't on his list, were given a lump of coal that I imagined to be that shit left in the grill after a barbecue. I couldn't believe the hype surrounding ole Saint Nick, nor could I believe the storyteller's next words.

"If you do what your mama tells you and continue to be a good girl, Santa Claus will bring you a daddy and he'll take real good care of you!"

I couldn't have been more than seven years old when I was told this story, but I knew from that moment, the person telling it to me and the story itself were both full of shit. It was my daddy who told me the story of Santa Claus during one of his charity dick visits. That's when my mom begged him for money to help with me and he agreed to throw a few dollars her way in exchange for a nut. Back then, I thought of it as charity work because he wasn't in need of Mama and her coochie, or the bonding time with me that always seemed to come with it. He had a wife, son, two daughters and a well-groomed dog named Molly, that everyone in our community loved.

"But, why can't you be my daddy?" I questioned, hoping he didn't detect the pleading in my words.

"It's complicated, Monique."

"My name is Monica."

"I know your name," was the lie he told, as he placed his hat on his head and grabbed his expensive, floor length, winter coat. "When you get older, your mama will explain it to you. Now, you be good, okay? And Merry Christmas. Maybe this is the year you'll get you a real daddy, one that loves you more than me."

He was out of the house before my mama could recover from whatever enjoyment she had gotten from him. Mama was a mistake he made when he was drunk and I was nothing more to him than an unwanted reminder. He made sure to make me feel that way every visit. Mr. 'Powerful, Black, Community Activist' and 'Religious Leader' slipped in his faith and knocked up the soul-searching neighborhood tramp. He told Mama to abort me, but she told him I was a blessing from God and vowed to never tell a soul who she'd laid down with to make me. She even moved to Fort Campbell, Kentucky with her older cousin who was in the army for a while to pretend she got knocked up out there. I was the secret that City Councilman Bishop Gerald Tims would take to his grave, all the while praying that God would forgive him.

That fat man he told me about wasn't Elder Flynn, I asked. I couldn't find him in the scriptures of the book my daddy taught his congregation from every Sunday, either. The Trinity made up of God and Jesus didn't include this Santa Claus character as the third piece. My name never made any list because I couldn't be judged by the term naughty or nice. I was created in sin and my birth went against everything that was good, yet evil didn't find me worthy enough to use, either. No, the good Bishop was wrong. I never received any nice gifts or lumps of coal and my 'real daddy' as he put it, didn't come that year, either. It took twenty-three years for my real daddy to show up...

December 23rd, 2018

Adventurous: willing to try new, unusual methods, ideas, experiences and exciting things. To take risks or to take on adventures that require courage.

I yearned to live out those definitions. Adventurous Monica sounded better than any man's last name prefaced by Mrs. But, I feared adventure. After walking away from my marriage, it took years to build my comfort zone. Adventure meant stepping out of that.

I wanted to be that man's everything, but never could. He was greedy and my love, nor my body, could feed his appetite. While I thought my 202 pounds on this 5'6" frame was a meal with plenty of leftovers, Thaddeus got himself 300 pounds of woman between two 150 pound, ugly, duck-faced bitches. All the while, he treated me like I was a midnight snack that he only ate when he was bored.

I played stupid. I told myself that 'working late' really meant he was on the clock but then, he tested my gangsta. He walked one of his sluts into my salon and tried to sweet talk me into doing her hair, free of charge. It wasn't until I started blow-drying and brushing the relaxer into her scalp that they both knew the jig was up. I still start my prayers off by thanking God that the cosmetology board didn't revoke my license and that aggravated domestic violence charge was able to be expunged. Showing my ass got me arrested and almost had the love of my life taken from me, doing hair. Yet, my silly ass took him right back. Maybe I loved loving him or maybe I loved the thought of being in love with him. Either way, I was willing to give him more love than I was willing to give myself. It took feeling our son move around in my stomach as the doctor told me I had chlamydia for the second time in three years to decide it was time to love me. I packed up everything that was mine, moved it to a storage unit and at seven and half months pregnant, I moved into my salon. It was the biggest adventure I'd ever signed up for. I wasn't comfortable in my decision because that meant I had to listen and trust myself. After 223 million mistakes, bad choices and wrong decisions, how in the hell was I supposed to find comfort in trusting myself? But, I did; I made it through a hard labor and a divorce by myself, with God's love giving me strength.

Things got harder before they got easier as I lay my mama to rest next. She had a bad cough that my Grandmamma was sure was the flu, but the doctors called it stage four breast cancer that had spread to her lungs. It was rough tucking her into her final bed with a two year old on my hip, but I did it.

My grandparents seemed to see my strength. My Granddaddy let me turn the old barbershop out in the country into my salon. They also gave me the three bedroom house they had spent the last 50, or better, years in. They packed up and moved to an assistant living facility, somewhere in Florida. I would have kept up with them if I had a choice, but they didn't give me one.

For the last eight years, I've played it safe. No boyfriends or overnight guests born with dicks and I have a self-pleasuring sex toy collection that could get me a page in the Guinness Book of World Records and I'm tired of all of it. The new year was approaching and that 'new year, new me' cliché had made its overused way into the salon and planted the notion of change in me.

"How many of these beautiful Malaysian inches do you want cut off this time? You spend $140 a bundle for 30 inches only to walk out of here with 18; you get on my nerves, Sharon," I said, slapping her across her legs with the A graded hair.

"No, the hell I don't pay $140 per bundle, not anymore. I fooled around and typed luxury hair in Memphis on my Facebook search bar and found this company called Val-Ree's Lux and Beauty Boutique. I snatched me up one of their bundle packages and some Mink lashes while I was there. I'm putting them coins I saved on paying your overpriced ass!"

"With the energy and muscle it takes for me to make you look like something, I'm not charging you enough."

"Whatever! And no cutting this time. I'm trying something different; it's time to switch everything up. 'New Year, new me' and I'm putting myself first. Mark my words; by this time next year, I'm going to have so many men begging for my hand in marriage that I'm going to have to move to one of those foreign countries where they'll allow a Queen to have five or six husbands," she giggled. "How I'm feeling about life, I might fuck around and have 7 or 8 of them when I'm done."

"Girl, you are a mess!"

"A hot mess; and when you stop pretending that little man is the only man you need in your life, you can get you two or three husbands, too."

"He is the only man I need in my life," I snapped. "He has my full attention until he graduates and moves out."

"Did you tell him that?"

"Tell him what?"

"All he has to do to escape your smothering is get his high school diploma and move out," she laughed, until she choked on her spit as I prayed her choking took her ass out. When the coughing stopped, she said, "Seriously, sis, I've been coming here for almost 10 years and you haven't had a man since Thaddeus left you."

"I left him!"

"Well, since you left him. Don't you think it's time for you to let someone love you and show you all men ain't like Thaddeus' funky ass? It's Christmas; if you open your heart to be willing to let someone in, maybe Santa will send you a good man. A man that will love you more than Thaddeus ever did."

Déjà Vu, I thought. The last person to tell me Santa would bring me a man was wrong and Sharon was, too. I didn't need a man in my life; what I needed was some dick that I could treat like a tampon. Stick in, let it do its thing and then discard it. I hadn't realized Sharon's words influenced me until the dirt road I travelled home on turned into a paved one 45 minutes later. When I looked up, I was on the less traveled side of the town or, as I called it, White Collar-ville - Mayhem, Tennessee.

Mayhem earned its right to be split from Memphis being that it was everything Memphis wasn't. No barbeque, no soul music and no poverty. Bad didn't have an address there and thanks to my grandparents, I did. Leaving Memphis was a farfetched dream of mine when I was married. A dream that never materialized into reality by the divorce and less than an hour's drive South East. The city was no bigger than 16 stop signs spread between 8 right turns, however, Mayhem's inner city compared to its country outskirts that I lived in felt like they were States apart. Crossing into the city limits was an adventure of its own, but with the success of my salon and online fashion boutique, I was ready for the voyage.

***

There wasn't a noticeable difference in the bar. It looked like every other bar I'd visited dipped in a snowy Christmas theme and jolly holiday music to match, but other than that, everything was the same. The same wooden, water-resistant counter top. The same bullshit chatter of sports failures, legends, and achievements. The same cheers of thanks as the bartender topped off glasses in hopes of a larger tip once the liquor kicked in. The same overpriced frothy beers on tap promising to be the coldest around and the same liquor labeled as top shelf to be sold at the price of a bottle of it at the store up the block. The same local team paraphernalia hanging near the pool tables and around the dart board with a visible, thin layer of dust to garnish the faded team colors. The same, the same, the same. Everything was the same and I was on a hunt for everything different.

"You gotta have a collar on that shirt to join us!"

The voice belonged to the bartender. I had been sitting at the bar nursing my second glass of Long Island Iced Tea long enough to decipher it, though I wasn't sure who he was talking to. At first glance, everyone seemed to meet the dress code plastered on the wall at the entrance that read: Collared Tops, Pants at the Waist and You Can Keep the Socks, All Ae Need is Shoes...and then I saw him. This beautifully long-limbed, wide-width, muscular creation, void of smile yet still handsome in his stern facial expression stood in front of the fireplace at the far end of the bar at least 200 feet away from me and instantly, I knew he was the adventure I needed. The hallow depths of his eyes lacked color and appeared to be black. They held no story and sang no song. Nor would those thin, tight lips encased in his beard tell his yesterdays or thoughts of tomorrows. The wind blew him in those doors; he didn't enter willingly because I knew anything that was mine, came with a fight. He was mine.

He didn't look familiar and the energy surrounding him didn't feel the same. It could have been the music, the date on the calendar or the Christmas stockings hanging from the mantel, but with embers crackling behind him, he looked like a roasting chestnut and I craved to be that open fire. I craved for his smooth, mahogany skin to touch mine, to press against my nipples as we attempted to get closer than we already were. I wanted him to cover the wide curves of my body underneath his height and width while he stroked in and out of me. Once he claimed his territory by marking his spot in me, we'd switch positions and he'd sit me on his hardwood to cover him in my glaze until a puddle formed in his belly button. I wanted him to fuck me like he was mad at me without reason. I wanted break up sex and make up sex, but I'd settle for some sympathy dick, too. The longer I stared at him, the more I craved this man…this strange, unfamiliar man to bang my back out. Thoughts of him touching me to pull me into his embrace became unhealthy as anxiety began to build to the brink of needing oxygen. I needed to step outside and get myself together, yet my body didn't move. I was in cardiac distress, but my chest wasn't the only thing throbbing and yet, I couldn't take my eyes off him.

"Is this better?" he asked, fumbling with the shirt he had balled in his hands. He shook it out, put it on like it wasn't plagued with wrinkles and took a seat at the end of the bar.

"A shot of whiskey coming up!"

"Let's make it a shot, in a shot instead, thanks!"

The white V-neck t-shirt he wore into the bar and ripped, loose-fitting jeans were covered in dirt. If his work badge wasn't dangling from his belt loop, you'd assume he'd been in a brawl and by the looks on the faces around me, that was exactly what everyone in the bar assumed.

"Rough day?" I asked, after watching him guzzle down the equivalent of a pint in shots.

"Is it that noticeable?"

"Not really," I shrugged, while inviting myself to the empty bar stool next to his. "Well, not in here, anyways. For a night spent at the bar, you're on target, but I was actually pretending that you and I were somewhere else."

"Wow," the look on his face matched his word. "Straightforward. You have my attention." He gave me a look full of curiosity as he summoned the bartender with a four fingered hand motion. "Whatever she's drinking, her next glass is on me. Now back to you, where were you pretending we were?"

"I don't know, the urge to join you took over me before I got to that part. All I can tell you is that I wanted to take you far away from here and even further from whatever it was that's plaguing you."

Pouring it on thicker, I batted my eyelash extensions and thanked the heavens for Long Island Iced Tea, it was doing a great job of aiding me through this. My determination mixed with whatever the hell the bartender put in this cup because I didn't see him brew any tea, had evolved into something lustful and soulless that I didn't like, but was definitely going to roll with. If it gave my dildo the night off, then by any and all means.

"It's almost Christmas and you're too handsome to look like you were already given coal."

"Girl, listen to you spitting game like you can handle me. You must've had one too many because you don't look the part you're trying to play. Maybe I should tell the bartender to hold off on that drink." He chuckled, revealing a smile that made my coochie tingle. I slightly gapped my legs.

"You could be right about the drinks. I've never said or done anything like this in my life, but do you really want to be right? I'm only asking because I'm not sure if I want you to be."

"You came over here to question if I'm interested in you?"

"No, the look on your face is what sent me over here; it matched the way I'm feeling."

"Sounds like you need to vent instead of working on your pick up game, then."

"And what do you need? I don't remember you disagreeing about having a rough day."

Holding his glass in the air as though he were making a toast, he said, "I got what I need to get me through the moment. I didn't come here looking for a fix for my problems. It will take more than Tennessee whiskey to straighten my shit out. Besides, I'm not in the mood to talk nor to listen." He shrugged.

"Good, 'cause neither am I!"

I placed my hand where his dick should meet the fabric of his pants and squeezed. He was softer than wet rose petals stuck in a bathtub's drain. I didn't release him until he hardened, I needed an accurate measurement of dick I was craving.

"I should scream rape!"

"You can, after you let me rape you."

Chuckling and shaking his head, he asked, "Aren't you a little concerned about my background, health or even mental status?"

"Not at all. I brought condoms, we won't be kissing or doing anything oral and you won't be around long enough for me to care about your past, present, or future. My 10 year old son is with his daddy until Christmas evening and then he comes home to open all $4,000 worth of gifts I put under the tree. He's the only full-time man I have in my life and I'm keeping it like that. If you're crazy and your crazy ass pops up at my house in the country, uninvited, I'll bury you in the cow manure and use your body as fertilizer. All I need from you is one night to give my dildo some rest."

"You have a 10 year old son?"

Out of all the shit I said, that was his response?

"Yes, I only have one child and he's spoiled. Are you asking because I mentioned his daddy? You don't have to worry about him; he's a deadbeat. I'm talking toe-tagged up and buried in late child support payments. He's remarried with no kids, that includes our son. The only reason I let Junior go with him is because he needs to see the type of man his daddy is for himself. At 10 years old, I know he can handle it. That boy has been begging to come home since I dropped him off. He said his new step momma can't cook." I laughed.

"I have a 10 year son old, too." He dug in his pocket, pulled out his wallet and fumbled through receipts to find it. He handed me a picture. "That's my Junior, little Titus."

The little boy was his father's twin, minus the beard and age lines. He had on a football uniform in the picture.

"He plays for the East Side Sharks in Memphis? My son ran all over them this season. He's a running back for the Mayhem Hawks."

"You're from here? Now I know you're pretending to be something you aren't. There ain't nothing but wholesome, country women in Mayhem; you were talking like you were from North Memphis."

"I am from North Memphis; I grew up on Chelsea Ave. I moved to Mayhem as an adult, but my grandparents were born and raised here. I spent all my summers as a youth in Mayhem."

"I'm Titus and you are? Wait, don't give me the name you came up with for your night at the bar. I want to know the name you go by in Mayhem," he finished and extended his hand.

Taking a deep breath, I placed my hand in his, defeated.

"Monica, the boring salon and online boutique owner."

"It's a pleasure to meet you, Monica; what brings you into Mayhem's city limits if you live way out in the country? That's about an hour's drive."

"Dick."

"What?"

"You heard me. It's been a while since I had some and I refuse to go a day longer, but you ruined that. I've been sitting with you too long to try to work the room for potentials now."

"Let me get this straight. Your amazingly gorgeous ass is single and can't get any sex? Were you born a man?" He shot his eyes at my neck; I was sure he was in search of an Adam's apple.

"No, I'm sexless and single by choice, a bad choice judging from the way I'm feeling now and you're going to get your feelings hurt looking for an Adam's apple. Those are being removed now."

"Are you kidding me?"

"Nope, if you can afford the procedure a surgeon will shave down the thyroid cartilage to reduce the size. Before you ask me how I know, it was on one of those crazy shows that comes on in the middle of the night on satellite T.V. I have no problem proving to you that I'm all woman."

We paused, gave each other an eyebrow raise and laughed like we were good friends, having the time of our lives at the bar. The conversation jumped around…technology, parenting soon to be teenage boys in this day and age, and why I didn't have a man circled through it a few times. When I finally shut my mouth to take in the wonderful time I was having with a man, fully dressed, he held his shot glass in the air a second time, this time to make an actual toast.

"To an incredibly beautiful woman who's on her shit!"

"I'll toast to that!" I excitedly held my glass up in agreement.

We toasted, talked, laughed toasted some more and when the bartender called out, "Last call for alcohol," we agreed that we weren't ready for the night to end. He walked me to my car, held the door as I got in, and then followed me home in his pick-up truck.

***

"It doesn't get more country than this. Is that a kerosene lamp?" Titus asked, as he followed me up the stairs on my porch.

"It is, and what does a city slicker know about kerosene lamps?"

"Nothing," he chuckled. "Read about them in high school history and saw them on A Little House on the Prairie. Does it work?"

"I'm sure it does, but I don't use it. This country girl has a thing for electricity." The motion light came on as we reached the top step. "Come on in and make yourself at home. I'll grab the bottles out of my room. If you don't mind, grab us a glass out the cabinet next to the refrigerator."

"You keep your liquor in your room?"

"Where else should it be kept?"

I shot up the stairs, nervous as hell and drunk. I had a man in my house, in my kitchen cabinet grabbing us glasses because I told him to make himself at home. Before I panicked, I went straight to the bathroom and ran me a bath. The smell of burnt hair and soggy panties weren't going to ruin my night. Sitting on the toilet, zoning in and out, I watched the bath salts metabolize in the water as the douche bottle floated under the flowing water still in the plastic bag it came in. It was time to give myself a pep talk.

"It's only some Christmas dick, Monica. It doesn't matter that you're enjoying his company or that he's sexy as fuck. Let him fuck the life back into you and then send him away. No talks of getting to know him or spending more time together. 'New year, new you' and that doesn't involve Titus becoming your new man, understood?"

"Hey, are you all right up there?"

His words scared the shit out of me and for a second there, I thought he overheard me talking to myself.

"Yes, I'm grabbing the bottle now. White or dark?" I yelled down back at him.

"Dark…whiskey if you got some, and I tightened up those pipes under the kitchen sink. I could hear the water dripping into the bucket you got under there when I rinsed out our glasses. That should save you a few bucks. You're welcome!" he chuckled, and I blushed like a school girl passing her crush in the hallway.

"Fuck, I'm in trouble!"

"What did you say? I couldn't hear you."

"I said, um…thank you for fixing it."

"No problem, beautiful, do you blow trees?"

"Do I blow what?"

"Trees. Oh, I forgot you're out here in the country and don't speak city. Do you smoke weed? I'm about to roll up. I can go smoke it in my truck, if you'd prefer."

He rolled up and we smoked; boy, did we smoke! After a few more glasses of whiskey and a couple of overfilled blunts later, I was spread eagle on my cedar wood dining room table being made love to, I didn't make it to the tub. A lot had changed in sex from when I had it five years ago and being made love to was one of them. One night stands, from my experience, meant being rammed with dick until both the people involved toes went numb and then calling it a night. If dick was sucked or my pussy was eaten, it was done in the freakiest form and fashion and I'd make sure he was gone, so neither of us would have to look into our nasty ass faces the next day. Titus licked me the long way slowly. He started at my clit and ended by French kissing my ass. He stroked my body with his body like a paint brush on an empty canvas, making me his new masterpiece and then he turned me over, cupped my 38 DD's in his hands and stroked me the long way, slowly. We told each other shit we both knew we weren't supposed to be saying.

"I want you inside of me forever; you think you can make that happen?" I moaned.

"You asked that like you have a choice in this situation. I made you mine before we pulled up. This ain't shit but consummation; give Daddy a kiss."

We kissed like we missed each other hundreds of times and how love was brewing, but neither of us confessed it. I should have stopped it when he fell asleep in me, but if felt so right. I woke him up instead and led him hand-in-hand upstairs to my bed, where we kissed until he was back hard.

"Fuck Thaddeus!" He slowed down his stroke some at me screaming out my ex's name, but didn't question my outburst.

Instead he whispered, "Yeah, baby, fuck that nigga, Thaddeus. This my pussy and you're supposed to be my wife. I'm even gon' help you raise that nigga's son; fuck Thaddeus."

I came harder than a rapper responding to beef on a diss track and then I passed out.

Christmas Eve 2018

I woke up to the scent of bacon tickling my nose and 22 text messages from my son. T.J. never texted me this much, but then again, he's never been away from me this long. I thought about turning the car around and brining my baby right back home, but he needed this time with his daddy. This past football season pulled on my heartstrings as I watched my son practice as the only woman in the bleachers. Listening to those fathers talk about their sons in their fatherly tone of love made me realize there's a level of love that I can't give T.J., no matter how much I wanted to. T.J. realized it, too. As the starting running back, he was asked to stay the night at the coach's house whose son was also the starting quarterback to prep for games and T.J. got to see the love and functions of a two-parent home. It wasn't long before he started to say things like, "I wonder if my dad played football and if he was a running back, too?" and "Coach even makes his son practice in the off season; I wish I had someone to work with me in the off season, too." Of course, I'd take off to throw the ball with him, however, he'd never accepted it. My shortcomings in love should have never affected T.J. and since they did, I reached out to Thaddeus.

"Now who did you say you were again?" Thaddeus asked, for the third time, and again, his background noise did a great job of overpowering my voice.

"Monica, your son's mother."

"Monica? My ex-bitch, Monica? What the fuck you want?"

"You mean your wife; I ain't been nobody's bitch!"

278

"There you go with that shit, always want to argue. I'm at work; what do you want?"

"We need to talk; it's about T.J."

"What about T.J.; is he all right?" For a split second, Thaddeus sounded like a concerned parent.

"Yes, he's fine."

"Then, why are you calling me? I don't have any money. I'm trying to get on my feet right now, but when my shit get right, I'll start paying you child support or whatnot."

"When you get your shit right?"

"Ain't that what I just said? I appreciate you not letting the white man get all up in our business and put his hands in my pocket. I do and I'm going to keep my word and send you a little something each month for our boy. Let me get my bread up first and I promise I'm going to come through that bitch like superman for my seed; it's just hard out here. I ain't just keeping a roof over my head; I'm providing for my wife and we're sending money to her mom left and right. I got him, though."

Praying was the distraction I needed from cussing his ass out, hanging up the phone and sitting in the bushes in front of his house with my gun ready to shoot his face off. To know that I was once in love with that man made me want to put the pistol to my own head. To learn to love yourself is a beautiful thing.

"Listen here, Thaddeus. I'm going to act like I didn't hear none of those tired ass excuses you gave on helping me to support our son and get to the purpose of my call. T.J. is damn near a teenager now and he needs his daddy."

"He been needed his daddy. What's so different now? I told you I wanted to spend time with the little nigga and you told me I wasn't shit," he yelled, cutting me off. "It must be convenient for you to let me in his life. Hell, you've always ran the show."

"What you're not going to do is twist my words and our son will never be, nor be referred to, as a 'nigga' by you or anybody else. I did say you weren't shit; that's a fact, but I never said you couldn't see him. You've been telling me you're getting on your shit. Hell, it's been 8 years. How much more time do you need?"

"Aye, fuck you, bitch. That shit you're talking is the reason I left yo' ass and the same reason you don't have a man now. Don't no nigga want a bitch with daddy issues and a fucked up mouth. You thought you were better than me because you could make a little money doing hair and I had to bust my ass at a warehouse and that's why I kept fucking off on you. How are you going to be my wife, but always tryna stunt on me like I ain't shit?"

"Because you ain't shit and I'm not going to go back and forth, arguing with you about your worth; there a reason I reached out. You got a decision to make and I need the answer right now. You're going to get T.J. for half of his Winter Break and at least once a month moving forward and you will continue to have peace or,"

"Or what, bitch? Your mama dead, your daddy out in these Memphis streets living his best life and you don't have no brothers or cousins to threaten me with; what you gon' do, bitch?"

"I'm gon' show you what a bitch is when I walk into juvenile court and file child support on you. I'm going to let them know you didn't adhere to the child support agreement we made at the time of our divorce and tell them how you haven't given T.J. one red cent. I'm also going to ask that we split custody. You get six months and I take the other, swapping out holidays each year."

"Man, what kinda ho gives up her son to try to teach his daddy a lesson?"

"Apparently, the type of ho you once married, so what's it going to be?"

"I can't just make a decision without talking to my wife about it. Having him in my life affects her, too. She might have plans for us for the holidays."

"T.J. isn't something you squeeze into plans. You make your plans around him and honestly, I couldn't give a fuck less about what you and your wife have to agree on. I need to know your decision before the courts close."

"Drop him off at my mama's house on the 20th and come back and pick him up on Christmas around four. You need to tell him that he ain't getting shit from me for Christmas; I'm broke."

"He doesn't need a dime from you; all he need is time, but if you hurt him, you won't have to worry about the courts determining how broke you are or aren't. You don't need brothers or cousins when you have hit man money." I hung up before he could say another word.

Checking T.J.'s text would have normally been my priority and it was, until I heard the baritone voice downstairs in the kitchen singing along classic to R& B Christmas hits. I wrapped my nakedness in the flat sheet and joined him in the kitchen.

"I see you can sing a little bit. I didn't know that radio still worked."

"I fixed the shortage in the wiring, now get out!"

"Get out?" I laughed, taken aback by the demanding tone of his voice.

"Yes, get out! If I'm in the kitchen, you should be in bed waiting for me to feed you."

"Is that how it goes?"

Chuckling, he said, "You asked too many questions you already know the answer to. So, let me tell you how it goes so we can get some clarity," he coughed to clear his throat. "When you allow me to be here with you, I'm in charge of breakfast and we will swap out dinner, but I'm cooking that pot roast you have in there tonight. That's if I'm welcomed to stay that long."

"You're welcomed to stay until I leave to pick up my son tomorrow evening. That's if you can stay that long," I teased.

"I can and I will. Now go get back in bed and lose that sheet; I gotta eat, too." He winked and then kissed me on my lips. I sashayed my ass back up the stairs and got into bed.

Breakfast was great and so was his because his tongue put me to sleep. My cellphone vibrating under my back is what woke me up.

"Hey, T.J."

"Mama, you got to come get me right now!" He shouted into the phone and sent my heart racing.

"I'm on my way, baby. Are you at your daddy's house or your granny's?"

"I'm at his house and bring a Cheeseburger combo with you."

"Wait, what?"

"She's killing me with her cooking. She said she was making fish, grits and spaghetti, but I can't tell which is which. Everything feels weird, has butter and sugar on it and is red. She trying to poison me, Mama. I'm not never coming back over."

Thank goodness, I thought and almost missed his next words.

"And they keep fighting because my daddy is whack."

"T.J., what do you mean they keep fighting?"

"Kimmy caught my daddy cheating on her and he bounced the other day. The coward hasn't been back since."

"Why didn't you tell me this when it happened? I'm on my way!"

"I didn't tell you because I wanted to see my daddy for he who really is and I wanted to see what you went through married to the buster."

"Watch your mouth, son; that's still your daddy. I've never talked bad about him to you and I'm not about to talk bad about him with you."

"I don't know why you didn't; he's everything you taught me not to be. He's lazy, a liar, a bad provider and father, and he's cool with breaking women's hearts. He's a punk; you don't have to agree with me. I stayed because a real man doesn't leave a woman alone when she's hurting. Kimmy is messed up over him and he doesn't deserve her tears."

I waited eight years to hear that the woman that willingly broke up my home was going through the same thing with the same man because I thought it would make me feel good. It was supposed to make me feel at peace that karma had gotten its revenge for my sake, but it didn't and my son was the reason why. Karma had a sneaky way of punishing everyone that seeks revenge and I finally understood why the quote said if you're seeking revenge, dig two graves. A part of me had just died, the hatred I felt inside for my replacement was nothing more than a memory.

"You're right; a real man doesn't leave a woman alone while she's hurting, so how about I send you some delivery and be there to pick you up around noon, instead?"

"I guess that's cool and maybe she could come and have dinner with us tomorrow instead of being alone."

"Hell no, but that was a very sweet gesture. I love you, T.J., you are my world, baby."

"I love you, too, First Lady. Pizza and a 2-liter, please. All she drinks is black tea and alkaline water."

"I got you, baby; call me if you need me."

"Yes, ma'am."

Taking a deep breath, I placed my phone on the nightstand and stared at the ceiling. Titus climbed on top of me and laid in between my legs missionary style but didn't penetrate me.

"I don't know what all occurred, but it sounds like you're doing a hell of a job raising that boy!"

"I'm trying to, but there's so much more that he needs that I can't give him."

"You can't let your uncontrollable shortcomings bury you with doubts, it will spill over into what you can give him. I'm with you. I believe every child should have a two-parent home, but the truth is, that's a lie. What good is having a two-parent home full of lies, abuse, drugs and violence? Sometimes, it's best to snatch up the child and go than to keep letting me hurt or see hurt from their other parent because they pitched in on creating them. Being born with a dick don't make you a good daddy,"

"Nor does being born with a coochie make you a good mother," I finished his sentence. "Is that what you're going through? Is little Titus' mother unfit?"

"My son's mother is a lot of things, but I don't know if the word unfit is doing her justice. Like you, I don't talk bad about her to anybody because at one time of my life, she was the love in it. What I will say is, my son comes first, and I'd catch a murder rap before I'd ever allow him to be hurt."

"Anything for our boys, huh?"

"Yep and I'm hoping that one day, we'll be able to add each other on our list."

He no-handed his way inside of me and I came before he completed his first full stroke. I was enjoying every minute of us. It was going to kill me to tell him that I never wanted to see him again tomorrow.

Christmas Morning

The music was blaring through the house, which meant Mr. Fix It was at it again. I called myself running speakers around the house a few months back, but they never came on. It was nice having a man's touch around the place. I decided after riding his face and screaming I love you that I would wait on calling whatever this was between us quits. There was a lot of potential there and seeing that I hadn't talked to him long enough to get to know him, I couldn't make a fair decision on what my heart really felt. Not to mention that condoms were only used once and seeing that I don't have sex, I wasn't on any birth control. I already had a stop at the pharmacy on my list for the morning after pill, but if he gave me more than a baby, I needed to be able to reach out and touch him without going on a manhunt.

"Good morning, beautiful." His words sounded like he had sang them.

"Good morning; how long have you've been up?"

"Since about six. I know you have to get your boy today and there were a few things I wanted to fix around here until my next invite."

"What all did you fix?" I asked, getting out of the bed.

"You'll see after breakfast; you know the rules. My time with you is limited, so can you stay in bed, please? I've already told myself it maybe awhile before we can do this again, at least here. I want to enjoy it while I can. I think I got one more gift in me to give." He winked, "Monica, Daddy loves you, too. I heard you last night, but didn't want to say it until I was sure. Yes, I love you, but the truth, is I don't even know you… and you don't know me. We have to mature whatever the hell this is between us. I'm not

286

saying we run off and elope, but we definitely need to give whatever this is a try. Do you agree?"

"This is so crazy, but yes, I agree," I said, shaking back the tears that wanted to fall. I was happy for the first time in a long time. Tears didn't deserve any of his attention.

"Good, we will work through all of this."

He kissed me and I could feel him absorbing my soul with his tongue. The last of my doubts and defenses washed away as we enjoyed the taste of each other's kiss. 'New year, new me' and the best part is that I had finally found my daddy.

"Let me check on this bacon, baby."

He left out the door and I grabbed my phone to use the internet search engine. I typed City Councilman Bishop Gerald Tims of Memphis, Tennessee in the search bar and hit enter. There he was, the first man that made me feel like I was his shortcoming. The first man that didn't care if he had my love because Santa would bring me a real daddy. The irony of it all was that the picture of him that made tears fill my eyes was of him, dressed in a Santa suit as the grand Marshall of Memphis' Christmas Parade. His wife, kids and that ugly ass dog were surrounding him. He had aged poorly, but the bastards looked happy. How could evil keep winning?

The hurt knocked me out, but I wasn't asleep for long. The smell of burnt bacon startled me out my slumber. I dashed down the stairs calling Titus' name with each step I took.

"Is everything okay, baby? I could smell the bacon burning. Titus?"

Smoke covered the kitchen, but the smoke didn't prevent me from seeing that Titus was gone. The cast iron skillet the bacon in was on top of an eye set at its lowest setting. At that heat it would take the bacon at least an hour to burn which made me think he had to have been working on something outside and set it on low to give him more time to complete the task. I took care of the smoking pan and then headed to the stairs to put on some clothes and meet him outside. I didn't notice it until I reached the front door, but my Christmas tree and the gifts under it were all gone. That motherfucka even stole the stockings that hung over the fireplace that said T.J. Hell, that dirty motherfucker had a T.J., too, Titus Jr. I ran out of the house, hoping I could see him up the road, jump in my car, and catch him, but if he wasn't in eye's view and with the straight shot, I could see downhill. That meant it was already too late; he was gone.

To be cute, that bitch lit the kerosene lamp on the porch, but the kicker didn't come until I walked passed the dining room table and there was a plate of beautifully cooked bacon and French toast waiting for me with a bottle of maple syrup and a note that read:

Mama Claus,

I don't know if you're reading this before or after you've called the police but, please know that I'm so sorry, baby. I really am! The police won't be able to find me; they've been looking for years. I'm not bragging and just don't want you to get your hopes up to be let back down. My name is made up. My fingerprints dusted away and even the ID I showed the bartender wasn't real. The only way they can tell you who I am or give you any information about me is if you plan on letting them have some of that love serum I left inside of you, but I have a feeling you won't because out of everything that was fake, what we felt for each other was real. You shouldn't have been the target of my Christmas thief, but you made yourself the target. You were way too vulnerable; you threw yourself at me as soon as I walked in which means, you've been hurt badly. Last night, after hearing you talk to your son about a man leaving a woman hurting, I didn't think I could go through with it. I didn't just see you as a woman hurting, I saw you as my woman hurting but again, you forced me to when you said, "Anything for our boys, huh?" It was those words that reminded me of the 10 year old boy that I birthed and never met. My son deserved a good Christmas like yours or even better after all the shit he's been through because of me. I love my son and this was supposed to be the year I spoiled him into knowing it, but it's hard to stay employed on the run and although it's a petty violation of probation, I promised myself that I was never going back into a cage once I was freed. I want you to know that I meant what I said about us maturing together and we will because I'm going to make this right. I know it seems fucked up that I robbed you on Christmas Day, but we will work through this like I said. I can't tell you when or where, but you will see me again because I love you, beautiful.

Love,

Daddy Christmas

ABOUT THE AUTHORS

Author C.J Hudson hails from the east side of Cleveland where he grew up surrounded by crime, violence, and drugs. Determined to not succumb to that way of living, he attended Kent State university for one year. An avid reader for the past eighteen years, C.J was introduced to urban fiction by his future wife when she gave him Carl Weber's Married Men. Although he enjoyed his first urban fiction novel, C.J craved to read about the type of street stories that he saw on a daily basis in the inner city. That's when he started going to Borders and searching out Street lit books. He quickly came across K'wan's classic novel Gangsta. He then went on a reading barrage and read everything from T-Styles to Triple Crown novels. Shortly after that C.J was laid off from his job as a machine operator. While laid off, C.J. decided to try his hand at writing. After writing his first manuscript entitled Skeletons, he wrote the manuscript that got him a publishing deal, Chedda Boyz. Since dropping his debut novel, C.J has penned eleven more novels. His social media handles are as follows:

Facebook: Author C.J. Hudson

Twitter: @Author C.J. Hudson

Instagram: authorcjhudson

www.authorcjhudson.com

E. Raye Turonek is a married, mother of five charismatic children. She resides with her family in Michigan, where she was born. Telling tales she's moved to tell, can take you to a place dark but intriguing, then horrifying yet somehow titillating, all while leaving you hanging at the edge of your seat. Or, it can make you feel as if E. Raye has taken you to a world of wonderment, to which you wouldn't want to escape.

On April 7th, 2016 Compelled To Murder became her first published work. The risqué, mystery suspense novel is much different than the adventure/fantasy novel she is currently working on. Compelled To Murder was previously written as a screenplay, one of two written by the author. Its original name was "A Reason to Kill," when written back in 2007. With the change from screenplay to novel, also came a completely different title and a refreshing new beginning.

This new author is looking to fulfill the readers need for a sensational experience that won't be forgotten!

Tito M. Bradley, a self-published author was born and raised in East Cleveland, Ohio and graduated from Shaw High School in 1990 with a certification in Welding and Blueprint Reading. Tito is 46 years old, a Police Officer and currently resides in Maple Heights, Ohio with his wife Maggie.

As a youth Tito had dreams of being a rap artist and formed his first duo group in 1988 with his cousin Jamal Cater, the group's name was "T&J", their song "This Beat Is Thumpin" was featured on a local compilation album. In 1993 Tito started his own record label (High Roller Records) and another cousin, Marcus Moss, joined the group which was now renamed "Total Destruction." The group released a cassette single with the songs "Hurricane" and "I'm Going Crazy" and within the same year, Tito wrote several R&B love songs which were presented to the R&B Group, Men At Large One of the songs written entitled "Will You Marry Me" was featured on the groups second album, "One Size Fits All."

Frustrated with the music business, Tito walked away and worked as a Welder/ Fitter for years in Cleveland's Steel industry. In 2005 Tito was bitten by the creative bug once again. During a card game with some friends, he got the idea to write about the topic of discussion, relationships. After years of research and interviews, his first book "We Got Issues, A conversation About Black Love and Relationships" was completed and released in 2009 under his own company, Bradley Publishing. The book was met with rave reviews and was featured in the Cleveland Call and Post Newspaper.

Tito began working hard to promote his books and while on a book promotion tour he ran into a former classmate who was an author of urban fiction. The reading of his friend's book motivated him to step into the genre of urban fiction. After developing an original story line, Tito wrote his second book "Bait and Switch" in 2013. "Bait and Switch" took the literary world by storm and his fan base grew even larger.

Tito was a guest on Terry Crumpton's "Hollywood in the Hood" TV Show along with other radio shows and public appearances. Tito even made his directorial and acting debut by filming and starring in a movie trailer for "Bait & Switch" which gave Tito national recognition and appeal. Selling books outside of the local circuit gave Tito the boost that he needed to take the game to the next level

In 2016 Tito released his third self-published book which went into a completely different direction. This book, a suspense thriller entitled "Reciprocation" about an unorthodox serial killer that can't be profiled.

Most recently, Tito has hit the ground running again with his fourth book "Blue Euphoria". This erotic novel has sent his fans into a frenzy. The promotion of "Blue Euphoria" is currently underway, but all four books are available on Amazon in paperback and in the Kindle format.

Facebook: Author Tito M. Bradley

Instagram: Author Tito M. Bradley

Email: Titobradley@yahoo.com

Danielle Bigsby, a native Nashvillian and self-published author under the Royal 4 Publishing Presents imprint has been a published author since 2015 with debut of Rivers Of Emotion. She then went on to publish Erotic Yet Exotic roughly a month later. She continued writing ultimately landing a publishing contract with Adore Publications in late 2015. She then went on to release Drowning In My Emotions which was a revised edition of Rivers Of Emotion with new material and Nasti Desirez (formerly Erotic Yet Exotic) under a newly acquired pen name, Nasti D. Shortly after she penned Deadly Pride: Loyalty Holds No Weight yet after doing some much needed research, she decided that would be her final release under Adore Publications. After several discussions that resulted in irreconcilable differences, the book was rejected.

Never being one to allow others the ability to control her destiny, she self-published the book the very next day. While the book was riddled with errors, it served as a valuable motivator going forward. Patiently waiting to regain rights over her previous releases, Danielle went on to self-publish the very first of many volumes to come advocating against gun violence titled Hood Love: Ain't No Loyalty In It. The book released New Year's Eve 2015 signifying her clean slate in the literary industry.

After regaining the rights to her previous works she went on to re-release them throughout 2016 with Drowning In My Emotions taking on a new, more inspiring title: Braving The Storm: Life's Cleansing Moments. She also released the second installment in her anti-gun violence volumes titled Hood Love 2: The Streets Still Ain't Loyal that year as well. Also in that same year, Nasti D began taking on a persona of her own.

2016 proved to be a big year for Danielle as she also traveled to her very first book event that year put on by the 556 Book Chicks in Atlanta, GA. It was her first time ever traveling outside her home state. Things got even better for her that year as she also attended the red carpet premiere of The Hackman web series put on by the Queen City Bullies whom she also happened to have an internet radio show titled Raw Sex Uncovered through. The show primarily catered to her erotic audience yet various wild, fun, entertaining, and educational topics were covered throughout the length of the show. Raw Sex Uncovered reigned as the #1 show on Queen City Bullies radio station for nearly a year or so before Danielle decided to hang up her microphone in exchange for more literary events and travel.

In 2017, Danielle also took on a new role as a publisher as she published both her daughter Danterryia Bigsby and son Te'Ontez Bigsby's debut titles: D is For drama/Diva and T is For Trying. It was in this same year that she also became a contributing author with her contributions to the Betrayed By Love, Adored By Lies and Our Book Of Poetry anthologies. Her literary travels continued throughout 2017 with an appearance at Meleah Solange (Indianapolis, IN) where she currently holds the title for being the author to sell the most books in one book signing. She also traveled to SOL (Silver Springs, MD) put on by Papaya Wagstaff as well as returning for the second year to the Atlanta Kickback put on by the 556 Book Chicks. She even went on to participate in her very first erotic poetry battle at the Queen City Bullies Sports Bar and Grill (Charlotte, NC) grand opening and walked away with the win.

Danielle also released new mater in 2017 with the release of From A Rock To A Diamond yet it proved to be a very humbling experience for her. Things didn't go so well and it nearly crippled her yet the outpour of love from readers, fellow authors, and supporters in the literary industry as well as some who weren't allowed her to pick up the pieces and journey on. From A Rock To A Diamond is currently under revision and will be re-released once Danielle feels confident with the final product. Wanting to end 2017 on a positive note, she released Desire 2 Be Nasti under her erotic alter ego, The Erotic Specialist aka Nasti D.

With the start of 2018, Danielle set out on the journey of improving her brand both publicly and in private. She has released both Hood Love 3: Take Heed To The Warnings and Hood Love 4: Warning Before Destruction this year which further showcase her dedication to advocacy against gun violence. Her literary travels have continued this year as well with her making her very first appearance at the infamous Hood Book Headquarters (Detroit, MI) owned and operated by Michelle Moore. It was there that she got the opportunity to meet the legendary author K'wan himself which is a moment she'll forever cherish.

Danielle Bigsby has no plans of stopping as she is continually writing and planning for future literary events. Her resurgence time and time again is both empowering and inspirational. It is also further proof that it's not about how many times you get knocked down but how many times you get back up! Social Media Handles:

FB: www.facebook.com/danielle.bigsby.92/

Instagram: www.Instagram.com/bigsbydanielle/

Twitter: www.twitter.com/R4_Pub/

Email: Royaldiva312@gmail.com subject line- Literary Business

Website: R4Presents.tictail.com (updated paperback books are available/on hand)

Juan C. Diaz is a graduate of Wilmington University, obtaining a Bachelor's Degree in Psychology; later obtaining his Master's in Psychology from Walden University. Diaz is the also co-founder of the online art magazine Neon Renaissance. He resides in New Castle, Delaware with his family.

Nisha Lanae found love in reading to escape a life of abandonment, homelessness and being the product of two addicts as a young child. As she grew older, the love of reading increased and the love of writing developed. By age 23, she had independently self-published her first novel titled Dice… The Queen of Murder. She now runs an indie publishing company Concrete Rose Publications, LLC where she has self-published 4 titles with many more on the way. Nisha believes adversity is only a fuel to keep moving forward.

Instagram Pendiva_nisha

Facebook Nisha Lanae

Email author.nishalanae@yahoo.com

Business website www. ConcreteRosepublication.com

 List of work:

Dice. The Queen of Murder.

Pounding the Pavement.

LAnd of Snakes

Ghetto Rose

Betrayed by love, adored by lies Anthology

Still a Ghetto Rose (Coming January 2019)

Scorned Heart Bruised Ego (Coming January 2019)

Raynesha Pittman is the CEO, Founder, Publisher, Author and the creative mind behind Conglomerate Ink and Rayn-Bow-N Productions. Raynesha didn't make it through storms, she learned to welcome them. After trading in her youthful days in California for adulthood in Tennessee, she is surrounded in the love of her six children and her Roq. With fifteen titles and more page turners in the works this traditional and self-published author is one you should get to know. Join her on Facebook and Instagram under Author Raynesha Pittman or follow her Twitter @ConglomerateInk. Most importantly, grab books. They are available everywhere books are sold. Her goal is to become a household name like Made in China, will you help?